Shards of Memory

Ruth Prawer Jhabvala

Shards

of

Memory

DOUBLEDAY
New York
London
Toronto
Sydney
Auckland

PUBLISHED BY DOUBLEDAY
a division of Bantam Doubleday Dell Publishing Group, Inc.
1540 Broadway, New York, New York 10036

DOUBLEDAY and the portrayal of an anchor with a
dolphin are trademarks of Doubleday, a division of Bantam Doubleday
Dell Publishing Group, Inc.

Library of Congress Cataloging-in-Publication Data

Jhabvala, Ruth Prawer, 1927–
    Shards of memory / Ruth Prawer Jhabvala.—1st ed.
      p. cm.
      1. Family—India—Fiction. 2. Family—New York (N.Y.)—Fiction.
    3. Family—England—London—Fiction. 4. Gurus—Fiction. I. Title.
    [PR9499.3.J5S33   1995]
    823—dc20   94-45311
    CIP

ISBN 0-385-47722-8

10 9 8 7 6 5 4 3 2 1

Memories, many of them not my own, are passing shyly and vividly through my chamber.

—RILKE, *Letters, 1906–7*

The joy of life . . . was just in the constant quick flit of association . . . between the two great chambers . . . of direct and indirect experience.

—HENRY JAMES, *Notes of a Son and Brother*

Part One
Antecedents

One

THE ORIGINAL MOVEMENT had no name, but after Henry's parents took it over, it became known as H & H, after their headquarters, which they called Head & Heart House. They both lived there, but Henry remained with his grandmother, whom he involved in his work. He was no longer editing the papers entrusted to him—his parents had removed them—nor interpreting the philosophy of the movement; instead he traced and followed its influence on the lives of certain individuals, mostly belonging to his own family. And it wasn't the movement itself that interested him so much as the personality of its founder: "the Master"—an appellation that Henry could not at first pronounce without embarrassment. But later he found it natural to think of him by that name—as natural as it was to think of his grandmother as "Baby," which was what everyone called her. He was grateful that she was there to help him, for no one knew as much as she did or could think back as far. He proposed taping her memories, which pleased her, although at first she fussed—who, she said, would want to hear anything she might have to tell. However, when he placed the tape recorder in front of her, she spoke into it spontaneously, fluently; she had even dressed up for the occasion in one of her smart afternoon outfits, with a rope of pearls wound around her neck.

Baby

I'm not really the right person to tell you anything because my thoughts—if I have any at all, my husband would have said—are not very orderly. If I tried to get things in order, I would have to go back to my mother and the Kopf family, or my father and the Bilimorias. Kopf and Bilimoria: New York via nineteenth-century Germany, and Bombay—here already you can see how mixed up everything is going to be, apart from the jumble inside my head. But these two families never really met—let alone mingled—except of course through me in whom they have come together, producing (as everyone will tell you) an average sort of person.

No, I can't see that I'm very different from the friends with whom I lunch and go to concerts. Although I have an Indian father, I could be taken for any little Jewish lady of a certain age. I like to wear bright colors and gold and other jewelry, and my hair is as black as that of my friends who have chosen that shade rather than blond or red. I did try red once, but I could see for myself, without having my husband kindly point it out, that it didn't suit me. But it remains my favorite color, so instead I've had my walls done up in red, which gives the place both an exotic and a cozy look. My grandson Henry says I crouch in here like a sorceress among her charms and spells, which in my case are the photographs of himself in all stages from a baby on, and of his mother Renata. I also have a lot of vases, crystals, clocks, inlaid boxes, and other jeweled things I've loved over the years. My pretty lamps sit among these objects, picking them out against the red walls so that they glimmer like precious stones scattered over the floor of some magic wood: this again from Henry—sometimes he says "magic wood," sometimes "bewitched forest." I don't know how he gets this impression of me as some kind of sorceress; maybe because I usually beat him at our evening games of chess.

Shall I start with my mother? Shall I start with my father? Or how they met, uniting not only Kopf and Bilimoria but two unsuited personalities? I've heard it said that the people most difficult to see in perspective are one's own parents. I've discussed it with my friends—we discuss all sorts of interesting questions over lunch, which might surprise people who see us having a good time in the restaurant, throwing our diets to the winds. We agreed partly—we could never agree completely, there are some who would rather slit their throat than agree with anyone else—but most of us did think that we were beginning to get an objective view of our parents, now that we ourselves are much older than they are in our memories.

My mother, Elsa Kopf, lived mostly in London, while I grew up with my father and my grandmother in New York, in the Murray Hill house where Henry and I still live. But it was different then, with maids in the attic and the kitchen and laundry in the basement. Now the basement is a very nice garden apartment, and the rest of the house is also divided into apartments, all rented out; mine is on the second floor. But at that time—seventy years ago—we had the whole house and it belonged to my grandmother, Dorothy Kopf. It was stuffed with furniture, pictures, carpets, and hangings, and probably this was what formed my own taste for such interiors.

My father's name was Hormusji Bilimoria, but he always called himself Kavi, which means Poet. When he met a stranger, he bowed and introduced himself as "Poet and Patriot," and then he laughed, which allowed the other person to laugh too, if they wanted to. He was wonderful company for my grandmother and me. He chose the concerts, operas, and plays we went to and afterward listened respectfully to our opinions—mine too, when I was no more than six or seven. My grandmother was as much a novice as I was, for her life with my grandfather Kopf hadn't been very cultural but had consisted mainly of eating meals with similar families: bankers, owners of department stores, and other such Philistines, as my mother Elsa called them.

Elsa had never been happy in her parents' house; she said it suffocated her. She was very different from the rest of the family, even in appearance: she was tall while they were all short, stumpy, and she had red hair and green eyes. In her youth she had wanted to be a concert pianist, and to escape the rest of the household, she would lock herself up with her grand piano, which she played very loudly, especially when her parents were giving a dinner party. Mild and good-humored with the lavish food of the Kopf household, the guests would twinkle and smile and say that yes, it was easy to see, or to *hear,* they joked, that there was a genius in the house. As the years passed and it became evident to Elsa that she was too complex to be a genius, her playing became even louder and more tempestuous. Fortunately, she had a wonderful piano teacher, Mme. Richter, who understood both her talent and her temperament. She was a Russian, a refugee of the Revolution; from a rich and cultured family in Moscow, she was now supporting herself by giving piano lessons to whatever daughters of good family she could find in New York. Mme. Richter belonged to a group who met to study and practice the teaching of their spiritual Master; and it was she who first really understood Elsa and opened up for her that other world Elsa had failed to find through her music.

Mme. Richter became my piano teacher too. I had no talent at all, but she never made me feel inferior to my mother, in this or anything else. She spent a lot of our lesson time writing letters to friends while sucking some very sweet bonbons that she loved. Afterward she collected her check from Dorothy and drank a glass of tea with her and Kavi. She had a very worn black coat, with a bit of fur left on the collar, and an old cloche hat that she never took off. She told Dorothy and Kavi about her many hardships—she supported a delicate daughter and a grand-daughter—and her check was usually larger than was due for my lessons. She was as tactful about my lack of talent with my father and grandmother as with me; she lovingly fondled my face and said I would do well, although she didn't specify in what.

As I said, it was through Mme. Richter that Elsa first learned about the Master's work. Mme. Richter had been among his earliest supporters, and she and her family had lived with him in what was his first commune. Afterward, along with other pioneers, they were sent to spread his message throughout the world, or at least in the more developed parts of it. Mme. Richter came to establish a branch of the movement in New York; but while the European chapters were flourishing, attracting wealthy people able to contribute time, money, and country houses, the New York one never managed to take off, perhaps because the Master himself, unable to get a U.S. visa, failed to make a personal appearance here. Mme. Richter and the other charter members were so short of funds that they couldn't pay the rent on a meeting place but had to convene in their own cramped living quarters. Mme. Richter did not even have an apartment of her own but roomed with her daughter in a run-down old house on the West Side. At that time it belonged to a German woman who lived in the basement and rented out the upstairs rooms to needy refugees. Mme. Richter had a second-floor room, which had once been (and would in years to come be again) a handsome parlor with a fireplace and tall French doors leading to a little wrought-iron balcony. But in her time—she lived there for years, her granddaughter was born and grew up there—it had peeling wallpaper and big patches of damp on the ceiling. When it was her turn to hold the meeting, Mme. Richter worked hard to make her place presentable. She took down the curtain on a string—it partitioned off her bed and was also useful for hanging clothes—and she borrowed chairs from the other lodgers. The German landlady pitched in too, and sometimes she attended their meeting, though usually still in her apron and house slippers.

I think it speaks highly of Elsa's character that, in spite of this shabby milieu, she at once recognized the importance of the Master's teaching. His portrait of course was there to inspire, hung prominently on the wall of Mme. Richter's room where it hid a mildewed patch—the famous portrait of him in collar and necktie and a big black mustache. News of Elsa's recruitment was sent to him; they were relieved to have something positive to report to the Master, for he was not pleased with their lack of success; also rumors of mischievous intrigues among them had begun to reach him, so that he had threatened to disown their group. But he approved of Elsa—young, beautiful, and of the Kopf family of New York—and after some months word came that she was to be sent to him in London.

This summons stirred up great excitement—in Mme. Richter and the other followers; in Elsa herself; and in Elsa's family, who didn't want her to go. But it all came to nothing, or nothing that anyone expected; for by the time Elsa's boat docked at Southampton, the Master had mysteriously taken off for somewhere else. But though she did not meet the Master, she did meet my father, Hormusji Bilimoria, already known as Kavi.

In a way, my father's family, the Bilimorias, were not that different from my mother's family, the Kopfs. They too were a large merchant family living comfortably in an overfurnished house— only theirs was in Bombay, by the Arabian Sea, with ocean breezes blowing through the verandas where they sat in carved cane armchairs. My father was the only son and there were several sisters, two of them unmarried and living at home. The days in the Bombay house were long, very long—Kavi described the many hours the family spent on the veranda, sighing about the heat and their digestive disorders while waiting for lunch to be served in the dining room. Here, still sighing, they helped themselves from the platters of rice, fish, lamb, and special egg preparations passed by the servants walking around the table on naked feet. Lunch took a long time and sleeping it off even longer; a woman servant crouched at the foot of each bed to fan away flies and massage arthritic limbs. Late afternoon came, the servants opened the shutters and brought tea and English digestive biscuits. Then mother and daughters began to get ready for their daily outing; the mother was fat, the daughters scrawny, but all dressed alike, in the daintiest white georgette and lace, with satin court shoes peeping out from the embroidered hems of their saris. They piled into the family carriage to be driven to the Taj Mahal Hotel, where their little marble table was always reserved for them. It was on the first landing, so that while drinking their pineapple juice, they could watch people go up and down the red-carpeted marble staircase. Many stopped to talk, and there was a lot of gossip, partly in English and partly in Gujarati, with the latest secrets that could only be whispered (this was always in Gujarati). But there were some haughty looks too, directed at enemies; these included a whole branch of their own family, with whom they were in litigation over property.

Kavi told us that, when he was small, he accompanied his mother and sisters on these outings, but later he went more often with his father to watch him play bridge at the club. He attended a Jesuit school and was driven there by the family coachman or, later, chauffeur, with another servant bringing his tiffin-carrier containing patties and Swiss chocolate. Sometimes he heard his family speak of the Indian Congress and "all those johnnies," their lips pushed out with the distaste they had for the entire Hindu population except their own servants. Kavi felt differently—even then, he said, his soul thrilled to words like independence and liberty, and he also studied English literature with Father Matthews and knew that Byron had died for Greece. But he could not speak of these feelings to his family, who would have thought him as mad as Cousin Soli shut up all his life in an upper story of the family house; instead he expressed them in English couplets full of Indian patriotism, which he read at playtime in the school compound to a group of friends. They crouched around him like conspirators, listening to his poems while eating the patties and chocolate he always shared with them.

Later, as an undergraduate in England, he met other kindred spirits. Those student years at Cambridge passed far too quickly, and although his family was eager for him to return home, he felt he needed more time to develop himself, both as poet and patriot. He moved to London where he wrote poetry and read it at meetings of Indian students and other supporters of the freedom movement. He was also published in pamphlets and newsletters and grew his hair long and wore a shawl. It was at this time he took the name Kavi—often ending his poems with a line addressed to himself: "O Kavi, in exile on the banks of the Thames, why do you let the Yamuna still fill your heart with the bittersweet flood of longing?" But in spite of this longing, he could not go home. There had been certain incidents—for instance, an Indian doctor, with whom Kavi had appeared on the same platform, had returned to India only to be arrested on arrival for engaging in subversive activities. Kavi realized that he could only be useful in London, and it was his patriotic duty to stay there. With his allowance from home, he rented a flat and furnished it in the artistic, semi-oriental style he liked (and later introduced into the Kopf house in New York).

Now it's time to tell how he and Elsa met, which was not very long after she had arrived in London to be presented to the Master. Although the Master himself had disappeared, the London group continued to be very active, successful, and highly organized. It was under the direction of Miss Cynthia Howard— she was about thirty-five at the time, with cropped hair and a monocle. There was an office where Cynthia conducted business affairs, but committee meetings of the inner circle were usually held in her own house on the edge of Hampstead Heath. Here she also entertained very generously—usually members of the group, but also giving more general parties where people could mingle with other groups, such as anarchists and students of oriental philosophies.

I grew up on Kavi's version of that party in Cynthia's house where he had first met Elsa. He never tired of describing the beautiful summer evening with all the windows and doors open to where the garden merged into the heath. The drawing room was soaked in summer scents from outside and from the perfumes of the women who had come to hear him recite his poetry. The sunset went on for hours—it shone on legs in silk stockings and on Elsa's red hair. I don't know if the light was really as golden as Kavi described it, or if this was the glow of his former happiness—everyone's former happiness, he said, because all the people there in Cynthia's drawing room were spending themselves and their money for something in which they believed. For some it was world peace—no more wars; for others, socialism or communism—enough for everyone to eat; for others it was independence from colonial rule—all nations free to develop their own great spirit; for some, vegetarianism—no more killing; for some, Esperanto—one world united by one language; and of course there was the Master's message, which promised not only a better World but a better Man.

I never heard Elsa speak of this first meeting, or how she came to marry him, but he must have been a very romantic figure for her; she couldn't have met anyone remotely like this young oriental poet, with his long hair and his shawl. She was much taller than he, and when they were first married, she took to wearing flat heels. I think that was the only concession she ever made to him, and she soon went back to her high heels, rising a head above him, which was the way I knew them. Their habits, like their personalities, were very different. She didn't care what she ate and was too impatient to sit down for it, walking around with a hunk of bread plastered with mayonnaise, and she swallowed hungrily like a wolf; whereas he had the appetite of a pampered only son and sat daintily cutting small morsels from small meals that he could never finish. In the mornings he liked to lie in bed for a long time—he called it his hour of inspiration—while she rushed to open the curtains and the windows and stood there breathing in the fresh winds of a new day. Then, leaving him daydreaming among his silk sheets, she would make her way across town in the Underground to Hampstead, to Cynthia Howard's house, with its little rooms and little staircases and maze of little passageways.

For a while, many years later, I shared Elsa's and Cynthia's life in this same house. By that time they were two very large women who quarreled fiercely with each other but could not bear to be apart. Cynthia suffered from gout and walked with a stick; when she did walk, that is, but mostly she sat in the upstairs study, in a leather chair by the fire, her foot propped on a stool, correcting the proofs of publications about the Master, her eyes screwed up against the smoke from the cigarette that hung from her lower lip. She wore a woolly cardigan and a big brown skirt that fell like sculpture over her knees. Her voice boomed up the stairs—usually to Elsa who was doing some other work connected with the movement in some other part of the house: "How the hell do you spell *differentiate*? Is this you or the bloody printer?" Then Elsa would come galloping up or down the stairs, and soon both their voices were raised to the roof as they hurled accusations against each other, insults and injuries going back twenty years, so that anyone listening to them would think that this was surely the end of their relationship, even if they didn't there and then murder each other. Only their cook, Katie, carried on placidly in her kitchen, for she knew that when she went into the study to take away the tea tray (sometimes with the china in pieces), she would find Cynthia in her armchair and Elsa on the floor by the stool with Cynthia's gouty foot on it, correcting proofs together and calling each other by their usual pet names.

When Elsa and Kavi had been married about two years—I'm going back to before I was born—he received some shocking news from Bombay. Kavi's father and uncle had been directors of a bank—two fine Parsi gentlemen, leaders of their community, trustees of many charities, members of the best club—but now their bank suddenly crashed, and it came out that they had for years been misappropriating its funds. Kavi's uncle fled to Burma—where he started a new bank and flourished all over again. But Kavi's father took another way out. One morning, just as the family was beginning to stir and the ayahs to open the bedroom shutters, a loud cry came from the butler standing in the door of the dining room, the tray with the breakfast dishes trembling in his hands. He was staring at the master of the household—suspended from a hook recently inserted into the ceiling for the installation of an electric fan. Dressed in his linen suit as for an evening at cards, Kavi's father dangled over the dining table; one shiny black shoe was still on, though the other had slipped off and lay on the cloth on which the butler had been about to place the toast racks and pots of English marmalade. Kavi took the next boat home to Bombay, and when he returned to England several weeks later, he was changed in many ways.

For one thing, he was poor now: the quarterly checks no longer flowed from Bombay into Grindlay's Bank in London to pay for his elegant life-style. Everything had to be given up and sold, and Elsa took him to live with Cynthia in the house on Hampstead Heath. Those two strong women now took charge of him and did their best to restore him. But he woke crying out at night, haunted by the memory of his father hanging in the dining room and what had happened to his mother and sisters. Their house and furniture and all possessions had been seized by creditors, and they themselves had to move from one relative to another until a little set of two rooms was found for them in a gray block of buildings run by one of the charity committees of which the father had been the esteemed treasurer. Here the sisters embroidered slippers and pickled mangoes for sale in a gift shop, while the mother, huge and forlorn, kept asking to be taken to the Taj Mahal Hotel to her place there at the top of the stairs.

Kavi wept and Elsa comforted him; I think this was the closest they ever came during the course of their marriage, and it was also the time I was conceived. I was born in a bedroom in the Hampstead house, and I'm told that Cynthia insisted on being present at Elsa's labor while Kavi trembled outside. The plan was that we would all live together and I was to be raised on principles laid down by the Master. But our household broke up when I was only three months old—I think Cynthia and Elsa had one of their monster fights, which ended with Elsa packing up Kavi and myself and sailing to New York to stay with her mother, Dorothy Kopf.

People are always asking me how I've managed to reach my present age and still continue to be called Baby. It was what my father called me while my mother was trying to decide on a name—or waiting for one to be chosen for me by the Master, who could not, as often happened, be located. When he was, and my name duly registered in London where I was born, everyone had gotten used to calling me Baby. Elsa did try to impose my real name, but as soon as she returned to England, my father and grandmother went back to Baby. For it was Kavi and Dorothy I grew up with, while Elsa made occasional appearances, which became less frequent as the years went by and she settled deeper into her work with the Master and her life with Cynthia. Whenever she was with us, everyone tiptoed around, wondering what her mood was—and it was usually bad, for she didn't like being here in her childhood home, which she felt to be very banal. She also didn't like the way I was growing up—for instance, the lack of progress in my piano lessons, where she was often present so that Mme. Richter had to stop writing letters and concentrate on teaching me my Czerny exercises. I'm sorry to say that it was a relief to everyone when Elsa went back to London. And yet, in a way, we did miss her presence in the house. For though it was oppressive, it was also challenging—yes, she was always challenging us for the way we lived and thought, so that while she was there we felt that perhaps we could do better. And I did try harder, at my math and chemistry and other lessons I usually couldn't stand, also at my piano practice, although without much improvement.

Mme. Richter said that the effect Elsa had on people, to make them reach higher and exceed themselves, was due to the influence of the Master. Dorothy maintained that Elsa had always been like that, quite different from the rest of the Kopf family and dissatisfied with everything they did and were. But that was just the sort of personality the Master was looking for, Mme. Richter replied, or who was looking for him. She herself was by this time completely disillusioned with the Master. He had withdrawn his support from her and the rest of the group in New York and had ordered them to disband—which was typical of him, Mme. Richter said bitterly, to turn his back on those who were not rich enough to be useful to him. She knew what she was talking about, she said, for she had met him in his earlier years, when he was nothing more than a poor refugee like the rest of them, and in his case of dubious origins. He had fooled her then, as he had fooled a lot of people since, but now she had learned what were the truly valuable qualities in human beings and they were not his. For it was not the exterior that mattered, flashy though it might be and impressive to other people, but what was inside a person—she mentioned her German landlady, a rough and rough-tongued woman yet full of kindness, a quality that Mme. Richter had learned to appreciate above all others, together with generosity. And here she often kissed Dorothy's hand and tried to seize Kavi's too, though he wouldn't let her but gallantly kissed hers instead.

Elsa and Cynthia used to refer to Kavi as "the Lily" because of his neither spinning nor toiling, but he made himself very useful in Grandma Dorothy's house. It's true that financially he was completely dependent on her; however, that was just a nice arrangement between them. In those days, I mean over seventy years ago, people had a whole staff of indoor servants—not like today when I'm lucky to have Griselda show up a few times a week—and besides the cook there was a parlor maid in black dress and apron, and a nursemaid for me, and a laundress, and a man to stoke up the boilers, and a chauffeur when Dorothy bought a car. Everyone came to Kavi for orders and he managed much better than Dorothy, for she was nervous and unpredictable, which made servants give notice till Kavi talked them out of it. He also kept up good relations with the tradesmen in the neighborhood, like the butcher, and the grocer who made up our special blend of coffee beans to be ground at home. Grandma Dorothy often entertained, mostly Saturdays and Sundays when members of the Kopf family and of Dorothy's own family, the Kellers, came for various meals. I never could keep apart the Kopfs and the Kellers—to me they seemed identical, though each considered themselves superior and didn't always have the best things to say about the other. But to me they all looked alike, including Grandma Dorothy: all short and plump, wearing clothes that were dowdy but well cut and of the best material. They talked a lot and ate a lot and the gentlemen made jokes, specially with me. I sat on their knees while they made clowns and mice out of their handkerchiefs for me, overwhelming me with their smell of cigars, cologne, and something elderly, something musty and masculine.

Kavi fitted right into this family of settled business people. He got to know the ins and outs of cousins and marriages, and of their illnesses and operations, and always remembered special diets. But he also brought something else of his own into the atmosphere. Until his arrival, Dorothy's taste had been the same as all Kopfs and Kellers, so that the pictures, carpets, china, and silver were almost identical. Kavi had lost his income but kept his taste for fine things, and he and Grandma Dorothy visited antique shows and auction houses, where she bought items he thought worth acquiring. Beautiful oriental objects began to be scattered among the furniture, which stood on legs as solid as the ankles of Kopf and Keller ladies. A Kashmir shawl was draped on Elsa's grand piano; and there were even some Persian miniatures, long before they became fashionable, so that fountains and roses blooming within exquisite borders were hung among the still lifes of dead lobsters that had been Grandma Dorothy's wedding presents.

Sometimes Dorothy persuaded her son-in-law to recite his poems to the family. I would sit in front, on a footstool embroidered with puppies and kittens, my arms wound around my knees; behind me the family sat in upholstered chairs, trying to keep as still as possible, though some of them had chronic breathing problems. I strained forward proudly toward my father the poet. He no longer wore oriental clothes—his shawls and white muslin had been replaced by velvet jackets, in burgundy or midnight blue—but his poems had remained oriental. He read with much expression and beautiful gestures of his small hands, and at the end he gave a modest smile, waving away appreciation as though he considered himself unworthy. But there *was* appreciation—and it grew as the years passed and the family became as familiar with the poems as with an old tune: for they were always the same poems, he didn't write any new ones, it was still "O Kavi! In exile on the bank of the Thames," except that he had replaced the Thames with the Hudson—"O Kavi, in exile on the banks of the Hudson, why do you let the Yamuna still fill your heart with the bittersweet flood of longing?" The family recognized both the lines and the feelings they expressed—who didn't know about homesickness, one aunt regularly said, why, even on a visit to her sister in Pittsburgh, she longed to be back home among all her own things. The uncles laughed, but Kavi defended her and said everywhere it was the same, missing the place or person you loved, the same loss and pain.

I used to hear Elsa and Cynthia scoff that, if he felt so much loss and pain, why the hell didn't he go home? This wasn't till much later when I went to stay with them in their house in London. I say their house though it was Cynthia's, but by then they were a couple and lived in it together. I suppose I could be considered a sort of pioneer for the following generations when it became very common to have two sets of couples as parents; although I think it would still be uncommon to have the father and grandmother as one couple and another the mother and her woman friend. But I never found the situation odd and didn't go around apologizing for it. I think I must have been what is called well balanced, and it's true that even in later years I've never suffered in the way so many of my friends have, with nerves and complexes for which they've needed expensive treatments. But my mother deplored my temperament, which she said I had inherited from the Kopfs and Kellers and certainly not from her. She regretted missing out on the important years of my education (or formation, as she and Cynthia called it): the original plan had been for me to spend alternate years in New York with Dorothy and Kavi, and in London at the Hampstead house. It's doubtful if we could ever have carried out this arrangement—if Grandma Dorothy and Kavi could ever have parted from me, or I from them—but anyhow the war made it impossible, and by the time it was over I was no longer a child and Elsa and Cynthia had lost their chance of forming me.

Shortly after the end of the war, Elsa cabled to say she was coming to New York to fetch me. We prepared ourselves for her arrival, which was however delayed because of her work. By this time she was an important figure in the movement, a principal

organizer, and we found her greatly changed. For one thing, she
no longer played the piano! This was a relief to me, for I too had
given it up completely, although Mme. Richter still came twice
a week, now mainly to pick up her check and drink tea with
jam. Elsa ran her fingers over the keys of the piano, remarking,
"It's out of tune" (it was, but none of us had noticed). She also
pushed aside the Kashmir shawl Kavi had spread on it—he
quickly settled it back, then hurried on behind her as she strode
around the house, checking up on what else was wrong. She
found plenty and became impatient with us—in this she had not
changed, she was still very impatient with people and things,
but now she knew how to put them right. She looked different
from how we remembered her: she had cut her hair, which was
more red than ever, having been touched up, and it sat tightly
on her head like a metallic cap. She seemed even taller than
before, and she wore a mannish coat-and-skirt suit, but pinned
to the lapel was a huge satin flower with tangerine petals and
jeweled pistils sticking out.

Since we were still happily living inside it, we had failed to
notice how much our household had deteriorated. It had become
difficult to get any staff at all, let alone the large one our house
needed. Elsa at once decided that it had to be remodeled and cut
up into apartments, one for us to live in and the rest to be rented
out. At the time we objected (she soon overruled us), but I must
say now I'm glad of her foresight and to have my own cozy
apartment here and rents coming in from the others. It was Elsa
who found the architect and supervised his plans; through her
work with the Master, she had become very experienced in
building, and in buying and selling properties. She usually
walked around with a briefcase stuffed full of papers; immersed
in her affairs, she squinted against the smoke from her cigarette,
for like Cynthia she now had one permanently attached to her
lower lip. If any of us happened to be in her way, she brushed us
aside as though she didn't see us, and probably she didn't, for
she rose high above us as she strode around on her giant legs. She
sent and received many cables and also booked transatlantic
calls, which usually came through in the middle of the night,

waking Grandma Dorothy so that Kavi had to spend hours trying to make her fall asleep again.

Grandma Dorothy had become so dependent on Kavi that she
wouldn't let him out of her sight. When he wasn't there, her
eyes hunted around the room for him, she even whined for him a
bit, so that when he came back, he flung up his arms and de-
claimed, "But here I am, here I am, here is Kavi the poet-slave!"
Then her face lit up, she clutched his small hand in her smaller
one and hung on to it for dear life. It made Elsa very impatient,
but fortunately something usually diverted her attention, like a
cable or a call. Also fortunately she was too busy to notice what
we had gotten quite used to—that is, Grandma Dorothy forgetting things or muddling them up, and no longer quite remembering who was alive and who wasn't. When that happened,
when for instance she asked after an uncle who had been gone for
twenty years, we would answer her in the most natural way
possible, as though he were about to come in the door. The aunts
and uncles humored her too when they came to visit; it was
nothing unusual for them and anyway some of them had become
just as confused.

Elsa decided that, while alterations were going on inside the
house, Kavi and Dorothy were to take up residence in a nearby
hotel. This arrangement did not include me because I was to go
to London to live with Elsa and Cynthia. Kavi tried to comfort
me—he said it was for the best, that it was time for me to study
something or other, and what was the use of living with an old
father and grandmother. Well, of course, I was unhappy to part
from them, but even more to part from a boy who played the
saxophone and with whom I was in love. It was my first time
and I thought it was unique and unrepeatable.

Elsa and I went to London by plane—another disappointment, for I had been looking forward to what might happen on
board ship. But no one, certainly not Elsa or anyone else of the
Master's group, had time for transatlantic voyages anymore. Before I go on to talk about London, I have to mention something
that happened with the piano teacher, Mme. Richter. Excited
about Elsa's arrival, she had been the first visitor to welcome her,

calling out in a high, cracked, joyful voice, "Where is she? Where is my little one, my own Elsa?" This Elsa came to meet her in the hall. Clutching a little basket full of Russian cookies she had baked, Mme. Richter raised her arms to fling them around Elsa's neck. But Elsa wouldn't accept her cookies or her embrace; she wouldn't even let her take off her coat or enter any farther into the house. Kavi and I, who had come to witness what we thought would be an emotional reunion, couldn't hear what Elsa was saying or see her expression as she said it, for she had her back to us. It was Mme. Richter who faced us—walking backward, as she was being edged toward the door; her cloche hat had slipped sideways so that her white hair streamed out as if standing up in shock.

What had she done? Apparently something too awful for Elsa to tell us, beyond hinting at betrayal of the Master. Kavi and I felt so bad that later the same day we secretly went to visit Mme. Richter where she still lived in the house with the German landlady and the rest of the refugees. We found them all gathered around Mme. Richter, who lay on the bed in part of the room that was usually curtained off; now the curtain had been pushed aside so that all could see her lying there suffering, lit up by the gray light made grayer by the dirty French windows. Her daughter, a pale young woman with strange slanting eyes, was applying compresses on Mme. Richter's forehead. The room, with its high ceiling and ornamental fireplace, looked decayed but aristocratic. So did the people in it—all except the landlady who, in apron and house slippers, sat four-square in the only armchair. Mme. Richter wouldn't look at us at first; she turned aside her face while the daughter changed the compress. Everyone was silent, even Kavi who usually had a lot to say; we all listened to a tap dripping into a basin. At last Mme. Richter told us that she blamed no one—only herself, for bestowing her love where it was not wanted. We had no reply, no excuse, and looked around for a place to put the envelope with the check, which Elsa had not given her time to collect. The landlady took it from us. Revived by a fresh compress, Mme. Richter managed to sit up and stretch out her hand—we thought it was for us to shake and be forgiven, but the landlady knew it was for the envelope. But we *were* forgiven, all of us, even Elsa; and apart from Mme. Richter's heart, which was blamed for being too affectionate, the only named culprit was the Master. Here everyone began to speak together. The mournful figures around the bed became animated; one old man with a decoration on his morning coat banged his stick angrily on the floor, till the landlady warned him about the ceiling underneath. They spoke bitterly of the Master whom they had once worshiped but who had abandoned them.

When I reached London with Elsa, the Master was again in some other part of the world, and I didn't get to meet him except in his portraits displayed all over the Hampstead house. The same portraits hung in the office, which occupied the two top floors of another house in Bloomsbury. I think the original idea had been for me to join the office staff—a bunch of volunteers and two harassed paid secretaries—to pack pamphlets or whatever, but somehow I never got started. I was supposed to take the Underground every morning to Tottenham Court Road station and then walk from there into Bloomsbury, and I did go to Hampstead station and sometimes even went down in the lift and on to a train, only to get off again because there was always somewhere else that it seemed nicer to be. London was in an unusual mood just then—some areas were devastated, there were vast bomb craters with fragments of buildings still tottering above the exposed foundations: but green shoots were springing out of them, some with buds of flowers on them. And the people were the same, worn out, worn down, but ready to start over. There wasn't too much food and even clothes were rationed so that for the lack of pretty dresses girls improvised, sewing long skirts out of blackout curtains and pieces of old tapestry.

During the war—besides their work for the movement, which had of course continued though the Master himself was absent—Cynthia had been an air-raid warden and Elsa a firefighter. They had tramped around in pants tucked into rubber boots, and although they no longer wore these, they still walked as if they did. They had also gotten used to blowing whistles and shouting out warnings, and their voices had remained commandeering even when they were only calling to each other up and down the stairs. Their cook and general help, Katie, had worked in a munitions factory, so that she too was used to shouting to make herself heard above the din of machinery. The house reeked of tobacco—all three of them chain-smoked—yet the atmosphere was somehow feminine, or female. Perhaps this was because Elsa and Cynthia had so many pet names for each other—"old thing," "Cynthing," "Elsakin"—and when they fought, they did so like women, calling each other bitch. Also there was the house itself with its many nooks, in each an ornamental piece of furniture; and all the vases were full of flowering branches plucked from the heath, for the garden itself was still under its wartime cultivation of potatoes and carrots, and had an air-raid shelter dug right in its center.

Elsa and Cynthia spent many hours walking on the heath—I think it gave them a sense of freedom to be able to tramp over that open space under an open sky. Of course, mental freedom was even more important to them, and it was on the heath that they had some of their most marvelous discussions. They often wanted me to go with them, but when I did, I always disappointed them. However hard they tried, they were unable to make me understand the meaning of the Work, and far from raising me to their level, I more often pulled them down to mine, for my stupidity so exasperated them that they became snappish and ill-tempered. There was the question of my name too—they said it was absolutely ridiculous for me to answer to "Baby" and tried to call me by my real name; but whether it was because it sounded so unsuitable for me or because I never recognized myself in it and failed to answer, we were soon back to "Baby," though every time they had to use this name, it set their teeth on edge.

London at that time was the perfect place to be in love, and I was in the perfect mood for it. I had very quickly got over the boy with the saxophone but not over the feelings he had stirred up, which I was eager to repeat. Unlike my mother (Elsa) and

my daughter (Renata), I've always been quick to smile at people
—I mean, strangers in the streets, sometimes I'm not even smiling at them in particular but just in general, because of feeling
happy. This is true even now—Henry says it's embarrassing to
go out with me—and how much more was it at that age, and at
that time in London with all those young ex-servicemen waiting
to be discharged and go out with girls and get married as
quickly as possible. No wonder I never made it to the office;
even if I got as far as Hampstead Tube station—and sometimes I
didn't—there was very likely some young soldier or airman on
the train, or in the lift going down to it, who thought my smile
was for him and started a conversation, during which it turned
out he knew of a new drinking club just opened or was on his
way to the London zoo, having spent his combat years planning
a visit to the gorilla there.

So I made a lot of friends and our phone never stopped ringing, and I went to afternoon clubs and pubs and parties and
dances and caught the last train back to Hampstead, escorted by
some young man, who then had to walk home all the way across
London. But that was what was so wonderful for everyone—after
the years of blackout and air raids to wander around freely in the
streets and parks and squares at night and watch the dawn come
up over Piccadilly. We were all ready to fall in love with each
other a hundred times over, and I nearly did; only finally it
wasn't with one of the young servicemen I met in any of those
places but with one nearer home—Cynthia's nephew Graeme.
He was a serviceman too, a wartime captain in the army, and he
still wore his very smart uniform and had all sorts of pips on his
shoulders and a Distinguished Service Medal on his chest and a
Sam Browne belt. He was to me the most dashing of all the
dashing young men I met, so that it was inevitable I should fall
in love with him. It really wasn't inevitable that he should do so
with me, but he did and spent the rest of his life wondering
why. We had nothing at all in common—except his aunt
Cynthia and, as I said, the particular time it was for us all.

When anyone is as English as the Howards—that is, Graeme
and his aunt Cynthia—they usually have ties with India that go

back for generations; and in future years Graeme often blamed this particular line of his ancestry for the attraction he felt toward me. He said it was so unreasonable that it could only be due to something instinctive, like a call of blood; and that most likely what had happened was that, during one of those endless hot Indian afternoons in the mofussil while the sahib was out quelling a riot in the bazaar, the memsahib had called in her lusty Goan cook. This was the sort of joke that particularly appealed to my husband—wry, half serious, and insulting (preferably to me). But it is true that, when we met, Graeme was very keen on India, having spent two years of his army service there. It had been an exciting time for him, and he had traveled around visiting nineteenth-century Howard graves in Lucknow and Meerut, and older ones in the South, and incidentally had become quite knowledgeable about temple architecture. He had made friends with many Indians, despising those of his countrymen who kept to their own little bourgeois social circles and their imperialist ideas. He was a great supporter of Indian independence and was glad to see the British Empire dissolve. Yet later he blamed the loss of empire for his own dissatisfaction, saying he had been born to rule people like me and not (another typical example of Graeme humor) to marry them. However, at other times he blamed me for not being Indian enough and grumbled that, if he had to marry an Indian, why couldn't it be one of those full-blooded South Indian girls who looked like temple sculpture and could sit on her own hair.

To this day when I think of a typically English person, I think of Graeme. This may have something to do with the time and place I met him, and also with my first impression of him in his British army officer's uniform. But mostly it has to do with his temperament, which I find difficult to describe because it was so contradictory. Basically, he was very morose, a terrible pessimist who thought life was unspeakably horrible; but it was a point of honor with him to pretend not to care and to be very stoical and make these jokes. In the beginning, when he was still interested enough in me to talk seriously, he told me about the Venerable Bede who had compared a man's life to the swift flight of a sparrow out of darkness through a span of light and—I can still hear Graeme saying it—back into unending darkness. That was how Graeme felt: as though he himself were that Venerable Bede (or rather, his bird). He was very fond of poetry and could recite reams of it by heart; his favorites were sardonic, bitter poets of the seventeenth century or the 1930s. But he also liked romantic poetry and would recite Shakespeare sonnets to me—walking across the heath, he would raise his face to the moon and say such exquisitely beautiful lines that I thought surely they must come out of an exquisitely beautiful soul and that I would love him forever. In some ways, he was very conventional—he couldn't bear not to be wearing the right clothes, and his shirts, cuff links, neckties, his shoes, his pajamas, his overcoat, everything had to be from exactly the right place; but he always had the air of not caring a damn what he put on. Most of his friends at that time were rather scruffy; they were intellectuals, or artists, or film critics with dandruff on their collars. Graeme himself had a conventional career: he had been in his last year at Oxford when war broke out, and when it was over, he went back to graduate and a year later passed the Foreign Office exam. He remained in the diplomatic service for the rest of his life, never rising very high and ending up as a deputy high commissioner in Calcutta. I can't say for sure about those years because I wasn't with him, but I know there was always something strange, suspect about what he did. Henry, my grandson—and his—says that of course Graeme was a spy. If he was, it would have suited him perfectly because it was his nature to be secretive, never letting anyone know his feelings or his activities, but misleading people about both, even when this was completely unnecessary. We were never divorced and he never remarried—"God forbid," he would say if the suggestion came up, shielding his face as though someone were about to hit him—but he was reported to have had many different affairs in many different countries. He wouldn't have been able to live without women, for he was physically passionate although this too he disguised, preferring to appear cool and indolent. On the whole, he disliked women—

I think because he needed them and he felt they took away from his self-sufficiency, which he liked to believe was total.

Whatever else he was and wasn't, the fact remains that Graeme *was* Renata's father, and it was through him that the Anglo-Saxon strain was added to the stock of Kopf-Keller and Bilimoria. This Anglo-Saxon strain was the predominant one at our wedding, which took place in Graeme's mother's house near Warwick. The Howard family had lived in the area for generations, but after Graeme's father died, the big house known as the Hall was sold to a boys' school and Graeme's mother moved into a much smaller place. Although she was not Cynthia's sister but her sister-in-law, she looked a lot like her and had the same manner and voice. They had been at boarding school together where, according to Graeme, one had succeeded the other as head prefect and both had remained head prefects for the rest of their lives. But while Cynthia devoted herself to the Master's world movement, Graeme's mother was busy with local affairs— she was for many years on the town council—and with her garden where she planted and dug till the last glimmer of daylight had gone from the sky. Thanks to her, on our wedding day the garden looked absolutely perfect; and it also happened to be a perfect day in June, with the air full of spices and scents, not only outside but streaming into the house through the glass doors, which had been left wide open to let the guests walk in and out, carrying their champagne glasses.

It was to please the Howard family that we had agreed for the ceremony to be held in the local church, where so many of them had been married over the years and also buried in the graveyard next to it. But it was to please myself too—I was mad with excitement to get to wear Cynthia's grandmother's veil, with little pink Howard children carrying my train. Graeme went along with it all—he was still fond enough to humor me instead of deploring what he later called my childishness—and Kavi had flown over from New York to give me away, bringing Grandma Dorothy, who was by now very disorientated and didn't really know where she was or what was happening. Kavi wore an Indian silk coat and I walked up the aisle on his arm; the organ played and made us feel exalted till we reached the altar where Graeme was waiting for us, standing there so tall and British and with his usual sardonic smile, so that we couldn't help feeling small, if only in size.

Several members of the Kopf and Keller families had also come over, on luxury liners: they loved transatlantic voyages, and having either sold their department stores and stockholding companies or handed them over to their children, they had plenty of time to attend weddings and funerals. It was strange to see them in an English church, or in Mrs. Howard's house and garden, instead of in their own overheated, overfurnished New York apartments. I had always thought of them as rather ordinary, certainly compared with Kavi; but now I realized that they too had something at least semi-exotic about them, with their large features and short, plump figures and the excessively expensive clothes they wore. The Howards loomed above them, as austere as rocks, and to address them they leaned far down toward them and spoke in that slow, kind way the English have with foreigners, although my family spoke nothing more foreign than American English. But if the Howards were a mountain range above the Kopfs and Kellers, then the highest peaks were Cynthia and my mother Elsa. These two wore voluminous wedding clothes and hats, and pinned to the center of their bosoms were the enormous insignia to which they were entitled by their rank in the Master's order. These were gold and in the shape of the sun with its rays, and they gleamed, glittered, and flashed like the eyes of a god watching over the marriage rites.

Here Baby's own account ends. She refused to go any further—maybe she regarded her wedding as a sort of summit from which she didn't want to come down. Or, more likely, the novelty of talking into a machine had worn off, and also interfered with her daily routine: for in spite of her advanced age, Baby kept very busy, with charity committees, and her masseuse, and lunches with those of her friends who were still left.

Now her grandson Henry had to rely largely on his own recollections, which were fortunately very detailed and stretched far beyond his own experience, for he had lived with his grandmother most of his life. He also had the advantage of being able to read to her what he had written every day, and if something didn't agree with her own memories, she challenged him. They often argued and sometimes quarreled, but they did in the end manage to get some sort of record straight between them. Later, Henry checked with everyone else still alive—his parents, and also Vera (Mme. Richter's great-granddaughter), though that was not until several years had passed, after Vera's marriage broke down and she more or less came back to him. Anyway, from here on the narrative is mostly based on Henry's research, and it starts with the birth of his mother Renata.

Two

WHEN RENATA WAS BORN, her parents had already separated. She was (accidentally) conceived in the course of their separation, one afternoon when Baby had gone to collect some more of her things from Graeme's flat in Washington, where he was then posted. Unfortunately he had been at home and could not resist taunting her in order to rouse her into losing her temper; he always loved doing this, though it was physically dangerous to himself and his possessions. Baby was apt to throw whatever came to hand, so before working her up, Graeme put everything fragile he had out of reach. Then, while she hurled objects at him, he ducked behind the furniture, shouting out "Fault!" or "Good shot!" When Baby was furious and in action, she was prettier than ever—and Baby was *very* pretty when young and quite irresistible to Graeme, especially when she tried to resist him and thumped her small fists against his chest. Their fights usually ended with them in bed together or, as on the afternoon that Renata was conceived, rolling around on the carpet.

Renata was born in New York and spent her early years there, with her mother, her grandfather Kavi, and her great-grandmother Dorothy Kopf, in the second-floor apartment that they had occupied since the remodeling of their house. Besides the members of the family and a general help, there were also a day nurse and a night nurse for Dorothy, who needed a lot of special care. Kavi was in his element, looking after his daughter Baby, his granddaughter Renata, and his mother-in-law with her attendants. Eternally youthful—juvenile, Elsa and Cynthia said— he appeared to have a second flowering around this period, both as an Indian and as a poet. After the one brief visit at the time of his father's bankruptcy, he had never returned to Bombay, but he regularly corresponded with his two sisters, who remained there in restricted but quite comfortable circumstances, thanks to the checks he sent them from a Kopf account he managed for Grandma Dorothy.

Kavi ran the entire New York household—he had even become an exquisite cook, mostly in the French style which suited his refined palate. But now in his later years he began to crave the foods of his childhood, and at his request his sisters sent him pages of Parsi recipes written out in their convent-trained hand-writing. He chirped as he hopped around in his kitchen—with age, Kavi had become smaller and more birdlike—he kept tasting the dishes he cooked up, wagging his head in self-approval. But though he appeared so merry, the poetry he had begun to write again was even more melancholy than his early poems of exile. "O Kavi! Shipwrecked on the river of Life in its surge to the Ocean, why could you not steer your boat with more skill?" "O Kavi! whose eyes are closing even as the moon rises pale in the heavens, was it only yesterday that they opened to the light of dawn?" This mood may have been evoked by the passing of the years in general, but also more particularly by the decline of Grandma Dorothy. She wandered around in her mind and in the apartment, which she sometimes mistook for the Hotel Palais at Biarritz where she had spent her honeymoon. She had diminished in size and become so tiny and bent toward the earth that she appeared to be growing back into it. This gnomelike figure, this fairy-tale paradigm of old age, was a natural part of Renata's childhood, and when Grandma Dorothy finally died, Renata calmly gazed at her—Kavi lifted her up to let her get a better view—laid out on her marriage bed with her jaw tied up, no more portentous than a frozen sparrow and not much bigger either.

Renata was the second child whom Kavi had brought up, some twenty-five years after his daughter Baby, and in the meantime he had grown not only older but wiser, in the sense of more philosophical. He now loved to occupy himself with large questions about human life, its meaning and purpose, and these he raised with Renata on their walks in the park or over chocolate milk shakes at their favorite soda fountain. Renata was very different from the child her mother Baby had been. Grave and thoughtful, she listened carefully to her grandfather and asked serious questions. When they were accosted by a poor person needing the price of a cup of coffee, the whole problem of poverty and riches had to be explained to her—not from the standpoint of economics, that was too limited a view for both of them, but in relation to a recurring cycle where the residues of one life were carried over into another, and humans, animals, and plants rolled around together in earth's diurnal course (to quote from one of Kavi's favorite English poets). And from there they ascended toward the planets and the stars and what went on out there beyond the reach of anything that Kavi, old though he was and not without experience, could even guess at.

Along with her grandfather, her mother played the most important role in Renata's childhood. These were busy years for Baby. Separated from her husband, her domestic arrangements taken care of by her father, she was free to devote herself to social and personal life and her many friends. Sometimes it was necessary for her to go away on trips with them—she always returned loaded with wonderful presents—but mostly she kept Renata close by her. She so much hated to be parted from her that, when she had an extended session at the beauty parlor, she would have Renata brought to see her there, so that Renata was quite used to the rich smell and heat and hum of these places as well as being petted by assistants and clients. Altogether Renata was used to people shrieking over her, for she was often taken along to noisy all-night parties; sometimes they were held at home, where she helped her mother's friends out of their fur wraps, while they pushed out their brilliantly painted lips at her and enveloped her in clouds of perfume and flattery. She did not care for being kissed by anyone except her mother and her grandfather—both lavish with their caresses—but she accepted it as part of social life, something that all Baby's friends did to each other, even to those they disliked. And some of them did it most extravagantly—especially the "Uncles" who so loved her mother that they stayed the whole night with her in her bedroom. When Renata visited them there in the mornings—"Leave off now!" Baby would shriek with laughter, turning away from an obtrusive Uncle to hug Renata instead; so that Renata never had cause to doubt that her mother would always love her best.

She also had the love of her father though she didn't know that, for he was awkward about expressing it. Actually loving someone, for their own sake rather than his, was a new sensation for Graeme. He came to see his daughter as often as he could, which was not difficult as long as he was posted in Washington. But later he came from as far as Istanbul or Kabul, taking a hotel room in New York so that she could be brought to see him there. After that he was rather stumped, having no experience whatsoever of what to do with a child. He bought front-row tickets for the circus, but she burst into tears at the clowns and had to be taken out; the same happened at the zoo where she was overcome by the expression on the face of a lion in his cage. Graeme bought every childhood classic he could remember— *Winnie the Pooh, Peter Rabbit, Peter Pan*—he read them aloud to her while she politely listened. Sometimes he asked, "Shall I go on?"

"If you want to," she replied and continued to sit deadpan with her hands folded in her lap. At the cinema, when he took her to see Donald Duck or Laurel and Hardy, it was he who laughed while she sat patiently waiting for him to finish enjoying himself.

He told Baby about their daughter: "That child has absolutely no sense of humor," to which Baby replied with a heartfelt "Thank God she hasn't inherited your particular brand." But

Graeme continued to make regular appearances all through Renata's childhood, spending a lot of money he couldn't afford —he was dependent on his Foreign Office salary—on air fares and hotel rooms.

Renata followed the family tradition of taking piano lessons from Mme. Richter, who seemed not to have changed, except that she had only a few strands of her white hair left and almost no teeth. Even her black coat looked the same, green with age and threadbare. Now she was always accompanied by her granddaughter, whom she was training to take over the task of earning their bread, the daughter being too sickly to do anything. Although only a few years older than Renata, the granddaughter was supposed to be teaching her, sitting beside her at the piano while Mme. Richter, sucking bonbons behind them, beat out time with her stick. If Renata made a mistake, Mme. Richter poked this stick into the granddaughter. Renata made many mistakes, she had even less talent than Baby, if that was possible. But she tried over and over, sitting very straight and stiff on the piano stool with her fingers on the keys equally straight and stiff. She was as desperate to express herself as her grandmother Elsa had been, and tears of rage came to her eyes because her hands would not obey her. Mme. Richter understood her perfectly; at the end of each frustrating lesson she kissed and praised her and told her she had a noble soul.

Elsa, on one of her visits to New York, came to the same conclusion about her granddaughter; she recognized her as a very different proposition from her own daughter Baby. Back in London, she reported her findings to Cynthia, so that both were eager to bring Renata to London and induct her into the Master's work. But Baby would not part with her, and Kavi too could not have lived without Renata. However, as she grew into adolescence, Renata became restless: besides the piano, other things too failed to satisfy her. Kavi had taught her to love poetry—anyway, *his* poetry—and for a while she thought she might study literature; but it was always difficult for her to pass exams, although she had more feeling for the subject than most of those who did. Painting too turned out not to be her medium.

She attended drama classes for a while, but these were worse than anything, for it was a torment for her to have to act out her personality before others. So it happened that when Elsa again visited New York—she now came more for the sake of her granddaughter than her daughter, let alone her ex-husband Kavi —she found Renata very ready to listen to her account of what could be achieved through the Work. Overriding Mme. Richter's warnings, and Baby and Kavi's reluctance to let her go, Renata decided to follow—more than literally—in Elsa's footsteps and accompany her to London to study the doctrine that had been such a guiding force in her grandmother's life.

The Master's work, as distinct from his personality and personal influence, has been expounded in the previous volumes that Henry edited and published. Here it is enough to say that the essence of the Master's teaching was: one step higher. Every student and follower of his had to endeavor to rise one step above his or her own emotional, intellectual, and spiritual development. This was very slow and exacting work; some people never seemed to make any progress at all—or hardly had they risen by long and laborious effort to that step above themselves when they fell back again and had to start over. It was really a whole lifetime's work—and more: "I want many lives," the Master used to tell them, "all your lives"—and the majority of the present followers had been with him twenty or thirty years at least and were now advanced in age if not yet in personality.

Perhaps it was this that, from the beginning, so disappointed Renata: that everyone was old—the same age as her great-aunt Cynthia and her grandmother Elsa. She was also disappointed in the prosaic domestic lives of these two elderly relatives, and it seemed to her that in spite of a lifetime of self-work, no transfiguration had taken place. They ate three comfortable meals a day, prepared by their cook Katie, and still fought ferociously with each other. Outwardly they were now mountainous and gray, so that Renata could not know that inwardly they had remained the fiery, passionate girls they had been. The other members were equally disconcerting: they spoke of higher orders of being but, as for their personality, seemed to remain where they were. They fought over rights and rank and who was to be elected to committees. And they were so very English—chilly, pinched, precise, and had to have their tea on time and just so.

In appearance, Renata herself was as English as any of them. She was tall and craggy like her father's family, with long limbs; there was nothing at all to indicate her Indian ancestry. She had her grandmother Elsa's green eyes and also a hint of Elsa's red hair, though by no means its full flame; Renata's tended to be gingery, which enhanced the impression she gave of being anemic—she was, slightly, maybe due to having shot up too fast in her early teens. Her father, who still came to see her whenever he could from wherever he was posted, was pleased with her looks —or would have been, if she had only known how to dress properly. He wanted to see her in English tweeds and camel coats, but instead Renata dragged around in shapeless cotton shifts imported cheaply from some underdeveloped country. She moved rather languidly, perhaps because of being anemic; her dress was often too long, or the hem had come undone, so that it swept the floor behind her. Whenever Graeme made an appointment with her, he was invariably there first—she was most unpunctual—and when he saw her approach, he had to turn away, sometimes groaning and covering his eyes. After she moved to London, he either came to pick her up in Hampstead or met her on the heath or in a park or street, never in his own club or the Café Royal or other such places where he would have liked to take her. She despised them—she wanted to be out in the open, preferably in wind and rain.

With her, Graeme lost all his usual calm and cynicism. He begged his mother to take her to live in her house in Warwickshire, send her to evening classes or wherever she could be made to learn something, anything, and introduce her into local society. Let her go to dances, make her *normal,* he pleaded. He almost wished she could be like her mother, like Baby, ordinary: but she was not; she was like her grandmother, like Elsa, extraordinary, at least in the sense of not being satisfied with anything that was not extraordinary. But Elsa too was concerned about her. Late at night, when Renata was asleep, Elsa would creak up the stairs of the old house in her nightgown—"Are you asleep, Cynthing?" She sat on Cynthia's bed, holding a mug of cocoa, talking about Renata who was not making progress in the Work, did not even seem to care about it. "But what *does* she care about?" Elsa demanded, as despairingly as Graeme, for Renata never seemed to lose her vague, rather dull look.

Here is a letter Renata wrote to her grandfather Kavi:

. . . Yesterday I had to go with Daddy, we went to a vegitarian (sp.?) restaurant which he hated and made his usual remarks which are supposed to be funny but really hurt peoples feelings and sometimes I don't know if he does it on purpose or what. He thinks I am very stupid so when I open my mouth something stupid comes out so I don't say anything and that makes him very mad and sarcastick. But tomorrow he has to go back to Kabul and I am sorry about it and wish we got on better but then we would have to be two different kinds of characters. I wish I could write to you that something wonderful and very great is happening here but it is not and I don't know if it ever will here, perhaps it is not the right place. Elsa and Cynthia are very *very* busy with the Work. Oh the Work, what shall I say. I go twice a week to lectures and three times for the exercise class where you are supposed to practice what they teach you in the lectures. Some of the phisical exercises are quite nice like we are supposed to learn to coordinate the right arm and left leg and vise versa (sp.?) to learn better phisical control and break old habits. But what they call the interior exercises which are also to break bad habits but interior ones like interior vises but what I hate is you have to think about yourself all the time which I think is incredibly boring. When your poem came yesterday just after I got home *exausted* from being with Daddy I read it *4 times* very fast like when you are very hungry you swallow food very fast . . .

Kavi's letter enclosing his poem had arrived by the afternoon post, which Katie as usual took upstairs to Cynthia and Elsa along with their tea tray. It was one of their favorite hours—they had several in the course of each day—by the fire in the upstairs study, Cynthia in her chair with her gouty foot propped on a stool and Elsa on the carpet, opening the mail and reading out whatever was interesting. Mellowed light from the declining sun pressed against the windowpanes, but inside the room it was much darker—the whole house was dark, surrounded by old trees—and they sat by the glow of little reading lamps and the flicker of their open fire in the grate. "Oh look at this," said Elsa, holding up Kavi's letter, "another epistle from the Lily to Renata!"

Cynthia took it, weighed it in her hand—it was quite thick— "What *does* he write to her?"

Both of them were dying to open it, to see what it was he had to say to Renata, what was the connection he had to her which they themselves had so far failed to establish. They knew he sent her poems—the first time she had in her enthusiasm read it aloud to them. They had reacted the way they always did to Kavi's poems—"another of the Lily's effusions"—and had not been careful enough to hide this from Renata. When she looked up and saw the expressions on their faces, instantly her own face changed, her green eyes glittered. Holding the poem close to her chest, she turned and left the house and did not return till long after dark. She said nothing then and nothing later, but for days they had to face her silent rage and learned to fear it. She was not like her grandmother Elsa, whose rages were a visible tempest, or her mother Baby, who threw things; everything was turned inward with her, as though she nourished a fierce flame in there to consume whatever deserved destruction. So now, when Kavi's letters arrived, they carefully propped them up on the hall table for her to see when she came in. She never again shared the contents with them, nor did they dare ask.

Altogether she was secretive with them. This was her nature, and so far the only people she had ever talked to freely were her mother and her grandfather. Anyway, it was they, far away in New York, who learned about her meeting with Carl, before Cynthia and Elsa on whose doorstep it had taken place. Renata had found Carl sitting on a bench on the heath, with his possessions around him: these consisted of his rucksack, his bedroll, and his manuscript. He was reading the latter when Renata passed his bench; he looked up at her and smiled—his beguiling smile, full of trust and innocence—so she asked him what he was reading, though it was not her habit to speak to strangers. He was so eager to tell her and it was so interesting that after a while she sat down with him—he bundled up his things to make room for her—and they talked about his manuscript. She realized at once that it was his life's work and that it was important not only to him but to the world.

He only revealed incidentally that he had nowhere to stay—but that didn't matter at all, he assured her, for it was still warm enough, almost, to sleep out, and anyway he had his bedroll. He loved sleeping out, and in any case he had no alternative. "You see, I have no money," he said simply and continued talking about what really mattered, that is, his manuscript. They went on sitting there till it got dark and time for her to go home. It turned out that he was hungry, not having eaten anything all day except half a loaf of bread, so she took him to a café in the High Street and bought him a fairly modest meal (even then, in the first flush of her youth and idealism, she was already careful with her money). Next morning she smuggled food for him out of Katie's kitchen, and they spent the whole day together, sometimes sitting on a bench, sometimes rambling over the heath, he with his rucksack and bedroll on his back and she carrying his manuscript. The next few days passed in the same way, Renata cutting her lectures and exercise classes, in fact, completely forgetting about them.

It started getting colder—autumn had set in, with a shower of wet leaves—and after he had eaten in their usual café, he walked with her to her street, where she knew of an empty house waiting to be sold. It was covered completely in ivy and had a large Victorian portico, where he settled with his bedding. She waited in her room for Elsa and Cynthia to go to sleep—it took a long time, she heard them talking in the bedroom under hers till after midnight—then she opened her window and gave their prearranged signal, which was a bird cry he had taught her. Leaving everything except his manuscript in the Victorian portico, he ran to her back garden and nimbly climbed up to her window, by way of a drainpipe. She stretched out as far as she could, first to take the manuscript, then his hand to help him jump inside. Since he had left his bedroll behind, she had to make space for him in her bed. They had the same sleeping habits—both lay on their right side, with no clothes on, the curtains and window open, for they loved fresh air. Both woke with the first light of dawn and he returned the way he had come. It was all perfectly easy and natural. She began regularly to attend her classes again, not for her own satisfaction but for Cynthia's and Elsa's; although now that she was getting involved in Carl's work, she had less interest than ever in theirs.

Here is another letter from Renata to New York, this one addressed both to her mother and her grandfather:

. . . Frankly I feel why should it be so interesting to improve our own character when what is needed is for the whole world to improve!! This is exactly what the person I met, his name is Carl, is working for and from the foundation up that is from the education of little children from their earliest years. It is very exsiting (sp.?) to be involved in this work but it needs organization and cash which we do not have but there is a lot of interest allready here in London . . .

The interest was as yet confined to her and Carl, but it was so fierce and fiery that they knew it must ultimately burn up all the dead wood around them. Meanwhile, Carl tramped from publisher to publisher, sitting in outer offices with his manuscript. Often he saw only a secretary, but even when he managed to get to an editorial assistant, he met at best with polite incomprehension. He expected it; he knew it was the inevitable reception accorded to anything as original as his ideas. Rejection only charged him up more—he quickened his steps, held his head higher, hurried the manuscript under his arm to the next publisher. He did not have a forceful personality; as with Renata, there was something bloodless about him—in his case, accentuated by his white-blond hair like that of a German child (Carl *was* German) and his pale eyes; but like hers, his eyes glittered with some inner passion. *Inner,* nonphysical—and this was also the key to their sex life: for they had some, though remarkably little considering their age and nightly proximity. Their excitement came from mental stimulation, their discussions of ideas, and it was this that occasionally overflowed into the sexual act, which remained incidental to them, almost perfunctory.

Renata was fully prepared to spend herself on Carl's ideas. At present, this mainly meant spending her money—like Elsa and Baby, she had an income from Kopf and Keller trusts. This was sufficient for a comfortable private life but not to finance a worldwide campaign for the reform and reorientation of every system of education. All she could do now was to feed Carl, give him a small sum for pocket money, and photocopy his manuscript with its constant additions and alterations—for this, she tramped a few miles to a place she had found that charged less than the others. But they were aware that soon they would have to start operating on a much larger scale. The prospect invigorated them: both had hope and faith, and Renata also had the example of Cynthia and Elsa and the superb organization they had built up for the Master's movement. Renata realized, and Carl agreed, that it was now time to inform them of the new movement that, unbeknown to them, was gathering momentum under their roof.

But then this revelation had to be postponed because everyone was thrown into a frenzy of excited activity: the Master was coming to London. He was making a worldwide tour of all the centers of his movement, and although this had in latter years become a seasonal operation, the rumor was that now it was to be the last: that it was to be a farewell visit prior to his intention of leaving his body. No one knew how old he was and only those who were very old themselves could make an approximate guess; but even they had met him when he was already intellectually and spiritually formed, and that was over half a century ago.

Yet when he appeared he did not seem old at all—let alone a

man in his eighties, which he must have been. He was short, thickset, bullish, pink-cheeked as if in vigorous midlife; and though his days and nights were packed with activity, he never showed the least sign of fatigue. Elsa and Cynthia, who were in charge of all the arrangements during his stay, had taken a vast furnished flat for him, put at his disposal by a shipping magnate, and here he received his callers and entertained at lavish meals mostly cooked by himself. He had many aides, and in some ways his style resembled that of a political leader, but he also functioned like a psychiatrist or some other kind of spiritual guide. A careful roster of appointments had to be kept, and for four hours every morning and three in the afternoon people were ushered one by one into his presence for their consultations, which were carefully graded from five minutes to half an hour. Only once did Elsa and Cynthia make a mistake in apportioning the time—whereupon he hurled a storm of abuse at them, and for the next few days took every opportunity to crush them with his sarcasm. Their meekness in the face of this undeserved opprobrium—they had erred by four minutes—was astonishing. It was as if they wanted to submit to his tyranny and accepted it as part of their training. They even appeared grateful for his concern, his help with their work on themselves.

He thundered and annihilated—it was his method with all his long-time followers; but he could also be wonderful company, especially at the evening meal to which he invited many guests. There was always one special dish made from some ancient recipe known only to himself; he filled their plates, explaining the properties of each spice he had pounded, and occasionally feeding some favored guest with morsels from his own plate. He sang songs, attempting to teach them the words and tune—both of mysterious origin—and he laughed at them when they failed to get them right. They tried and tried and tried again, but when they had almost mastered the song, he switched to a completely different and even more difficult one, so that they had to begin all over again. He also told fables, featuring animals, plants, and heavenly bodies, interesting and beautiful in themselves and with a kernel of meaning that had a direct bearing on the problems with which he had taught them to wrestle. These suppers went on for hours; they were all gathered around his circular dining table, with its marble top and golden claw-feet, and he opened bottle after bottle of every conceivable liquor, of which he drank the lion's share. By the end of the meal —it was usually early morning—everyone was in a strange, exalted state, feeling in a befuddled way that they had been raised above themselves. His eyes gleamed with his characteristic expression, benign yet mischievous, and his cheeks were a little pinker than usual. When he decided that the meal was over, he rose abruptly, sometimes upsetting a glass. Turning his back on everyone, he partly shuffled, partly staggered to his bedroom—it was the only time he showed any sign of age—followed by some of his aides; it was their task to undress him where he had fallen facedown on his king-size bed and was, very often, already asleep. Everyone else also rose from the table, completely silent now, as though with his exit the energy had gone out of the air, and they dispersed thoughtfully, each extracting his own particular lesson from the occasion he had devised.

With Renata he was quite different again. She was fitted into his schedule of appointments and, as a great privilege, was received in his bedroom very early in the morning. It was a sort of levee—not that he received her in bed: he was sitting on the side of it, freshly shaved and fresh all over in spite of his heavy drinking the night before; his bald head shone, his white mustache bristled, so did his white eyebrows over his slightly hooded, slightly slanted eyes. He wore what with anyone else may have appeared as an ordinary, if rich, dressing gown; with him, it became a royal mantle. He had one small naked foot laid over his knee and was pleasurably cracking the toe joints. He looked up at her and smiled, infinitely benevolent; with a generous sweep of his hand—all his gestures were sweeping, generous —he invited her to sit beside him on the bed. "Closer," he said, and she moved up closer. They were not alone in the room, one or two aides were there, and every now and again he gave them some command in an unknown language. But even if they had been alone, she would have trusted him. Although he exuded power, energy, sexuality—yes, at eighty—all these were now damped down for her benefit into paternal care and goodness. He asked her about her classes and exercises, and seeing her hesitate, he encouraged her to be entirely frank with him. He himself surmised that perhaps they were not right for her, so that it might be necessary to devise some different program. But to do that he would have to know her more intimately—although on that last word he laid his hand, small and compact like his foot, on her thigh, she understood that he was neither exhibiting nor referring to a sexual intimacy but something on a different level altogether. Enveloping her in a loving smile, he encouraged her to gaze into his Tartar eyes—they were pewter-colored and seemed to hold no reflections. What nationality was he? She couldn't even guess and had heard many alternatives.

She had no objection to opening her heart to him, as he was inviting her to do: except that her heart held only one interest—for Carl's educational program, for his manuscript. She was deliberating whether it would be right to mention it to the Master, who, after all, was selling a rival program; she thought that perhaps she should first consult Carl. The Master was silent, giving her time to reflect; his hand was still on her thigh, lying there so innocently that she had forgotten about it, even though at that moment she was remembering all she had heard about him from Mme. Richter and her circle. But now that she was actually with him she did not believe any of it; no, not even when he raised his hand from her thigh and laid it on her breast. Next he was holding both her breasts, not fondling them but more like a doctor, examining them; and then more and more like a doctor he raised the lids of her eyes. "Give me your hand," he said; she did so and let him feel her pulse with expert fingers. She remembered more stories about him—stories about his astonishing medical skills exceeding those of any doctor, for he had performed cures in cases that medical opinion had pronounced hopeless. He knew certain secret functions of the body just as he did of the mind; indeed, for him body and mind were inseparably bound together, and Renata concluded that his physical examination was to determine what mental exercises to prescribe for her. She was wrong.

"My poor child," he said.

"What?" she asked.

He said, "Don't you know?"

"Know what?" But she felt sure that he had diagnosed her secret; that is, her dedication to Carl's cause; and in a way he had.

"You're pregnant," he said.

"You're kidding," she replied, surprised into an uncharacteristic bit of slang.

He sent the two aides away in order to talk to her in absolute privacy. He was laughing at her: "I can see how you wouldn't know. You're the sort of girl who menstruates with complete irregularity." He said this so naturally that, although rather prudish, she cheerfully confirmed that this was so. "Moreover," he went on, "you never even know when you should be due." This too was true: menstruation was so objectionable a process for her, holding nothing but nuisance value, that she deliberately forgot about it between each cycle. "I think you'd have preferred to be born an angel with no bodily functions at all."

"Oh yes!" she cried, pleased to have someone formulate this vague desire for her.

"Unfortunately I can't help you there," he said, his eyes dancing with amusement. "Now: was this some immaculate conception? No? Then there is some young man—I hope he's young? And I hope you know who he is."

"Of course I know," she said indignantly.

"Yes of course. You would not be promiscuous. Really I'm surprised you've even brought it this far. I took you for a virgin. Tell me, did you by any chance ever desire to be a nun?"

"It would be fabulous," she said, her eyes glittering.

"My poor child," he sighed again. "Perhaps you'd better bring him here to have a talk. No, don't be afraid: no one is going to give away your secret."

"I'm not afraid," said Renata, raising her head proudly. But she was perturbed; she did not like the news she had heard; if anything like that happened to her, it would bring her down from the realms where she wished to dwell.

Carl took the news calmly—or rather, with calm pleasure. "Oh really? How exciting," he said, and after a decent interval went on talking about his experience that day with a publisher. So then Renata also became calm and stopped thinking about her pregnancy as anything very momentous. But Carl was eager for an opportunity to talk to the Master and wanted to go right away, not realizing what a complicated business of schedules and appointments a visit there entailed. Elsa and Cynthia were delighted, and proud too, that Renata should be asked for again (they weren't told about Carl) and fitted in an appointment with her as soon as possible. It was another private audience in his bedroom, only this time he wasn't sitting on his bed but in an armchair, with a little table in front of him and a basket of mangoes beside him. The furniture in the bedroom—in the taste of the shipping magnate to whom it belonged—was luxuriously comfortable, all of it without contours like one vast cushion into which to sink. But whatever had been left behind of its owner's personality had already been effaced by the Master's ambience: his photographs of himself, his mandalalike charts, his Caucasian hangings and rugs (not used for prayer)—not to speak of his own forceful presence. The smell of the mangoes, like very sweet turpentine, pervaded the room, and he explained that they had just been flown in for him from Bombay, where they were in their short season. He ate them by punching the interior into a pulp, which he then sucked out from a hole in the top. He did not offer any to his visitors or his aides but enjoyed them by himself.

Poufs were placed on either side of him, which were so soft that they collapsed and slowly sank under Carl and Renata's weight. Carl did not notice—he had opened his manuscript and was explaining its contents, lisping as he always did when he was excited, his German accent getting stronger and more incomprehensible as he got deeper into his abstract, abstruse arguments. Renata knew from experience how hard these were to follow on a first (or even subsequent) hearing, but the Master seemed to take them in his stride—if he was listening at all, which may not have been the case for he appeared engrossed in savoring his mango. He didn't interrupt Carl but let him go on, and on. Carl became entangled in the depths of his argument and his accent, so that even Renata, so familiar with both, had to strain to make sense of what he was saying. Once she glanced at the Master, to check if he was managing to follow, but all she could see was the smile under his long white mustache, now stained orange with mango; and when he caught Renata looking at him, he smiled more and then winked at her. She felt a spasm of annoyance, though she was not sure whether this was directed at the Master for not taking Carl seriously, or at Carl for continuing so obliviously to thresh around in his deep waters. The Master noticed her change of mood at once, he stopped smiling and leaned toward Carl and his manuscript with a show of interest, asking to see the title page. He read it out, " 'Education as Elevation,' " and repeated it, rolling it on his tongue together with the mango; and suddenly a spurt of mango juice burst out of his mouth onto the page—"Oh! Oh! Oh!" he cried in distress and quickly tried to wipe out the stain with his fist, thereby spreading it wider, deeper, and more indelibly into the paper.

He didn't on that occasion—or, it may be said at once, on any subsequent one—ask questions about the manuscript. What he did ask was, "What are you going to do about it?"

Of course they thought he meant about the publication of the manuscript, and they were elated by his interest—he was very influential and also had his own printing press. Both began to speak at once, but he interrupted them: "No, about *that*," and playfully pressed one finger into Renata's belly.

He was amused that neither of them had given the least thought to the problem. "It's going to grow," he told them. "It's going to go big—big—big"—and with both hands he showed how big—"and then—*boom!*" His laughter made the same *boom* sound.

Renata's pregnancy did grow, but not the prospective parents' interest in it. Their prime concern remained Carl's manuscript, and eager to follow up their meeting with the Master, they kept asking for another private audience. This was not granted; in fact, Carl never met him again and Renata only when he was surrounded by other people—at lectures, general meetings, and sometimes when she was invited to one of his evening feasts. Then he always had a sly wink for her, in reference to their secret; and he never forgot to propose a toast to "the coming generation," raising his glass toward Renata. Everyone else joined in under the impression that it was Renata herself they were toasting—not unnaturally, since she was forty to fifty years younger than the rest of the company. She was no longer required to attend either the inner or the outer exercise classes: the Master himself had absolved her, telling Elsa and Cynthia that he had a different plan for Renata. He did not tell them what this was, but they were very much gratified by his interest in her. Elsa began to regard her appraisingly—failing to notice her expanding waistline but wondering what special qualities her granddaughter had inherited, maybe from her. She could not yet discern them: Renata remained vague, unfocused, passionless— very different from what Elsa herself had been, and still was, though in her sixties.

Winter had set in, and Carl needed a less hazardous shelter than climbing up the drainpipe to Renata's bedroom. Although in practical matters as vague as Renata and with his mind somewhere else, he always tended to find what he needed. He rented a back bedroom in a rooming house, which was cheap enough to satisfy Renata's frugal nature. Here, apart from his occasional excursions to publishers, he spent his time working on his manuscript—entirely happy, wearing a scarf around his neck against the cold and mittens he had made himself by cutting the fingertips off a pair of gloves. He could only light the gas fire when Renata remembered to bring shillings for it. He was also dependent on her for his food, which she purloined from the Hampstead house or bought ready-cooked—he accepted whatever she gave him, for he was no more concerned about food or personal comfort in general than she was. Their interest in each other was equally temperate: sometimes she came to see him and sometimes she didn't, and what he principally noticed about the latter occasions was that there was no food and no shillings for the gas meter.

It was at this point that Graeme came to London for a Foreign Office briefing and, as usual, wanted frequently to be with Renata. She submitted to these meetings with her father in the same stoic way as she had as a child; but now that her judgments were more rigidly formed, he had an exasperating effect on her. She deplored him—everything he was and stood for—and he deplored her in the same way; but he loved her, so that whereas for her their meetings were just something to be got through, his feelings about them were more painfully mixed. He hated the places she chose for their rendezvous—such as, for instance, the vegetarian restaurant where she took him one winter's day when she was about six months pregnant. It had wooden tables and benches and they were served by an amateur waitress who did not clean the table properly or get their order quite right. He was sarcastic with the girl, which made Renata feel ashamed; and she rebuked him, "She's not some coolie, you know."

"If she were, she'd know her job a damn sight better."

This remark, delivered in his most clipped accent, fitted in with her view of his entire personality. He drove her wild. He hadn't taken off his overcoat but sat wrapped in it as though protecting himself against contamination. She even felt that he included her in his general distaste—and it was true that he hated to see how perfectly this place suited her. The other customers and the waitresses shared her anemic quality, as well as the thin-lipped rectitude of those devoted to a cause, even one no more positive than not eating meat. Only the pictures on the walls were wholesome—apple-cheeked children biting into hunks of whole-grain bread, and peasants dressed in primary colors toiling waist-high in fields of golden corn.

Graeme had never admired horsey women, county women, committee women, Englishwomen—they had been the butt of his humor—yet now he longed for his daughter to be at least a little bit like them. If only, he sighed to himself, she could be induced to dress properly, or—he glanced at them—sometimes to clean her fingernails. Giving up on her appearance, he attempted to change her personality by engaging her in some sensible activity. Every time they met, he proposed a job he had heard of for her, or brought along the prospectus of some educational course: to restore pictures or antiques, to train with a veterinary surgeon or an auctioneer. She barely glanced at the pamphlets or listened to him; it annoyed her that her own father should be so ignorant of her character as to bring her these mundane proposals.

Today it was an assistant's job at the India Office Library—hardly had he pronounced these words when she exclaimed: "That's the last place I'd be seen dead in!"

He didn't ask why; he knew why, he had heard it often before. How the British had stolen everything of value out of India—stolen books for their libraries, art objects for their museums, a nation's culture purloined: before Independence, he himself had had similar feelings about the Empire, but in the intervening years these had been largely transformed into nostalgia. He didn't argue with Renata, for he was always afraid of exacerbating her irritation with him. He did so want her to at least tolerate him. And in the present instance, he also felt somewhat ashamed of his change of attitude—of his middle-aged nostalgia as compared with the idealism of his younger self. And of course there was always her final retort on this subject: "You forget, of course on purpose, that I happen to have an Indian grandfather."

He did often forget—looking at her, it was easy to forget—but he said nothing because she never liked to be reminded that in appearance she had taken after him and his family. He half turned away from her on their uncomfortable bench, only to be met by the sight of people who embodied everything he deplored in her.

"Why do we always have to meet in places haunted by these shades of Hades. They're not even dead, only half dead—naturally, feeding on this pap, what else can one expect"; and he irritably pushed away the plate the waitress had just dumped in front of him.

"Isn't that typical," said Renata. Her teeth like his were gritted. "Only what you eat is right, only what you do is right, and only what you are. Everyone who is not like you is to be condemned and despised, including of course me."

How easy—how nice, he now thought—it had been with her mother! With Baby, he could drop as many invidious remarks as he liked till she blew up in the most attractive way, soon to simmer down and forget whatever it was that had made her explode. But Renata took everything dead seriously; and she never forgot. And today she seemed especially testy with him; also, he noted, especially dowdy, as though she had put on an extra layer of those loose rags she wore. She even seemed to have gained weight, which did not suit her; and for the first time ever she was hungry, not only finishing the disgusting milk concoction they served here but ordering another. In placing it in front of her, the waitress had left a moist ring on the table; Graeme automatically wiped at it but desisted when Renata hissed, "Don't: you'll hurt her feelings."

He summoned his small stock of patience and said, "All right, so we rule out the India Office. But what else is there? Do you have anything in mind? You have to do something, Renata."

"You seem to be absolutely sure that I do nothing; also that I have no ideas of my own or plans or any future at all, but you'll see."

"I shall be delighted to see. But couldn't you let me in on them a little now? Before I go back to Kabul? You would set my mind at rest no end."

"I can't tell you now."

"Why not? Why not, Renata?"

"Not now."

"Then when?"

"When the time comes."

She had flushed a little, blood gently flowing under her very pale skin. Unlike the rest of her, her face was not swollen but looked somewhat pinched.

"You're not, by any chance," said Graeme in his cool way, "pregnant? . . . I see," he said at her response—or lack of it, for she was totally silent. "Is that what you predicted I would see, when the time comes?"

"No! That's not it."

Actually, Renata had not been sure what she had been referring to—Carl's educational scheme or her pregnancy. But now that Graeme had guessed the latter, she was absolutely sure that it was the former she had meant. Anyone could have a baby, but not everyone could change the world.

Three

WHAT STRUCK Baby and Kavi as extraordinary was that Graeme, who was really a bachelor type, should discover Renata's condition before Elsa and Cynthia, who lived in the same house with her. It was he who communicated the news to them that he and Baby were going to be grandparents, and Kavi a great-grandfather. Kavi was the only one whose joy was unalloyed. But then Kavi rejoiced a great deal nowadays. He had not become childish—on the contrary, his mind had sharpened—but he was childlike, unjaded, and could take great pleasure in everything that happened. When he heard about Renata, he was so exultant, he jumped up and marched around the dining table, shouting out salvos of applause.

Baby left for London at once, and Graeme received her at the airport. They had not met for several years but resumed their normal relationship immediately. He blamed her for what had happened—"But I wasn't even here!" she protested.

"It's all that fucking around you did while she was growing up."

"Oh well," she shrugged, rather complacently.

"I suppose you're still doing it," he said, and as always she was very much aware of the way he was looking at her, his sarcastic smile not unmixed with appreciation. She worked hard at her appearance, so she had reason to feel confident, sitting with him in one of those roomy London taxis, pretending not to notice the glances he threw in her direction. But when he saw her fixing her little hat a bit, his smile changed to that smug expression he wore when he had somehow got the better of her. Of course it made her want to thump him, which he knew very well, so they were back to their usual form with each other. They swayed side by side on the high pearl-gray upholstery, he with his legs crossed and his trousers hitched up just the right degree. He was carrying his rolled umbrella, and once, while she was checking up on her lipstick, he slyly poked her with the tip. "Oh sorry," he said as she snapped her compact shut with the force of a slap. So they rode along.

Graeme had to return to his posting in Kabul, and Baby took charge. It was inconceivable to her how Cynthia and Elsa could have failed to notice Renata's pregnancy. Under the rags and shawls in which she enveloped it, her body was visibly misshapen while her face had become very pointed and paler than ever. She looked rather like a Florentine painting of the Virgin Mary in the same condition—which may have been the reason why everyone forgot about the young man who was responsible for it. Renata herself seemed to have forgotten; when Baby asked her where he was, she clapped her hand before her mouth: "He must be starving!" She hadn't been to bring him any provisions for two days. She ran down to raid Katie's kitchen and threw everything into a paper bag. When Baby said she would go with her to meet him, Renata didn't mind, she said all right.

It was a really squalid place she had taken for him, with only one WC for the whole house full of lodgers and no bathroom at all. His room was a small oblong with a metal bedstead in it on which he was sitting working on his manuscript. He leaped up when his visitors entered—he was extremely pleased to see them, and not only because of the food they had brought. Baby realized that, like Renata's, his mind soared above material matters. Altogether there was a resemblance between them which was more spiritual than physical—though it was physical too, especially in comparison with Baby herself, wrapped in her mink and a mist of perfume. Carl fell on the food at once—he was truly very hungry; while he ate, he was at the same time explaining his life's work to Baby, and failed to notice that she couldn't understand a word. Nor did she try very hard—she already guessed that she would hear it very often in the future (and so it turned out). Renata too was not listening but was absorbed in her own thoughts, her hand laid absentmindedly on her pregnant belly. Although they sat side by side on the bed, she and Carl seemed as remote from each other as from the rest of the world. And these two were to be parents of a child! Baby understood there and then—in the next room, another renter was having a fight with his girlfriend, furniture was being thrown about—that someone would have to look after that child and those two on the bed as well, and who could that be except Baby herself.

Renata agreed to return with her mother to New York, and Carl was excited by the prospect of going with them, although Renata saw no reason why he should—"What for?" she asked. His face fell, so that Baby felt sorry for him and thought how insensitive it was of Renata not to realize that he would want to be present at the birth of his child. But it was not the child that was on his mind, it was his manuscript, and he eagerly urged his case—that England was too cramped in every way to receive his ideas, which needed a large, open country like America. "Oh all right," Renata agreed, not very graciously, but he gratefully pecked at her cheek in pure friendship and was ready to start at once. So was Renata, she didn't feel she had anything to keep her here. That was her nature—as it was Carl's too—there was nothing to keep them anywhere. They were like those plants with roots that need no earth but freely flutter in the air or any other element.

But Elsa and Cynthia were strenuously opposed to the child being raised by anyone but themselves. Informed by Baby of what had been happening on their doorstep, they showed only mild surprise, followed by total approval. Baby found her mother and aunt changed by age—though changed is the wrong word, on the contrary, they were very much the same only more so; that is, their personalities had petrified, become monumental. Cynthia *was* like a monument—enormous, immobile, enthroned on her chair by the fire with her swollen foot propped up. Elsa had remained highly mobile—she now moved around for both of them, charging up and down the stairs or flinging herself into their little car to hurtle off on some errand. She had retained her perfect health, including her teeth, and wore glasses only for reading; she was big, strong, and muscular, partly from exercise but mostly from the inner discipline with which she curbed her passionate nature. And if they were monumental physically, they were even more so in their minds, which had hardened into rocks of certainty. They at once laid out an elaborate program for the upbringing and education of Renata's child—it amazed Baby to hear these two aged women talk as if they still had a whole lifetime to put at the disposal of a newborn baby. For evidently this was their intention: to devote themselves to him, as though he would somehow bring their work to fruition. Baby did not know what was on their minds—and did not find out till many years later—but she fully understood that she would have to rescue her grandchild not only from incompetent parents but from these two formidable ancestresses.

It was useless to argue with them. She knew that the only way was to appeal to a higher authority: it was her general policy, when she failed to get satisfactory service—say, in a store or a bank—to go straight to the top person. She asked to speak to the Master. Elsa and Cynthia laughed at her, they said she was crazy to think she could just walk in to see the Master as though he were an ordinary human being. But Baby didn't see what else he could be and acted as always when the lower ranks wouldn't let her get up to the management—she brushed past them and walked right into the inner office where she was usually very well received. And that was what happened here too. The Master's flat was in one of those big luxurious blocks with a lot of porters guarding the entrance, and carpets, and plants in gilded pots. She had no trouble at all with the porters—who knew at once that she was not the type to be kept waiting—nor with the person who opened the front door, and it wasn't till she was actually inside that anyone challenged her. She kept right on opening doors with an air of authority while they came sheepishly behind her, their protests growing more feeble as she penetrated deeper into this enormous flat.

Led on by the smell of frying spices, she tracked him to the kitchen where he was concocting one of his feasts. He made no fuss when she barged in, acknowledging that having got this far, she deserved to be there. He was in a collarless white shirt that may have been a sleeping garment, and he looked very rosy and healthy. If she hadn't known him from his photographs, she might have mistaken him for the cook. He stirred around in the simmering cauldrons and, after tasting from his wooden spoon, called to his assistants for various spices. Baby knew about spices from all the cooking Kavi did, following the recipes sent by his sisters from Bombay, so she could make some intelligent comments. This put them at once on a good footing. But actually they were on that already: the moment she had entered the kitchen, his eyes had lit up with an expression that was familiar to her. Yes, against all expectations, the Master was the type who liked her, and in a very healthy straightforward way like a man making no bones about being attracted to a woman. She always felt relaxed with that sort of person. They spoke about spices, and she explained how she knew about them, thereby also explaining that she was partly Indian, which he liked. He let her taste his concoction, and when she boldly suggested an improvement, he followed it. And all this before he even knew who she was or what she wanted. When finally she got around to telling him—how she wanted to take Renata away to have her baby at home—he was very receptive to the idea and said it would give him the opportunity to visit Baby in New York and get to know her better. It was one of many gallant things he said to her that afternoon.

Carl accompanied Baby and Renata back to New York and moved into the apartment with them. He took it for granted that he belonged to their household, though he seemed to have little personal interest in the members of it—that is, Baby, Kavi, and even Renata herself. But he was always polite, serene, and grateful for whatever was given to him. When Baby suggested that it might be a good idea for him and Renata to get married before the baby was born, he was perfectly agreeable. It was Renata who was reluctant, not so much on any principle but as though she considered it a superfluous act, or simply a waste of time. This summed up her whole attitude to Carl: he was there, all right, but she did not feel she needed to do any more about him. That suited him quite well. While she remained in the same bedroom she had had as a child, he slept on a sofa in the living room. With his own set of keys to the front door of the house and of the apartment, he was free to come in as late as he wanted without disturbing anyone. Sometimes he didn't return until the early hours of the morning, and when they got up, they found him fast asleep and fully dressed on his sofa. There was the same tranquil smile on his face when he was asleep as when he was awake. He made no secret of how he spent his days and nights—was in fact eager to tell them: how he walked around the streets and parks, sitting down when he was tired and talking to people. He was delighted with the city, which was everything he had hoped for. Although so charged with dynamic, even demonic energy, the streets were also full of people who had somehow escaped or evaded the currents of activity and were at leisure to listen to Carl read from his manuscript. Some of these were tourists, taking in the sights of which they took him to be one; there were a lot of very old people who sat half dozing in the sun; there were those who had nowhere to live and spent their long days squatting in doorways; there were others like himself with ideas to expound, to argue and discuss on some bench in a dusty square or on a street island between two streams of opposing traffic roaring by; still others brooded alone about the state of the world, and some of these hatched plots of how to draw attention to it by killing some famous person like the President. At night he went way downtown where there were many young people trailing around the streets, gazing into store windows displaying antique clothing, or eating a midnight meal in an open-air restaurant where Carl could join them. Or he himself would sit at a corner table inside a café, writing in his manuscript; sooner or later there would be someone interested to know what he was writing about and also to pay for his cup of coffee, if he happened to have spent all his pocket money.

Renata meanwhile went her own way, mostly accompanying her grandfather. In recent years Kavi had developed the habit of visiting the Indian restaurants that had begun to open here and there around the city. He liked to go for a late lunch and to stay on long after the other customers had departed. Then the waiters put on records of songs from Hindi films. They sat eating their own lunch near Kavi's table, confiding in him their troubles and their hopes—how they were being taken advantage of for their illegal alien status; how they planned to start a restaurant of their own and bring over their families to work in it. Kavi recited his poems, striking a chord in them, for they shared his heartrending nostalgia for a place they didn't really want to go back to. Here Renata too became imbued with India, though she had not encountered it at closer quarters than in this restaurant with the ingrained smell of curries and the Hindi film songs playing. She was so happy here that she accompanied Kavi every day; and every day she grew more pregnant, so that the waiters were very shy with her and did not dare glance higher than her feet.

Perhaps it was because of being steeped in this atmosphere during the last months of her pregnancy that Renata gave birth to a remarkably dusky little boy. Or he may have been a throwback to his Bilimoria ancestry, bypassing the Kopfs and Kellers, the English Howards, and Carl's Protestant German family. Anyway, Henry was definitely dark, born with a lot of black hair —when he finally did get himself born, and that took a long time. Renata's pains started in the night, and Baby and Kavi took her to the hospital. When Carl got home, he went to sleep immediately and failed to notice that everyone was missing till he woke up at noon. He didn't worry about it but went out again and again came home very late and dropped off into his peaceful sleep. And still Henry hadn't been born and Renata begged to be allowed to die. The doctor had theories about natural birth, which Renata shared and in a more detached mood would have defended fanatically; but at last, on Baby's insistence, a cesarean was performed, and so Henry was delivered and was received by his delighted grandmother Baby and great-grandfather Kavi. Carl too was delighted when they returned and woke him up—it was about ten in the morning—though being very tired he fell asleep again at once, the smile on his lips more joyfully serene than ever.

This remained Carl's attitude to Henry for some time—a happy acceptance of his existence, with no further strings attached. Indeed, nothing was expected of him; he was given no share in his son's existence except the accidental one of procreation. Renata continued to refuse to be married to him and registered Henry under her own surname; he also carried the names of his great-grandfather and his grandfather: Henry Hormusji Graeme Howard. So Carl didn't come into it at all except that he remained part of the household. Henry knew that the man sleeping on the living-room sofa was his father, but this word meant little to him; the important paternal relationship for him was with his great-grandfather. Kavi was in his element— another child to bring up, his third generation. Refined by age down to his essence, he was very thin, his pale ivory skin stretched to transparency; this gave him an appearance of frailty, though he remained as spry as ever. His mind was crystal clear, and so was his spirit—cleansed of every mote and speck of dust, leaving only the pure light of wisdom and goodness to shine on Henry's childhood.

Besides a great-grandfather, Henry also had a grandfather, and Graeme took this role as surprisingly seriously as he had that of Renata's father. Prior to retirement, he was now permanently posted at the Foreign Office in London and often managed to come to New York. Then he did the same as before with Renata —took a hotel room and spent the day entertaining Henry. But Henry was a very different proposition from his mother. Whereas Renata had been passive and unresponsive, Henry was interested in everything, and wanting more of it. Graeme couldn't take him to enough places or read him enough books: always Henry's bright eyes were on him, asking is that all? Then what? And Graeme would laugh and try harder. Graeme thought Henry was completely English; secretly he saw him as he himself had been in his youth when he had read metaphysical poetry and won a Distinguished Service medal. He accepted his grandson's dark complexion and slightly slanting eyes as disguising an English spirit; it was less confusing than with Renata, who looked so English and wasn't.

"Aren't you going to kiss me?" Henry demanded, looking up —far up—at Graeme when it was time to say goodbye. Graeme looked back at him, amused, pleased: yes he wanted to kiss him, even to lift him and press him against his heart, beating with such unwonted emotion. But there was Baby, his ex-wife, to whom he had delivered Henry home again prior to his own departure.

Baby was watching him derisively as if she knew—well, probably she did, damn her—how his feelings battled with his reticence. So all Graeme did was to bend down from his great height and swiftly touch his lips to the boy's hair; but before he could straighten up again, Henry's arms were around his neck and Henry's kisses all over his face. Graeme felt himself go very red—he liked to think from the effort of bending down and Henry's arms choking him; but Baby was laughing outrageously, and then she loosened Henry's arms and said, "Now it's Grandma's turn"—and at once Henry jumped up to wind his legs around her waist.

It was to be expected that Baby would drown her grandson in love, as she had done with her daughter. Sometimes they were like lovers. When Henry came to his grandmother's bed in the mornings, she pretended to be asleep so that he could wake her up, sprinkling water on her face till she burst out laughing, revealing herself to be wide awake, and he tickled her in revenge. He helped her dress, seriously advising her on her outfits, and she pretended to listen though she had already made her own decision, for this was an area where Baby imperiously ruled for herself. She often took him with her to her lunches, teas, and other engagements, and he had learned prettily to prattle, which she enjoyed enormously and the other guests pretended to, though secretly wishing he would disappear. She took him to all the usual children's entertainments and scanned the columns for new ones, so that no circus, marionette show, magician, or Christmas spectacular was unvisited by them—Graeme, himself in search of amusement for his grandson, often found himself perplexed, since Henry had already seen everything. Baby also took him to shows that she herself wanted to attend, even when they were quite unsuitable for his age; but he enjoyed them and was ready with comments, which were often amusingly inappropriate. Altogether he had become her favorite escort, a role that he took seriously, opening doors, ushering her into theater seats, even learning to light her cigarettes with a grown-up flick of her little golden lighter.

What was unexpected was Henry's relationship to his mother, or rather, hers to him. All through her pregnancy her attitude had been one of such detachment that it could be construed as indifference. But as soon as he was born—perhaps it was due to all she had suffered in the process—she became obsessed with him. She read every available book on infants and the stages of their development, and if he deviated in the slightest—didn't sit up early enough or failed to crawl—she was certain that something was wrong and dragged him off to specialists. Having read about the best sleeping position for babies, she would get up six times in one night to rearrange him into it, ignoring his cries of rage and discomfort; she stuffed food into him that he was not ready to digest; to strengthen his ankles, she made him wear boots that hurt him; and as soon as summer turned into fall, he was in a cap with earflaps and stayed in it far into the following spring. She was too anxious about him ever to enjoy him; but then, enjoyment did not enter her conception of this relationship, which had grown—ingrown—into the depths of her being. And he responded in kind: he loved Baby and Kavi, even

Graeme, freely and easily and had a good time with them; he never had a good time with Renata, and his love for her was almost painful. If she went out on her own, he was furious even though he didn't miss her, and when she returned, he would attack her, kicking her shins while she tried to defend and justify herself. He suffered because he couldn't be proud of her. She wore no pretty clothes like his grandmother, nor smelled as nice. Moreover, she didn't seem to know anything and had only the vaguest answers to his questions. Unlike other children's mothers, who had husbands or boyfriends, she trailed around alone, looking forlorn and odd. She *was* odd, and it enraged him. He would watch her, wonder about her, his eyes following her as she moved around a room, lost in her own thoughts; when she became conscious of his stare, she would look back at him, startled, wondering in her turn about him and the hostility of the gaze he turned on her.

As if all these near and dear ones were not enough for Henry, there was also the extraordinary interest shown in him from London by his great-grandmother Elsa and his great-great-aunt Cynthia. But to explain this, it is necessary to go back to an occurrence at the time when Henry was born—this birth taking place, by a coincidence too marked to be ignored, on the same day, perhaps at the same hour, as the Master's departure. The Master had been in his usual state of perfect health, so the event had been unexpected to everyone except himself, who had predicted it. The last supper around his marble-topped dining table had been a specially festive one. Cynthia and Elsa had been there of course, crammed in tightly with all the others—the Master alone spread himself in an armchair, while for the rest there was only room for a narrow upright seat. That was one of the charms of being around him: however old they were, in his presence each became a disciple, a young aspirant, a fledgling soul. It was one more reason why they were all so keen to do work for him, and the more menial it was the more eagerly they threw themselves into it. Even Cynthia, who was almost as old as he was, forgot her gout and gladly enrolled herself as his kitchen maid—

or one of them, for cleaning up after the Master was a job for a team. He was an elaborate cook and an astonishingly fast one, reaching up here and there in all directions for only he knew what spices and ingredients; but when he had finished, every pot and pan in his pantry had been used, the kitchen floor was ankle-deep in refuse, and the walls were splattered with grease. But afterward the mood around the table was excited, expectant, for everyone knew some wonderful fare was to be offered to body and soul.

So it had been on the evening of the last supper—indeed, expectations ran even higher than usual, the Master having chosen, for some unknown reason, to appear in full evening dress: frock coat, cravat with enormous diamond pin, and patent leather pumps. He had grown exceedingly stout in this last year, and his clothes were so tight that he was forced to sit up straight and straitened instead of, as usual, half sprawled across the table. As the evening progressed and great quantities of fiery food and liquor were consumed, his face swelled out above his collar and grew red as a demon's; a weaker man might have been tempted to undo his top shirt stud, but the Master continued to bulge and sweat in full regalia, pouring glass after glass down his constricted throat.

Everyone awaited the theme to be expounded over the table—for he always had one, and often it was connected to a particular person present there. This was a privilege, though usually a painful one, for compliments had no place in the Master's training program. So it was with both pride and apprehension that Elsa heard her name pronounced. She knew nothing good could be said of her: why else was she here, at his table, under his tutelage—she who, after all his years of work on her, was still as unformed, as unworthy as the day she had first come to him.

"So you're going to be a great-grandmother," he said to her. It made her gasp, it was so incredible: she, Elsa Kopf, as wild and unruly under her crop of white hair as she had been as a flaming redhead—and Cynthia next to her giggled and surreptitiously kicked her ankle under the table.

"A great-grandmother," the Master repeated, and he too was smiling. "And what are you in reality? A chick that hasn't even managed to peck itself out of its shell." Elsa dropped her eyes, she squirmed, yet she was joyful too, for she felt like a chick, young and downy in his masterful hands.

He was tender with her. This was by no means his usual method—at this point his mood might very well have darkened, his smile giving way to his terrible frown; he would begin to draw up his indictment, which was of course completely unanswerable, even if anyone had dared to answer. But today it was not her he blamed, it was himself—"Yes because I haven't done enough for you. I've failed. I've failed all of you, since no one, no, not a single one"—here he glanced around the table and they all had to drop their eyes as his rested on them: his slanting, pewter-colored eyes, now popping awesomely because of his tight collar—"not a single miserable one of you has managed to hatch a soul."

They were silent. He continued, "And now what's going to happen to you? What will become of you? Who will take care of you now, who will carry you in his arms, feed you with whatever pitiful pap you're able to digest? Is there anyone willing to pick up the burden that I'm at last getting off my back? Has he come yet? Is he born?"

What was he telling them? That he was leaving them—but also that he was leaving them to one who was about to be born? They had no time to speculate. Sunk in his regret for them, the Master tried to comfort himself with the succulent meat dish he had prepared. He put a morsel in his mouth—and next moment the earth itself seemed to burst asunder: he spluttered frantically, flailed his arms so that glasses of red wine spilled in all directions; everyone jumped to their feet in horror at the terrible retching sound he made to dislodge the piece of meat stuck in his throat. They surrounded him, fumbled to unbutton him, but the eruption continued and now he clutched in his agony at the tablecloth, bringing all the plates, dishes, glasses, bottles, and decanters crashing down with him. Some guests lifted him, some carried him, while others did their best to strip off his tight-fitting clothes; but still he heaved and retched and swelled till, unable to explode, he imploded. By the time they laid him on his bed, six people carrying him, the storehouse of treasures within his vast cranium, which held God only knew what secrets of what worlds, was shut up forever.

Four

THIS EVENT took place simultaneously in time with Renata's anguished labor. When two days later news of Henry's birth reached Elsa and Cynthia, they were too stricken and too preoccupied to appreciate its significance. Since the Master had died in London, his funeral was their responsibility, as well as making arrangements for the members of other groups who arrived from all over the world to attend it. The Master had left no specific instructions about who was to take even temporary charge of his organization. It turned out to be the survival of the fittest, for by this time most of the principal members were exceedingly old, and in fact two of them collapsed and died as a result of the strain of traveling to the funeral, the emotion of the funeral itself, and the dissension that broke out immediately afterward. At the end of a few weeks, most of them were glad to get back home, leaving Elsa and Cynthia in possession of the field in England. They gave up the Master's flat and carried his effects to their own house in Hampstead. By far the most important of these were his personal papers. Although there had been publications about him and his work written by others, he himself had not published anything during his lifetime. His teaching was direct—person to person, heart straight into heart—in accordance with the ancient methods on which it was based. However, there were always people taking down his sayings, and he himself had dictated more than one version of what was rumored to be a spiritual autobiography, a guide for the perplexed.

Five years passed, which Elsa and Cynthia spent reading, sorting, and collating the mass of material that had accumulated in several black trunks with brass nails hammered around the edges. It was wonderful work for them, seated by their fire in the study, with the curtains open to catch the last glimmer of light fading over the heath, and Katie bringing in their tea. But they realized it was work for more than a single lifetime, let alone one already as far advanced as theirs. Other hands would have to take up when theirs left off: only where were those other hands? As the years passed, distressing news reached them from all quarters of the Master's groups breaking up with internal rivalries, deaths, or people just getting too old. Yet the Master's work could not die any more than a tree when its leaves drop off in the course of the seasons. The sap must rise again, buds sprout on the branches. As with all living things, there would be a new birth; and it was then they remembered the last words the Master had uttered: "Has he come yet? Is he born?"

At first they did not dare speak of their surmise, not even to each other. Yet it must have dawned on them about the same time because when the moment came, each of them was ready for it. This was at their usual teatime, when Katie came in with the tray and the afternoon mail, and they had to clear a space among the surrounding mass of the Master's papers. They were glad to pause. Elsa poured and stirred and handed Cynthia her cup; Cynthia, nearer the fire, held out their crumpets on a toasting fork, and when they were ready, Elsa buttered them. The cushioned room, glowing with the fire and little reading lamps, filled swiftly with the aroma of butter melting on hot bread, their Earl Grey tea, their cigarettes. It was not yet time to draw the curtains, for although it was dark inside, a deep apricot light still glowed in a portion of the sky, with the crowns of the trees etched against it, each leaf in detail.

"A letter from what's-her-name—Baby," said Elsa, pronouncing the name with her usual irritation. She extracted the envelope from the rest of the mail without enthusiasm, she didn't expect much from her daughter's letters, they were too rambling and trivial for her taste. So it proved today—Baby babbled on about the weather, Renata had a cold, Kavi had baked a cake, and darling Henry insisted on wearing a bandage around his head, pretending to be a wounded soldier: and here are some photos of him, isn't he too gorgeous not to eat? Elsa picked up the photos—her interest in a five-year-old was limited, even if he was her great-grandson; she looked, then looked again closer under the reading lamp, then handed them to Cynthia. Cynthia, after the first cursory glance, had the same reaction; and soon they were studying the photos together, holding them under the lamp. They said nothing—but at this moment the same thought began to stir in each of those two white heads, as close together now under the lamplight as they had been through a lifetime of living and loving.

The photo they pored over most intently was a close-up of Henry's face. What was remarkable about it was the way he did *not* look: that is, not in the least like his pale, abstracted parents, Carl and Renata. Henry was a dark and shrewd little boy—of course there were the Indian ancestors, yet it wasn't exactly Indian that he appeared, but something else, difficult to define. The most perplexing of all were the eyes, which were partly hooded, partly slanted—Elsa and Cynthia exchanged glances but no words. They put the photos back in the envelope but soon had them out again, and again their heads were bent over them under the lamp. By now it was quite dark outside, but they were too preoccupied to draw the curtains; and any belated passerby on the heath might have been startled by the sight of them framed within their lighted window, like two sibyls hunched over some mysterious brew to distill its potent emanations.

During these years Graeme had got into the habit of visiting them once a week. His mother had died in the course of his last posting, so Cynthia and Elsa were his only close relatives in England. He was very familiar with their household, having spent weeks of his vacation with them as a schoolboy. Of course at that time they had still been in their prime, and although entirely committed to the Master's program, they had led a very worldly life, with numerous entertainments to lighten their serious pursuits. Graeme remembered one particular night—it was New Year's Eve, and he must have been about ten—when they had come to show themselves off to him; both were in costume, in tails and top hats, gardenias in their buttonholes, carrying canes with silver knobs. Cynthia had done a little dance routine to amuse him, which ended with her sticking out her seat, huge in striped pants, coquettishly in his direction. Applause and laughter followed. But when they came home many hours later they had had a fight and screamed at each other on the stairs. Graeme, who was supposed to be asleep but wasn't, having sat up to drink a toast at midnight with Katie the cook, crept out to look at them over the banisters: far from the immaculate swells to whom he had said goodbye, they had returned looking like two crumpled drunks. Elsa snatched off Cynthia's top hat, which sat askew over one ear, and threw it down the stairs. Cynthia plucked Elsa's gardenia and stamped on it. Graeme couldn't see who struck the first blow, but they began to slap each other's faces in quick returns like a tennis match. Their nephew watched this with interest, which dissipated when instead of slapping they were suddenly kissing each other mouth to mouth (this would have been fascinating to him if it had been a man and a woman—sex!—but now it was just soppy). Their arms wound around each other, their mouths still glued together, they began to walk up the stairs, and at their approach Graeme scurried off to bed. They ascended to Cynthia's bedroom past various portraits of the Master—there were so many of them all over the house that his eyes always seemed to be following them, and usually in benign if sardonic consent to whatever they were doing.

Now, fifty years later and at the end of his career, Graeme came every Sunday for a traditional roast beef lunch, then stayed on for tea and supper. He was comfortable with them, and they pampered him. His own bachelor flat in central London was bleak and lonely—as was his whole existence; having mostly lived abroad, he had few friends and was without standing in his office where everyone, including himself, counted the days till his retirement. A sardonic loner, a traveler to unknown destinations, Graeme had come home to an appreciation of having a family. It was the main topic of conversation between him and Elsa and Cynthia—their Sunday afternoons were not unlike those at Grandma Dorothy's, when Kopfs and Kellers had exchanged information about each other. There was no one in all the world except Elsa and Cynthia who could understand that peculiar expression of amused exasperation Graeme had when he spoke of his ex-wife Baby ("Baby!" he exclaimed at the very name, and Elsa exclaimed with him). Or when he spoke of Renata, frowning here too but with exaggerated exasperation, ashamed of his own unrequited love.

"And Henry?" they asked him, leaning forward eagerly, that time after they had seen the photographs.

"Oh yes," said Graeme coolly, suppressing the pleasure that suffused him. "Bright little chap."

"Who d'you think he takes after?" they asked, and they too spoke as casually as they could manage.

"No one, I'd say. No one that I know of. He's his own man. Sui generis," he said, unable not to smile at the absolute uniqueness of his grandson.

"You don't think he looks the least little bit like the Lily?"

"The Lily? . . . Oh you mean Kavi. Well it's true Henry's dark, but that too in his own way. Incidentally, the Lily is a misnomer because Kavi does quite his share of spinning and toiling in that extraordinary household."

Following a longish pause, taken up with careful pouring of after-lunch demitasses—"And a chocolate mint, Graeme dear, we know you love them . . . À propos 'extraordinary household,' would you say it was altogether the right atmosphere for little Henry to grow up in? If one thinks only of what is best for the child?"

"Oh don't worry about Henry: he has them all where he wants them," smiled Henry's grandfather.

Another long pause was here in order, if only to suppress signs of excitement. "Does the child have a strong will?"

"I don't know too much about children," said Graeme. "But he certainly knows what he wants and gets it."

"Ah." Cynthia and Elsa leaned back in their chairs. After a while they were confident enough to ask a more leading question: "Would you say he showed signs of being a natural leader?"

"A Master?" It was Elsa, always the more headlong of the two, who went this far.

It was a mistake: Graeme grew more guarded; Graeme drew back. Lulled by the domesticity of their household, he had forgotten the eccentricity of their preoccupations. Not that he in the least held these against them; he felt that people were perfectly entitled to their own madness—as long as they didn't try to involve him, or, by extension, his grandson.

"For heaven's sake," laughed Graeme. "He's five years old and has plenty to contend with. Imagine what it's like to have Renata for a mother—I know what it's like to have her for a daughter—" He frowned, he laughed. "Her latest fad is one of those new cameras—Polaroid? whatever—with which she stalks around the house in search of someone to photograph, and her most frequent victim is poor Henry."

"Did she take these?" They drew out the photographs, ever at hand.

Graeme flicked through them, and he too stopped at the close-up and gazed back into Henry's foreign eyes.

They watched him, quite desperate for some comment that would give them further elucidation. Finally Cynthia said, "He doesn't seem to take very much after his father."

"His father?" Graeme looked up in surprise; like everyone else, he was in the habit of forgetting that Henry had a father.

"Yes. What's-his-name. The German boy." Then Cynthia was daring: "He *is* the father, isn't he?" she asked.

Graeme had lit his post-prandial cigar; it made him look very comfortable. Examining its glowing tip—"We have Renata's word for it and no reason whatsoever to doubt it."

"Of course not," said Cynthia and Elsa.

Several more years passed. Cynthia and Elsa had grown immensely old, as had the other members of the Master's groups. With no one energetic enough to carry on the practical work, the centers folded one by one, and their properties were repossessed by the bank or dissipated in litigation. If it had not been for Cynthia and Elsa, the Master and all his works might have been extinguished; but fortunately they were there to keep it glowingly alive. They continued to work day after day on his papers, and the more they read, the more excited they grew—rejuvenated too, at least in their minds. But in other ways they were beginning to be conscious of their age, especially Cynthia, who was so gout-ridden that she could hardly move, and also very heavy, for she continued to love her food. It drove Elsa wild to see her so immobilized when her mind was still bright and frisky—as it had to be in order to catch, hold on to, and interpret the Master's words. This was their work, of the utmost urgency, and there were only the two of them left to do it. "Get off your fat rump!" Elsa would yell at Cynthia, tugging at her from one side with Katie, almost as old as they, heaving from the other, till they got her to her feet where she stood swaying on her stick, panting with the effort, shaking all over with laughter, for Elsa was still yelling at her to get going, get moving, get yourself in shape, you silly bitch! Elsa put all her strength into this—for the Master's sake, and for her own, for what would she do, Elsa thought with desperation, if Cynthia were no longer there beside her. And so she spurred her on, insisting that their days must continue as they always had done. The walks over the heath were replaced by motor drives, and a major task was to get Cynthia in and out of the little car that Elsa still drove with reckless speed; and when this was achieved, Elsa hugged Cynthia wedged in beside her, almost crushing her with her affection, making Cynthia wheeze and laugh.

"But at my back I always hear/Time's wingèd chariot hurrying near"—it had become Graeme's habit to murmur these lines or others like them during any lull in conversation; or muttering to himself as he strolled in the street with his hat and rolled umbrella, or stood on the escalator taking him deep into the bowels of the Underground. He continued to travel to New York at least twice a year and to report on these visits at his Sunday lunches in Hampstead. Photographs of Henry continued to be scrutinized through different kinds of spectacles helped out by magnifying glasses. But how long it took for a little boy to grow up—so much longer than for an old woman to grow older. As they continued their daily study of the Master's papers, their impatience mounted: it could not be that all this would be lost and no one left to disseminate it. They felt the Master's words, still warm with his wisdom, crying out to be uttered again by a living mouth. They could wait no longer—Cynthia was about to turn ninety! It was still possible to get her into the car as far as Harrods, but certainly impossible, however willing her spirit, to get her as far as New York. The next time Graeme returned from one of his visits there and delivered his report over Sunday lunch, they asked him outright: would it not be a good idea to acquaint little Henry, who was after all partly English, with the land of some of his forefathers?

They had chosen a good moment—or perhaps (who knows) it had been chosen for them by a force of which they were only the conduit—for it so happened that Graeme's thoughts were tending in the same direction. He had not been as pleased as usual with his grandson's progress. Henry had again left his school, for the second time by his own decision (one school had voluntarily declined the honor of teaching him further). He said he wasn't learning anything there he couldn't learn better by himself. His father, Carl, approved—the natural absorption of knowledge by children was (as far as anyone could make out) part of his thesis on "Education as Elevation"; but he was the first to regret it, for it meant the end of his peaceful slumbers till noon on the living-room sofa. Henry was up early and saw to it that everyone else was too. He and his great-grandfather Kavi fed whatever hungry animals, birds or cats, they could find around their high-rental neighborhood. While his grandmother Baby sat at her dressing table taking off her night lotion in order to apply her day lotion, he spoke to her about various subjects on which he felt she should be informed ("No really, darling, isn't that fantastic—do you prefer this blush on me with my hair or ivory, are you sure, Henry? You're not trying to make me look a fright?"). He addressed mathematical conundrums to the sleeping figure on the couch, and when Carl responded by hiding his head under the covers, Henry pulled them off him. There were frequent mornings where Henry ran through the apartment dragging away the bedclothes, while Carl, his shirttails flapping around his bare legs, ran behind him in protest, and when he caught up with him, they fought like two children—Carl always won, but only because he was bigger.

It was assumed by everyone, including the household help and Henry himself, that he was the most intelligent and indeed generally superior person among them. Graeme shared this opinion: he found his grandson to be an interesting mixture of the precocious, volatile, oriental child that he was in appearance and the stubborn, strong-willed, sturdy English boy he was not. His home environment developed the former aspect: Henry knew everything better than everyone else, and he was completely autonomous, eating what he liked when he liked, which was never at regular mealtimes, and going to bed only when he was exhausted, usually around midnight. Graeme felt it was time to develop his grandson's alternate aspect. Henry was nearing the age when he could be admitted to one of the great English schools—Graeme himself had been at Rugby, as had his grandfather, his father, and many uncles and cousins. The problem was how to extricate Henry out of his adoring household. The only one willing to let him go would be his father; as for the others, Graeme did not feel he could even mention it to them. He realized that his best approach was through Henry himself—and in such a way that Henry would appear to have had the idea on his own. The boy was just young enough and Graeme still sufficiently the diplomat—sufficiently, anyway, Graeme thought sardonically to himself, to get around a twelve-year-old grandson

—for this ploy to work. Henry came to the conclusion that an English school might be an interesting experiment to try out at this stage of his career; and since the decision was his own, it was of course final. Baby and Renata were beside themselves.

Renata said, "What if I should die and you ten thousand miles away?"

"Three thousand four hundred and fifty-eight," this boy corrected her.

So it was that Elsa and Cynthia got their wish. Henry came to London and moved into the house in Hampstead with them, into the flowered bedroom on the third floor where Renata had slept and where, in fact, he had been conceived. He was everything that his great-great-aunt and great-grandmother had hoped for. He was also out to please and treated them to the bright chatter and gallant manner he knew to be suitable to their age group. They could not suppress their delight in him and kept exchanging glances, which he caught, so that he heightened his efforts, almost as pleased with them as they with him. He did not neglect Katie, still cooking in her basement kitchen, and devoted some of his time to her entertainment and instruction. Whereas in New York he had kept his own hours, here he fitted right into the routine of the house and was at the table for all three meals, seating himself after drawing out the ladies' chairs, and complimenting Katie with exclamations of "Katie, you've done it again. De-*li*-cious!" He also spent many hours in the study while they worked on the Master's papers; sunk deep in an armchair so that only his legs in knee socks stuck out, he was engrossed in a book, quiet as a mouse and apparently oblivious of how they glanced at and whispered about him, almost as though the work they were engaged on had reference to him. And indeed, in those hours they very often came close to what they themselves called "spilling the beans." They managed to restrain themselves before him, but at night they couldn't sleep for excitement, and hardly had they retired to their respective bedrooms when Elsa would emerge again to sit on Cynthia's bed, talking and planning for hours. Henry could hear their voices coming up through the floorboards, though too deep in his own reading to let himself be disturbed. His reading was rather like himself: it was still partly childish— there were many English children's classics in the house, some of them original editions dating from Cynthia's childhood—partly adolescent, with adventure stories set on various planets; and he was also on his first reading of *War and Peace* and *Crime and Punishment,* swallowing everything with the same indiscriminate appetite. He lay on his side, propped on his elbow, luxuriating in these hours when everyone left him alone—unlike in New York where his mother or grandmother kept coming in, with nothing more interesting to say than how late it was and that he was ruining his eyes.

The only fly in the ointment was Graeme. Besides joining them for Sunday lunch, he also turned up for supper several times a week, unable to keep away from his grandson. His presence upset the prevailing harmony, for he kept insisting that Henry was here not to enjoy life in Hampstead but to go to school. He ignored the superior smiles this evoked from Henry himself and the women of the household, all of whom knew how far Henry was beyond anything any school could teach him. But Graeme persisted. He was willing to concede to them that Henry was too precious—in both senses of the word—to be entered at Rugby or any other public school; but he had begun to research some of the smaller, more progressive boarding schools and brought along prospectuses for them to study. They put off the day: they said there was still so much for him to see and learn in London; the weather was too cold; let it be spring and they would motor down to inspect some of Graeme's suggestions. Graeme said all right, they could have the winter, but after that—yes, yes, they cried, of course Henry would go to school! Relieved at the reprieve, they couldn't wait to get Graeme out of the house and only just kept from sticking out their tongues at his retreating back before returning to their lovely time together within their cozy home.

But it was as if a term had been set to their happiness and they would have to make the most of this one winter. Cynthia and Elsa, long since deprived of their own strolls over the heath, felt that Henry needed fresh air, and bundling him up in several layers, they sent him out with exact instructions where to walk. This was always within sight of the house, for who knew what dangers lurked for an innocent child among those rambling paths and behind the brambled bushes; but it was also for their own benefit, so that they could watch him from the house while he walked up and down, his gloved hands in his pockets, his head under his cap sunk into the scarf they had wound around him. They nodded encouragement from their window, for he looked a miserable figure. He *was* miserable—Henry preferred Nature in print, or in paintings in a gallery. And it was cold and unlovely out here, with the winter wind sweeping unimpeded over the bare earth and through the black branches of trees stripped of leaves and birds, and over the sky which looked like frozen water. He kept glancing piteously to where he could see them standing in their window; he waited for their signal to come indoors, which came earlier every day for they were as eager for his return as he was.

They also looked forward to their daily outings in the little car. Henry took a leading part in heaving and pushing Cynthia into the front seat beside Elsa. Katie waved goodbye from the front garden as they set off with a jolt, caused by Elsa's driving, which was always bad, especially when she was impatient with Cynthia. They took Henry to the same places they had taken his grandfather as a boy, the same round of Madame Tussaud's, the zoo, and the usual museums, always ending up with Henry seated, as Graeme had been, in front of a very tall ice-cream sundae called a Knickerbocker Glory. Henry's favorite destinations were the big London museums where he could leave Elsa and Cynthia seated in one of the picture galleries while he ran off to enjoy himself among sabers and mummies. And it was within the vast Victorian pile of one such museum that Elsa and Cynthia had their most conclusive conversation yet about the future and Henry's role in it. They watched him as he ran off and saw him stop before a marble sculpture in the middle of the next gallery. The sculpture was of a nude Achilles, and Henry looked very tiny as he stood craning his neck in front of it; yet framed by the doorway as within a triumphal arch, there was something in the composition of hero and Henry together that made Cynthia nudge Elsa. "Well," she said, almost teasingly, "are you sure now?" and more teasingly, "Absolutely sure?" Elsa smiled, laying her hand on Cynthia's, and both were silent and deeply satisfied. Whereas Henry had left them to go and view, among other treasures, his favorite exhibit, which was a life-size model of an Indian tiger devouring a British officer, his two companions had chosen to seat themselves in a gallery of restful English pictures. These depicted pastel interiors where women with bobbed hair—not unlike themselves in their youth—sat smoking cigarettes, their crossed legs shining in silk stockings.

" 'Has he come yet?' " Cynthia quoted.

And Elsa capped it with " 'Is he born?' " Yes, they were sure: he had come; he was born.

The single topic now during their midnight sessions was how to hand over the cherished burden the Master had left them to the rightful successor. They were tempted to take the most direct way and open everything up to Henry himself. It was absurd, they agreed, to say he was too young: if one counted in years, yes, but certainly not in maturity of understanding. There were, however, other considerations—trivial ones, like the question of school. It was useless to appeal to Graeme. They tried and found him adamant: Henry had to go to school. Then they ventured further—time was so pressing, so fleeting—further than they should have done with Graeme, who was not born to understand. They began to make allusion to the future role that awaited Henry, even hinted at a prediction to be fulfilled. They saw Graeme's jaw tighten, his eyes became a steely blue: "Isn't it next week," he said, "that you're going to Surrey, to what's-the-name of that school?"

"Springdale, Graeme dear. We are both motoring down with the dear boy, it's all arranged."

"Good," Graeme said. "Let's stick to that, shall we."

They exchanged glances, giving him up as a hopeless case. Each understood that since Graeme could not be relied on, they would have to act on Henry's future alone—from beyond the grave if necessary, so that next day they would be paying a visit to their solicitor. But when they spoke to Graeme, it was only about the excursion to Springdale: *"So* looking forward—it will be a delightful drive, if only the weather is kind to us."

It was a rainy, slippery, ugly day when they drove off to inspect the first of the proposed schools. In other ways too it started badly because, whenever the weather was like this, Cynthia's gout was worse than ever, and it was extremely difficult to get her up and into the car. By the time this effort was completed, everyone's nerves were frazzled. Even Henry, usually of the sunniest temperament, was gloomy; partly of course because of the purpose of their excursion—they all knew it to be utterly futile, there was no point in his going to any school. They were in such a bad mood that Katie was glad to see the last of them; it was too wet to wave goodbye so she hurried back into her kitchen to comfort herself with a cup of tea, glad that *she* wasn't crammed in that little car with them and all their bad temper.

This did not improve as they drove through London and got stuck in midweek traffic jams. Cynthia and Elsa were beginning to snap at each other, and by the time the outer suburbs had been reached, they were no longer on speaking terms. The last London Underground station was left behind, and now they were out in what passed as open country—very flat around here, mostly with small factories, interspersed with rows of suburban villas and occasionally some brindled cows in a green field. Not that much was visible through the shroud of rain that enveloped them and dripped off their windshield wipers sweeping desperately to and fro. Elsa had to keep clearing the glass with a handkerchief, and when Cynthia offered coldly to do it for her, she accepted with an equally cold "If it's no trouble to you."

"None at all."

"Thank you very much."

Henry, desperate with boredom, tried to do the *Times* crossword puzzle—always a frustrating affair for him, since he could never get the English references, and it made him feel stupid to witness the ease with which Cynthia solved them (and Henry hated feeling stupid).

In the front seat, Cynthia and Elsa continued their chilly exchange—"May I trouble you for a match?"

"Certainly, if you can bear to grabble around for it in my handbag."

Henry asked, "What's 'A floral harvest temporally potential'?"

After only a few seconds, Cynthia said, "Rosebuds."

"Why?" Henry said.

Cynthia laughed. " 'Gather ye rosebuds while ye may.' It's obvious."

"How?" Henry said, frowning with frustration.

Cynthia shrugged, smiled slightly, suggesting it was too easy even to explain. That made Elsa mad and she shouted, "Yes, how!" ready for a row, which Cynthia, as bored as everyone else, was glad to give her.

"My dear," she told Elsa, "use your brains or whatever you have."

"Oh yes. Of course. Only you have them. English brains. Crossword brains."

"What's 'He laughingly gives you advice'?" Henry tried to divert them.

"Don't," Elsa advised him. "It's an utter waste of time and effort."

"Hardly *effort,* for a halfway intelligent person," sneered Cynthia. To Henry she said, "Samuel Smiles, dear."

"No halfway intelligent person would waste a moment of their time on such rubbish. Give it to me, darling," Elsa said to Henry, holding out her hand for the paper. "I'd much rather you sat back and had some good thoughts."

Henry willingly handed her the newspaper, but Cynthia was enraged. "How dare you tell the boy what to do or not to do! Give it back to him at once!"

"I certainly shall not! It's going right out the window!" Elsa shouted and began to roll down the glass. Cynthia leaned across to snatch the *Times* away—now upset on her own account because she hadn't read it yet. Henry put his hands over his ears: having witnessed their love fights before, he preferred to absent himself. They continued to struggle in the front seat while the rain and wind poured and rushed through the window Elsa had half opened. Henry kept his ears covered and stared over their heads at the windshield wipers; in spite of their furious activity, they could only part the curtain of rain for seconds at a time. It was during one such second that Henry, looking straight ahead into the windshield, saw the shining breastplate of a removal truck loom up and swim monstrously through the waters toward them; but since his ears were still covered, he didn't hear anything.

Cynthia was killed outright, Elsa died later in the hospital, and Henry had to remain in the hospital, in the county of Surrey, where the accident had occurred, for several months before he could be moved home to New York. There too he remained in various hospitals and clinics—not for months but for years, so that by the time no one could medically do anything more for him, both his childhood and his adolescence were over. Henry was a man, but probably a very different one from what he might have been if there had been no accident. He was badly crippled, and through the years of repeated surgery and lying in contraptions afterward, he did not gain what would probably have been his proper height, so that the upper part of his body appeared overdeveloped in contrast with the rest of him. His head, magnified by a full black beard, looked especially large. This disproportion was a fitting outward sign of his inward condition: too disabled for any youthful physical activities, Henry had had to develop other faculties.

The main principle of the Master's teaching had always been that his students must work on themselves. Henry had had no alternative but to work on himself, first to endure, then to overcome. When he emerged from all his operations and courses of therapy, he was a fully formed personality: fully self-formed, for there had been no more question of schools. Tutors came and went to give him the rudiments of an education; on this he had to build as best he could by himself. The doctors had predicted that he would always have to be in a wheelchair, but Henry was determined not to be. Just as he had gone through various schools as a boy, he now went through therapists, then dispensed with them and trained himself. He was willing to put himself through every kind of effort and anguish, and as a result, he eventually triumphed: although, to anyone unfamiliar with the circumstances, it may not have appeared a triumph, for Henry limped very badly, dragging one hip and leg behind him, so that it was painful to watch him.

It was generally expected by his family that he would do something extraordinary, though no one knew what this might be. His father Carl had hopes that Henry would carry on his work, and with this end in view, he lent him his manuscript to study, "Education as Elevation." But when Henry gave it back, his only question was about the faded, still faintly orange stain on the title page. "It's mango juice," Carl replied, but when Henry asked how it had got there, Carl waved the matter away as too trivial to explain.

It was more than half a century since Elsa had swooped down on the family house to cut it up into apartments, and so far Baby had retained only one of them for herself and her family. Now she took the tenant of the adjoining apartment to court and won her case on the plea that she needed the space for her crippled grandson. She had the partitioning walls knocked down, re-uniting the whole floor the way it had been in the days of the Kopf family. But whereas then it had been two enormous reception rooms with several side rooms, now the same space contained the whole of Baby's apartment as well as the adjoining one, remodeled to accommodate several more bedrooms. The new arrangement was most welcome to Carl. He had never complained about having to sleep on the sofa—on the contrary, he was grateful—but of course it was preferable to have a bedroom of one's own, especially with Henry coming home to live, perhaps again to disrupt his father's morning sleep. As soon as the new rooms were ready, Carl moved himself into one of them—the smallest, which he humbly acknowledged for his own.

By the time Henry came back home, his great-grandfather Kavi had grown so frail that he appeared to be completely whittled away. Unable to go out—his legs were very shaky—he remained mostly sitting on his bed, a tiny, shriveled sage in white muslin. Instead of reciting his verse, he summoned up odd shards and fragments of the past—memories that had formed in the chrysalis of his mind to emerge and fly about on their own. For instance, he spoke of someone called Safiya, who was beautiful beyond imagination, with eyes like velvet pools and hips like strung bows and breasts like ripe mangoes. Also her cousin who treated everyone to spicy chickens and evenings with the singing and dancing girls. But there was one evening in a deserted house, lit only by candlelight—the candle flickered and went out, and then Kavi was in Cynthia's house in Hampstead, reciting poetry in a room where the setting sun shone on red-haired women in short frocks of pleated silk.

These were the last sparks of Kavi's mind that still hovered above his almost nonexistent body. Slowly they too faded as, with his daughter Baby on one side, his granddaughter Renata on the other, and his great-grandson Henry at the foot of his bed, he sank into his final darkness. Renata brought her camera for one last picture of him—it was the only way she had to hold on to anything, to prevent it from dissolving into the vague mist in which she lived. Afterward, however, after Kavi had died and they had cremated him, she destroyed those pictures for they could have been of any dying old man and not of the Kavi they wanted to remember.

Carrying the urn containing his ashes, they took a train up the Hudson and got off at a pretty river town. Here they hired a boat to take them out among all the other painted pleasure boats nimbly darting around. They had brought a tape they had of Kavi himself reciting, and amid "Frail Bark of Life," they scattered his ashes over the river where they seemed to disappear not into the water but into the blaze of light reflected on its surface.

Part Two
Legacy

Five

HENRY NEVER had to worry about earning a living. Before their last fatal ride, Cynthia and Elsa had visited their solicitor in order to change their wills and make Henry their principal heir. It was, Baby commented, as if they had known in advance that they would owe him this compensation. Graeme thought so too, with approval, though it made no provision for him and left him with little more than his pension to live on. He didn't mind, his needs were few, and his only important expense was his trips to New York, which he tried to make at least twice a year, to see his family. He became an expert in cheap transatlantic fares and perched with dignity on a narrow seat among indigent students, still in the correct traveling attire he had worn as a diplomat seated in first class.

Henry came into his money at eighteen, but when he reached the age of twenty-one, he had another important communication forwarded from England by Cynthia and Elsa's solicitor. Enclosed in a plain envelope was a triple-sealed one: Henry opened it, read it, and laughed—surely not the right reaction to a document that came to him from beyond the grave. But anything to do with the Master had always appeared to him somewhat ludicrous, maybe in reaction to the solemnity with which Cynthia and Elsa had surrounded his name. The letter they left Henry had the same note of reverence with regard to the Master—and now, even more ludicrously, this was transferred to Henry himself: for the letter was nothing less than an annunciation—of Henry as the Master's successor, chosen by the Master himself just before he choked on his piece of meat.

Henry did not divulge the contents of the letter to anyone else. But during the next few days he read it several times more: for there was one line that gave him pause, one word rather, and that was where they referred to Henry not only as the successor of the Master but as his son and successor. No doubt they meant it in a spiritual sense, but for Henry it was a reminder of his own strange and hitherto unexplained appearance. He continued to keep the letter to himself, but it had raised some questions that had not troubled him before.

These new reflections were focused on Carl. Henry didn't see much of his father, for at this stage Carl had not yet changed his habits: he was out most of the time, tramping around the city with his manuscript and his head full of ideas he had himself generated in there. When he came home at night, or in the early hours of the morning, he ate whatever food had been saved for him, and if there wasn't any—if it had been thrown out by the help, or inadvertently eaten up by Renata who was as nonchalant about meals as he was—he went to sleep hungry and uncomplaining. Henry began to wait up for him. He studied his father, watching him hunched over the kitchen table, eating so rapidly and hungrily that Henry asked him what he had had all day.

"Nothing"—Carl gestured with his hand—his mouth was full—"no time," he explained when he could, adding, "no money," with a smile to indicate that this didn't matter at all.

"Why didn't you ask for it?" said Henry, for he too regularly provided for his indigent father, who took as naturally from him as from the rest of the family.

Carl shrugged. "Too many more important things to think about. What's the matter? What are you looking at?"

"You," said Henry. "I'm looking at you."

"Oh I didn't know I was so very beautiful," joked Carl in his

Teutonic way. But he was disturbed by his son's eyes fixed on him—those slightly hooded, slightly slanted eyes, so different from his own.

"What are you asking me?" Renata asked Henry.

"If you slept with him."

"With the Master? You must be crazy."

"So Carl really is my father?"

"I guess," said Renata, not with real enthusiasm.

Henry too was perhaps not one hundred percent enthusiastic, but he was ready to accept Carl. He discussed it with his grandmother Baby that evening while they were playing chess.

"That's what Renata always said, so we have to take her word for it; and Carl's. Poor Carl," sighed Baby, out of habit at the mention of his name. She had grown fond of him over the years.

"And there's never been another candidate?"

"As your father? . . . No," she drawled this negative out slowly and not altogether convincingly, so that Henry prompted her:

"But?"

"But," Baby said, quite unexpectedly cornering one of Henry's bishops.

"Now *how* did you do that?" he asked in genuine admiration; whereas he was a meticulous, scientific player, she was careless and intuitive. They had played together since he was seven years old, and she usually won. Every time she made one of her startlingly clever moves, as now, she cackled and leaned over to pat his bearded cheek; it was a hangover from when he was small and she had to comfort him for losing.

"But I'll tell you the truth," she continued. "We all found it very hard to believe her."

"Ah," Henry said. "And did you suspect anyone else? *Was* there anyone else?"

"Not that I knew of," said Baby regretfully. "But of course we didn't know about Carl either. She simply produced him, and then produced *you,*" and again she leaned over the chessboard to pat his cheek, in gratitude for his existence this time.

"Don't let's play anymore," he said.

"Because you're losing."

"No, because what you're telling me is interesting."

"I wish it were," she said. "I used to hear my friends talk about *their* daughters—getting engaged, getting divorced, joining the Peace Corps, whatever. There wasn't anything I could tell about Renata because all she ever did was take these long walks by herself and come in with her hair blown about. I wouldn't have been surprised if she'd said she'd—eh—with the wind and the rain."

"Copulated with?"

Baby began to laugh. "But the Master put it down to immaculate conception."

"The Master?" Henry began to tidy the chess pieces back into the box. "Did you know him?"

"Did I know him!" Baby laughed again and stretched. "If you're really not playing anymore, I'll go to bed." Aware of having thoroughly aroused his curiosity, she got up and went toward the bedroom—slowly, however, even at one point standing still to say "Good night," regarding him teasingly over her shoulder. When he had put the chess set away in its proper place, he followed her into her bedroom. She had just stepped out of her dress and was standing by the mirror, regarding herself in her underclothes. "You might knock," she pouted at him. But he knew she was not too displeased to be seen, for she was still plump and pretty, her legs shapely in black nylon.

"I'm not looking at you," he promised, and sat with his back to her till she got her nightclothes on and came to sit next to him.

"I met him when I went over to get you and Renata." Describing how she had made her way into the Master's flat— "He liked me," she said with girlish satisfaction, bending the nape of her neck to let her grandson undo the clasp of her pearl choker. "And I may say in a very nice way, without being ashamed of it—you'd be surprised, Henry darling, and I hope sincerely you never grow to be like that, but there are many, many men, your grandfather Graeme among them, who absolutely hate any woman who attracts them. Graeme just could not forgive me for that—I mean, he'd do anything to avenge himself for liking me, even though it didn't last more than five minutes."

Steering her away from his grandfather, "What did the Master say to you?" Henry said.

"What did he not say!" Baby replied. At first she smiled, but then she sighed, with nostalgia for something no longer available. "Men who know all about women do really make the best lovers—and presumably the best husbands, though obviously I have no experience of that, having made the mistake—"

"Oh please not Graeme again."

"All right, darling. But I'm sure *you* will make a wonderful husband for some very lucky woman."

Henry gave the rueful smile that was his usual response to any reminder of what couldn't be, and anxious to return to the original topic, he asked, "And did the Master know all about women?"

"Yes he did, darling. He was a very healthy man—I was really surprised, because everyone around him was so the opposite. I mean, the way they treated him and let him treat them, that was so *un*healthy. But I think it's the reason he liked me—one of the reasons—because for me he wasn't the Master or anything ridiculous like that but only—"

"A man to go to bed with?"

"You're talking to your grandmother! And even *if*—it was his idea not mine. I was really surprised: everyone looked on him as this great saint and philosopher, but there was only one thing he was vain about, and that was how many children he had fathered."

Henry was silent for a while; then he asked, "How many?"

"He wouldn't tell me exactly. 'Guess,' he said, and when I couldn't, he held up some fingers. 'Seven, Master?' Then he stuck up some more. 'Nine, ten?' 'I think we need a couple of zeros in there,' he said and he smiled in such a smug way under his mustache. It made me laugh at him but it was really rather sweet."

"Sweet," Henry repeated. "You're the only person I've ever heard use that word about him."

"Well he was to me," Baby said. "And he was very sympathetic when I asked his permission to take Renata home with me. Though you may very well ask: Why *his* permission? What business was my daughter of his?"

"Yes, what?" Henry keenly took up the question. When she shrugged—everything to do with the Master's work had always been beyond her, and only the Master himself had not—"Could it be," Henry suggested, "that Renata *was* his business? And, by natural extension, my unborn self?"

She was speechless—thunderstruck—but only for a moment. Then she laughed. "Get that right out of your head! Renata was definitely not his type—nor he hers, but of course no one has ever been her type. Anyway, there was nothing—nothing—nothing going on between him and Renata."

"Not even once?"

"Not even once. I said get it right out of your head."

But he could not. And it was Renata herself who reopened the subject with him, after brooding about it for several days. She spent these days—as she did increasingly—roaming the streets with her camera. No longer confining herself to her family, she now took pictures of whatever happened to catch her notice outside. When she returned from these expeditions, she did not look as though she had been roving in the city streets but over some heath where she had given free rein to her wild thoughts; so that Henry was reminded of what Baby had said, about copulating with the wind and the rain.

Renata stood in his doorway. She twisted one foot around the ankle of the other; she was always shy with him. She had something to say; it was about the Master. "He was the first person to tell me about you."

"Why don't you come in?" said Henry. She gladly did; he wasn't always so welcoming. He liked to keep his room extremely tidy, and claimed that she only had to enter to throw it into disorder. It was true that she tended to drop hairpins and bits of Kleenex, also to pick up things absentmindedly and put them down in the wrong place.

"What did he tell you?" Henry encouraged her.

"That you were—that I was carrying you."

"You didn't know?"

"How could I?"

"Then how did he know?"

"Oh he was weird." Having said this, she thought she had said a lot.

But Henry wanted more precise information—indeed, all she could tell him about the Master and her meetings with him.

"It's so long ago," she pleaded, "and I didn't know him all that well."

"But well enough for him to tell you about me."

"That's what's so weird." She began her usual business of picking up what was nearest to her—it was a book he was reading, and she fluttered through some pages without taking in a word. He removed it from her and replaced it where she had found it. If he hadn't known her, he would have thought she was hiding or avoiding something; and even knowing her, and that this was her usual manner, he wasn't sure that she wasn't.

"You just have to tell me exactly what happened."

"Nothing *happened.* It's only what he said and did—"

"Did?"

"Yes, that's what's so weird. Eerie."

"You have to tell me."

She squirmed a bit more, twisting her leg around the bracket of the chair. Henry himself was in his wheelchair—he usually was, at home, it allowed him to maneuver himself around more easily. The white metal bed was specially designed with gadgets to save him from getting out of it or to make it easier when he had to. The room had a spare, functional, medical aspect, which he had gotten so used to during his years in hospitals that it had become his habitual ambience. How different it was from the Master's large, soft, luxurious bedroom—which Renata now tried to recall in order to remember what had gone on in it. She described to Henry how the Master had taken her pulse, had gazed into the pupils of her eyes, had slowly let his hand travel over her womb upward to feel her breasts—"And then?" Henry asked.

"Then he told me you were coming."

"And you believed him?"

"Well why not? I didn't know. I always got so mixed up with the dates; I still do. I can't help it."

She looked at him in apology—for her vagueness, which she knew he hated. And indeed he found it particularly trying in the present instance—he thought irritably that the sexual act might have taken place while she was too abstracted to notice. "You're sure that's all he did?" he pressed her.

"Yes I'm sure." She bit her lip. "I think . . . I told you it was weird!" she defended herself as he groaned.

"Weird—weird—what was weird?"

"*He* was." She fell silent and could be seen searching around in her thoughts. Henry tried patiently to await the outcome. "You know, I've thought of something," she said at last and paused again. "And it's come to me before only I never told anyone because I knew they would laugh at me. *You*'ll laugh at me."

"I'll try not to," he said, trying above all to remain patient.

"He had such powers that even with what he did—it would have been enough to—"

"To impregnate you?"

"Or to change what had already happened."

"And you think that's why I look the way I do and not in the least like Carl?"

"I told you it was fantastic. I told you you'd laugh at me."

Henry did not laugh; the matter was too serious for him. Fortunately, around this time Graeme made one of his periodic visits to New York, and Henry decided that he was the one person with whom to share his secret. Taking the fateful letter, he went to visit Graeme in his hotel. This was in a run-down part of town, where people wrapped in indistinguishable cloths lay within the doorway of little shops gone out of business. He found Graeme's hotel midway in a block that had a Salvation

Army hostel, a Chinese laundry, and a watchmaker who also sold secondhand jewelry behind the barricade of a rusty metal grill.

When Henry handed the letter to Graeme to read, he saw his grandfather's jaw tighten. "Yes," said Graeme grimly, "they tried to tell me some such rubbish."

Henry had found him in bed. The room was tiny, with a minute shower cubicle and an enormous TV set; the view was into a well between fire escapes descending from rain-stained brick buildings. But in spite of these dingy surroundings, Graeme preserved his usual aplomb, even when he got out of bed and revealed himself to be trouserless. Since there was no chair, he hospitably swept his hand toward the bed for Henry to sit on. But the bed was too high for Henry to manage by himself, so Graeme had to help him—almost to lift him like a child and adjust his useless leg. When this was done, Graeme's face was very red, only partly with effort, and he had to turn aside from his grandson. But Henry, who had long since accustomed himself to his situation, at once continued to talk about the letter: "But what did they tell you?"

"All I remember is that I cut them short as soon as was decently possible. Or not even decently—the whole thing was so immensely irritating."

"But did they say I was the Master's heir—or his *son* and heir?"

"Preposterous," said Graeme, with more feeling than he usually showed.

After a pause, Henry said, "You prefer Carl then as the candidate?"

"Equally preposterous; and the whole thing taking place on Hampstead Heath—what is one to believe? Not that one would not believe anything of Renata, then as now. I'm surprised actually that she never did become one of the Master's—what's the word?—groupies. The wrong generation, I suppose; he catered to a different type."

"That's what Baby says."

"What does *Baby* say?" Graeme said, at once assuming his ironic tone.

"That Renata was not the Master's type."

"And how would Baby know that, I wonder."

"Because she herself was."

Henry couldn't help laughing at the memory of his grandmother's triumph when she had made this admission—and now also at the sight of his grandfather's expression: startled, *displeased.* He saw that Graeme was about to make some more searching inquiries, but Henry did not wish to pursue the question of whether Baby had slept with the Master. After all, it would not be via his grandmother that the Master might turn out to be his father.

Instead, looking at Graeme perched uncomfortably on the windowsill because there was nowhere else to sit, Henry became suddenly indignant. "Look here, you shouldn't be in this dump. If you don't want to come home, I'll find you another hotel."

"But this one is so delightfully cheap."

"You don't have to think about that," Henry said, growing more heated. "I've got money—actually *your* money, left to me because of some freak notion that I still don't understand."

Graeme laughed and patted Henry's shoulder. He felt absolutely no affront—didn't give his accommodation a thought. But he was sorry for his grandson: he knew that there were trunks full of the Master's papers waiting in London to be shipped to New York, so that Henry could take up the work where Cynthia and Elsa had left off. Graeme felt almost guilty that it was Henry and not himself who, along with the money, had inherited the burden of the Master's mission.

Six

THE MASTER'S PAPERS arrived in the black, brass-studded trunks that Henry remembered from Cynthia and Elsa's house; they also filled several suitcases and cardboard boxes, and some of them were in open bundles tied with string. Henry had them stowed away in the apartment, mostly in his own room where he installed metal shelves from floor to ceiling, cleared his closets of all but his most essential possessions, and accommodated the overflow under his bed. He also made his grandmother empty part of her linen and luggage closets and his mother provide further space in her room. They were thus awash in the Master's teachings.

Henry began his work by arranging the mass of papers into categories. The most important were the Master's own papers, comprising various versions of his autobiography, all unfinished and all contradictory. He had also left notes on his philosophy, either dictated or written out by himself at those café tables all over Europe that had been a favorite location for conducting his affairs. Then there were the official records of the various groups —business and committee meetings, financial transactions—and the publications issued from their presses. In addition, there were heaps of more private papers, private journals that the members had been required to write and submit to the Master: these were considered his property, a record not of their progress but of his, as embodied in the work he did on them. However, they remained mostly in bundles tied with string, none of which appeared ever to have been opened, let alone read by him.

All these papers were written in a variety of languages—predominantly English, Russian, French, and German—so that Henry had to engage an assistant to help him both to sort and to translate them. He hired Vera, whom he had known since they were both children. She was the daughter of Mme. Richter's granddaughter and had often accompanied her mother when she had come to give Henry his piano lessons. Vera had grown up in the refugee households that had been the ambience of the Richter family ever since their transmigration to New York, so that she knew many languages without ever having studied them. Even after Henry's piano lessons ceased, Vera was brought to the house by her mother Irina who came now on social visits and, incidentally, to collect the check that Baby continued to make out to her. Sometimes, when the mother was unwell, Vera had been sent by herself, but she was very awkward and blushed furiously when the envelope with the check was slipped to her—unlike her mother who had learned from Mme. Richter herself how to carry off the business with grace.

Baby enjoyed having Vera in the apartment all day, but Renata was very critical of her. "She's so ordinary," Renata complained.

"But that's what men like," Baby incautiously replied.

"Not *Henry!*"

"No not Henry," Baby quickly agreed, though secretly she thought otherwise.

"He could never, never care for anyone who didn't have very special qualities. And she doesn't."

Baby kept quiet. Oh no, she thought to herself, she's only young, she's only pretty, she only loves to be alive—and these seemed to her the most special qualities in the world.

Vera's days usually ended with her tidying away the papers and consulting Henry about the next day's work. Often friends were waiting for her downstairs to take her out for the evening. Once Vera had a new spring coat, made for her by a friend who was setting up as a designer. Baby admired it and Vera showed it off to her, how it was green one side and rose the other so that it was really two coats. "Oh how charming!" exclaimed Baby, meaning Vera as much as her coat, which was made with great flair out of pieces of very cheap material. Baby came to the front door of her apartment to watch the friends who had come to call for Vera. They exclaimed at the coat and Vera modeled it for them, wrapping it around herself and stalking her legs in proud elegance—only she couldn't keep it up, she started laughing and so did the others and then they all ran out the door and down the street.

Baby turned back into her apartment. Henry's door was open and he was sitting in his wheelchair among the Master's papers, his head bent over a very large book. He looked quiet and self-contained. Baby went in and stood beside him and stroked his hair, which was as dark and curly as his beard. He let her do it for a while before telling her not to. She recognized the book as his copy of Plato—he sometimes read aloud from it to her and she liked it, mainly for the atmosphere among the lively high-minded young men, not unlike Henry himself, all fired up over the immortality of the soul. Yet she also longed for other young companions for him, ones who were actually alive now.

She asked, "Where was Vera going, did she tell you?" He held up a warning finger and turned a page, but she went on disturbing him all the same. "Last night they were in one of those clubs they go to, two of their friends were the cabaret act, the place was packed she said, but it was all their own friends who only ordered the minimum; the management wasn't pleased but they had a lot of fun. They always have fun. She said I should go with them one night, can you imagine?"

"Why don't you?"

"Why don't *you?*"

He kept his finger on the line he was reading while he answered her, "Those clubs are usually in some cellar with a lot of steps to maneuver. And Vera's friends like to hop from club to club, whereas I don't hop; so I'd be a nuisance."

"You a nuisance," she jeered. "Why, Vera would be so happy to have you along, and so proud."

He looked up at her and even took his finger off the line. "Now what makes you think that?" She tousled his hair instead of stroking it, then bent down to kiss it. "Wishful thinking in your case," he went on. "And in Mother's case—the opposite."

Baby stopped kissing, straightened up, was surprised. "Has she said anything?"

"Does she ever say anything? She *looks:* she has taken to standing in the doorway and staring in at us with her Gorgon eyes until I have to tell her to go away. I don't know what Vera thinks; I don't even know if she notices—she carries on as if she didn't, so either she is a bit stupid or quite clever, I'm not sure which." He paused, for it was a question he *had* pondered.

"Did you see her new coat? . . . I'm only asking because she looked so pretty, really adorable. All right, I'm going—" but he had already returned to his reading.

As the work of sorting the Master's papers progressed, they grew into more and more separate heaps, which began to spill all over the apartment. Vera and Henry had to open up Kavi's room, left empty since his death. Vera began to spread papers in there for Henry to work on, and she also stowed away some of the files and bundles for which there was absolutely no space left in Henry's overflowing quarters.

Besides Renata, Carl too began to look in on them working together. There had been a change in Carl: no longer eager to rush out and spread his ideas on the streets of New York, he lingered around at home. Although it was an improvement on years of sleeping on the sofa, his room was too small, even for him, to stay in all day. One afternoon he came to Henry and Vera with a brilliant new plan. He explained to them that the Master's ideas on human evolution needed the basis of Carl's own ideas on education: for how could a human being develop unless provided with the potential for development from earliest childhood? Abstract theories always excited Carl, so when he spoke of them he became impassioned in a way that surprised Vera. Hitherto she had regarded him as one of those shadowy figures—mostly poor relations on sufferance—who had also flitted through the refugee households of her own childhood. But now she saw him transformed, alight with the cool blaze of a higher philosophy. He suggested bringing his manuscript into Kavi's room and working in there side by side with them at integrating its principles with those of the Master. Having put forward this suggestion, he smiled at them—his shy, hopeful smile, which touched Vera; if she had known him better, she might have solicitously brushed the dandruff off his shoulders. She was surprised that Henry made no effort to show enthusiasm for Carl's proposal. Carl did not try to press his case, but said, "Think it over," and quietly shuffled off in the bedroom slippers he wore in the house, partly because his feet were tender, partly so as to move noiselessly and not disturb anyone.

"I don't see why not," Vera urged Henry, and when he remained noncommittal, "I mean—he *is* your father."

"So they tell me," Henry said, uncommitted on this point too.

"You don't know how lucky you are. To have someone willing to own up." She pretended to sound rueful but was actually laughing. Vera's own father had not been identified, and she had never missed him, growing up perfectly happy in an all-female household presided over by the dauntless spirit of Mme. Richter. Whenever Vera caught her mother looking at her tearfully, Vera assured her, "It doesn't matter, Mummy." But Irina was determined to feel guilty over Vera's illegitimacy. She would not reveal anything about the father except that he was Irish (later it turned out that this was all she herself knew about him); if the subject came up—and when she was about twelve Vera couldn't resist some interest in it—Irina became withdrawn; if pressed, tears began to make a still passage from her eyes down to her feet. So Vera had soon decided that the question wasn't worth pursuing.

"Never mind about fathers," said Henry. "What about grand-fathers? *Great*-grandfathers?"

Vera laughed. "Do you really think he was?"

"He said he was," Henry said, also amused. "Or hinted, rather —as with a few hundred others."

They were talking about the Master. It was a theory they had developed, in the course of their research into his papers dating back to his first communal household, which had included the Richter family. There had been several pregnancies during that time, with fathers not quite accounted for. But that was a common occurrence in these makeshift families, then and later, with young boys and frustrated older men: some of these had been ready to assume responsibility, but whether they were or not, the Master was *always* ready and was even displeased by counter-claims. Since no other father had ever stepped forward for Mme. Richter's daughter Sonia (that is, Irina's mother), Vera had no alternative but to acknowledge him as her great-grandfather.

"So do you think we're related?" Henry asked Vera, pleased to imagine himself as linked by blood to this straight young sap-ling.

"How could that be?"

"Well—you only have to look at me," Henry pointed out.

"Yes isn't it odd," said Vera, taking this injunction literally. She studied his dark face with her candid gaze and concluded, "Are you *sure* Carl is your father?"

"If he weren't, Renata would be the first to disclaim him."

She continued to bathe him in the light of her serene scrutiny. "You've got a nice face, no really, I mean it. I like your beard." She put out her hand and touched it.

"Baby is trying to make me shave it off."

"Oh no never!" cried Vera with such personal concern that he felt flattered. "You'd be nothing without it—I don't mean noth-ing, of course I don't—Henry," and soothingly she touched his shoulder. "I mean you wouldn't look what you are which is absolutely different from everyone else."

"Is that good or bad?"

"It's very good," she sincerely assured him. "You're more intelligent than other people—*I* think anyway, though you might ask who am I to judge that, seeing as how I'm not all that wonderfully intelligent myself." She said this placidly, not in the least desiring to be contradicted; and when all the same he did so, she continued, "Anyway, not educated, I haven't even been to college—"

"Neither have I."

"But you for different reasons," she said. "With me, even if Mummy could have afforded to send me, I don't know that I'd have gotten much out of it. I like reading books but not to study them—like, I love the things you give me to read, but if you were to ask me anything about them afterward, I wouldn't know what to say. So I'm really grateful, Henry, that you never do ask when I give them back."

"I'm always scared you didn't read them or didn't like them, that's why I keep quiet."

"Oh no no absolutely not. You have not yet given me anything I haven't read all the way through except *Moby Dick,* and I've really, really liked everything. Thank you," she beamed on him.

Henry thought for a minute, after which he hazarded, "If we were related, I'd be your great-uncle."

"Certainly not! What an idea!"

They worked it out again: if the Master were Vera's great-grandfather via Mme. Richter, and Henry were his son via Renata: except that Renata, the most truthful person in the world, said it was Carl—"So we may not be related," Henry concluded, regretful in one way, but in another not displeased that the field between them should be clear for friendship only.

While Carl, changing years of habit, lingered around at home, it was now Renata who stayed out all day. But whereas Carl had talked to everyone willing to listen, Renata, stalking the streets with her long strides, was solitary, remote, taking in the scene not through her own eyes but through her camera. Sometimes the people she photographed attacked her—mostly verbally, but not always. Once, in the doorway of a shuttered store gone out of business, she clicked her camera at what appeared to be no more than a discarded old coat with a battered hat sunk into it: but suddenly this bundle stirred, heaved, and rose in vengeance, and she found herself grappling for her camera with a big black man, his bloodshot eyes rolling, and white tongue flapping in a grimy grayish face. When he kicked her shins, she kicked his, and after much tugging and pummeling, it was she who won and retained her camera. He sank back into the doorway, head drooping, still muttering obscenities. She stood above him, clutching her camera and indignantly telling him that if he didn't want to have his picture taken, he could have refused politely, like other people. She was willing to discuss the matter but he waved her away, not wanting to be disturbed further inside his pit of misery.

But there were other occasions when people didn't mind passing the time of day with her—maybe because that was literally all she expected from them, seating herself beside them when she was tired, sometimes accepting coffee in a plastic cup. One man, cooking up a little meal for himself on an old bucket under a bridge, offered to share his food with her, and feeling hungry, she accepted. He was a courteous host, also told her his story, how he had come to the city to be an actor but hadn't found work and had suffered some mental trouble. It began raining, so she continued to shelter under the bridge with him while he entertained her with reciting some Shakespearean soliloquies— or tried to but couldn't because, he explained, there were people in New Jersey who had wired some electrical appliance to let off shocks inside his head. Renata wondered how this could be done but did not regard it as impossible. That may have been the reason why people not so willing to talk to others didn't mind doing so to her: nothing that they told her was inconceivable to her, and she also perfectly understood how it was possible to have nowhere to go except in a doorway or under a bridge, and to be alone. Some days she didn't feel like talking to anyone, and when tired of walking, she too found an empty doorway to rest in; she might even have been talking a bit to herself, since there was no one else. One time she was moved on by a policewoman, and another time she had to get up in a hurry because of a gunfight breaking out between two dealers just a couple of doors away from her in front of a liquor store.

The day she had the fight with the homeless man, her shins were full of bruises. She didn't tell anyone, but squatting on her bed, she hitched up her skirt to examine them dispassionately and, equally dispassionately, cursed her assailant. She didn't really blame him—she knew how rage could take possession, it had possessed her too and she had kicked and punched him ferociously, so that probably he was as bruised as she was. She heard someone gasp—quickly she pulled down her skirt and looked up to see Carl. "What happened?" he asked, still gasping.

"Why do you come in without even knocking?"

"You left the door open. Let me see. No, let me."

She tried to stretch her skirt down as far as it would go, but he held her hand where it clutched the hem. "Don't touch me!" she warned.

Again he cried out at what he saw. He got up at once. "Wait! Don't move." She looked defiant but stayed the way she was till he came back with cotton and medication. In some places the skin had broken and he swabbed them with disinfectant—"I'm not hurting you?"

"Of course not," she replied with scorn, though it was stinging horribly.

Patiently, tenderly, he tended her and she watched him, and when he asked again what happened, she told him, though without making much of it. But he looked grave. "You shouldn't," he said.

"Shouldn't what? He attacked *me*, I didn't do anything."

"It can be very dangerous."

"Bullshit. He was just a poor old man who didn't want to have his picture taken."

Carl did not reply but continued to apply balm to her legs. She looked at the top of his head bent solicitously over her shins. His always thin hair had thinned more, revealing his skull, which was very white and looked frail and vulnerable, as if one blow would crush it. Had anybody ever attacked him in the streets where he used to wander so freely, she wondered—was that why he no longer went out? She hid her concern under the usual irritable manner she reserved for him. "Haven't you finished? You're carrying on like you're a frustrated nurse or something."

"Yes," he replied, "I always wanted to be a doctor but the exams were very difficult to pass. And you know I'm not practical. It's a pity. I would have liked to help people very, very much. But it's not in my temperament. Yes now I have finished but tomorrow you must let me do it again."

"I'll see how I feel," she said, pulling down her skirt.

"That is how I became an idealist: because I couldn't do anything practical for humanity, I wanted to work in philosophy. And people used to listen to me: when I went out to talk to them, they saw that yes, this man has an idea, he believes in it, perhaps it is a good idea and we can learn something from him. So they listened. I was like my late father—a teacher, an *Oberlehrer*—but the school where I taught had no roof and no walls, it was the whole world. I don't know if anyone learned anything—when the wind blows, when the birds sing, they do because they have to, they don't ask is anyone learning from us. I was the wind, I was the birds, yes funny isn't it." He smiled for a moment with his small teeth set in pale gums; but next moment he said, "And today what happens: they kick and kill you."

"It was just one old man and anyway I think he was crazy."

"Today people are crazy. Poor people are crazy because they have nothing and rich people are crazy because they have too much. And all hate so much that they have poisoned the whole earth, the air is poisoned, the water is poisoned, all of Nature is poisoned, and human nature is poisoned. Och," he ended up in a groan of disgust and despair.

For the first time in years Renata looked at him with attention. When she had first met him, he had amazed her by the purity of his ideals and the way he had given over his whole life to them, not caring for himself at all. Now the pure ideals had been destroyed for him, yet he himself remained the same—

older, more worn and wan, but just as intense. He had also retained his *transparent* quality, which was even physical, so that it seemed possible to look through him: this may have been an effect of his very pale skin and eyes.

"Did anything ever happen to you?" she asked him. "Did someone attack you or mug you or what?"

"Oh me," he smiled. "What does it matter."

"It *does* matter," she said, grinding her teeth in her fierce way. She imagined him with his manuscript, his smile, ready to engage in a deep discussion among strangers met in the city, and how they may have turned on him, attacked him, robbed him, torn his manuscript—"Where's your manuscript?"

"It's in my room. In the drawer. It is safe."

"Are you sure?"

"I don't take it out with me anymore." He clamped his mouth shut in a way that convinced her that something *had* happened and that both he and his manuscript had been threatened. But he would not say.

"Well you be careful," she said.

He smiled. "I think when madmen kick you in the shins, it is you who should be careful." And he stopped smiling. "Very careful. Because if you're hurt, we shall all die."

"Who'll die?"

"*I* shall." He put up his hand to touch her hair, which she wore long and loose as she had done as a girl, though it was turning very gray. He asked, "Where's Baby?"

"She's gone to the theater but she'll be home soon."

"Should I lock the door?"

"All right. If you want."

When he had done so, he came back to her and they sat side by side on the edge of the bed. They turned their faces to each other and brought them close till their lips met. To anyone else it may have appeared a passionless kiss—both had very thin lips, like straight lines—but it was enough for them. True passion for them lay elsewhere and was not carnal.

Baby came home from the theater and went straight to Henry's room to tell him about the play. She was still wearing her velvet cloak because she was in such a hurry to talk to him, and she unfastened it while she described her evening, starting with the pretheater supper she and her friends had had at a favorite little place—no, before that, when the hired limousine had come to pick her up and how terrible the traffic had been— and so on, right through the evening, with all sorts of asides and details as to what her friends had been wearing and how it did or did not suit them. While she talked, she also eased herself out of her shoes and then her earrings, which were pinching her lobes. After describing the play, she gave him her opinion of it, based not on reviews, though she had carefully read them, but on her own astute common sense. Nevertheless, she qualified it with "Of course I might be wrong, and as for Rose and Estelle, they're good girls but with not too much up here. If only you'd been there to tell me what to think." He occasionally accompanied her to the theater, but even apart from the business of maneuvering himself there (though she always managed to make it easier for him than anyone else), he preferred to stay home and have her come in this way and describe everything. But quite suddenly she grew tired and yawned while she took off some more jewelry, and he said she had better go to her own bed, there was no room for her in his. Gathering her things together, yawning more widely, she asked incidentally where was Renata, where was Carl—

"They've shut the door," said Henry.

She paused and looked at him. He nodded. Whenever it happened that Carl and Renata shut themselves up together—and that was very rarely indeed—a respectful hush stole over the apartment. Carrying her shoes in her hand, Baby walked in stocking feet past their door, casting a quick glance at it before disappearing behind her own. Henry too was thinking about his parents—it gave him satisfaction to imagine them together, like two aquatic mammals that had fortuitously found each other before swimming off again in opposite directions, each to a different far-off sea.

Seven

W HAT'S HAPPENED to your father?" Baby asked Renata.

"What do you mean, happened to him?"

Renata had not noticed that Graeme had failed to make his regular visit to New York. But Baby was very much aware of his absence—not that she missed him, no one made her as uncomfortable as he did, but she had got used to his appearing every few months.

"Don't you think you ought to find out?" she urged Renata.

"You know how Daddy hates people checking up on him."

This was true. It may have had something to do with his secret work, although Baby remembered that, even before he had joined the Foreign Office, he had liked to cover his tracks; and similarly, since his retirement, no one was to know where he was or what he was doing, though it may have been nothing. Baby had sometimes telephoned him—just to inquire how he was and when he was coming—but he had not appreciated her calls, mocking her concern till she slammed down the phone. Then she sat by it, fuming, waiting for him to call back, which he never did; but in his own good time he appeared, unannounced, and as casually as though he had just sauntered across the Atlantic.

Getting such an indifferent response from Renata, Baby turned to Henry. "Well call him," said Henry, but she wouldn't; she said she was too old for that sort of thing—too old to be worked up, she meant, the way only Graeme knew how. So Henry called instead and got no answer. She made him try again, and an hour later again, although in the meantime she had herself dialed secretly, with the same result. So it went on the next day and the next: all they heard was the phone ringing in what was presumably an empty flat. Baby had never seen this flat, although both Renata and Henry had—Graeme had taken it many years ago, when rents were low, to have somewhere of his own between postings. Baby made them describe it to her, just to have some idea of the place in which she could hear the phone ringing.

"But isn't there anyone—no one?—to clean or look after him or anything?" She was getting very upset; Renata too was by now showing concern.

Henry said, "Maybe he's off on some secret spy thing."

"He retired ten years ago," Baby said. "He's over seventy."

They realized there was no one they could ask about Graeme. He had no friend they knew of; no one who could tell them anything about him. Baby began to cry a bit; then she became angry. "It's his own fault for always being so horrible to everybody." By everybody she meant herself. Henry agreed that it was Graeme's own doing—not his fault but his choice: to be solitary, unencumbered.

Once he had told Henry about trekking in the Himalayas. It was not clear whether he himself had done this—probably not, for he had no vocation for mountain climbing, so it must have been something he had heard about from someone else: but in describing the thin air, with no sound, no birds, no vegetation, nothing except snow and ice on sheer cliffs and in deep gorges, he said that was the landscape for him, the world he wished to inhabit. But when Henry tried to convey this impression to Baby, she became furious. "He might not want anyone but he's got us. *We*'re there. So maybe I'm only an ex-wife, but that's something, isn't it, that's not nothing; it's not snow and ice."

She tried calling again, but still there was no answer. She decided that one of them would have to go to London, and that it would have to be Renata, whom he would really want to see. Renata agreed; she even went to an airline office and bought an economy ticket on which she would have to stay a minimum of ten days. It was only on the way home that she realized it would mean she would be away from Henry for ten days—their longest period of separation since he had been sent to England as a child; for when he had been restored to them after the accident, she had vowed never to be parted from him again. The airline ticket in the cotton pouch slung across her chest weighed on her like a millstone; she longed to get rid of it. Who would look after Henry? The answer—Baby—did not satisfy her: Baby had so many social engagements, Baby was old, he needed his mother and Baby was only his grandmother. These thoughts darted in and out of her head, exciting her so that her strides grew even longer than usual; her gaze was abstracted and she crossed the road on the Don't Walk sign, oblivious of the shouts of infuriated drivers. But as she neared the house, turning off the crowded avenue into the quieter street, there was a sight she did not miss: this was Henry emerging from the house with Vera. They were out on a walk, which happened sometimes when Vera, saying she couldn't stand reading about the Master one more minute, persuaded Henry that they both needed fresh air. Renata hid under the canopy of an apartment building and watched them from across the street. She saw that Vera was doing her best to slow down her steps, which were naturally quick, to enable Henry to keep up with her; and he was propelling himself forward as fast as he could, with one hip and leg dragging behind him. Nevertheless, he fell back so that she had to stop and wait for him; she was taller than he was and much fairer, and he looked very squat and dark as he labored behind her. Renata did not notice that a doorman had come out of the building where she had taken cover, nor did she hear him ask if he could help her. When he had said it a third time, she looked in his direction, but her narrowed eyes were so green and glittering that he dared not ask again.

When Renata told her mother that she could not leave for London, Baby decided to go herself. She wasted no time. She got down her matching luggage—long disused, for since Henry's accident no one cared to go far from home—and was soon settled in her luxury airline seat (no economy ticket for Baby), her feet stretched out and a mask over her eyes to enable her to sleep. But she could not sleep, for she was getting quite excited. It was twenty-three years since she had been in London—the last time was when she had gone to fetch Renata, on hearing of her pregnancy. That time Graeme had been waiting for her at the airport.

This time there was no one to meet her. She soon had a porter take charge of her luggage and get her into a taxi to be driven to Graeme's address. It was very central, near Marble Arch, and if he had not had it on an old rent, would have been far beyond his means. The first and second floors had been let out to offices, and no doubt the landlords were waiting for Graeme to vacate, one way or another, to rent out his flat at its present market price. It was very early in the morning—Baby had taken an overnight flight—and the offices were shut. There was one milk bottle in the entrance, and just as Baby's taxi drove up, the front door opened and someone stooped to take in the milk. It was Graeme. He looked up and saw Baby sitting in the taxi. He was in his pajamas and dressing gown. She scrambled out of the taxi—one little foot emerging first in its perfect pump—and said angrily, "Why the hell don't you answer your phone."

But it wasn't the phone that made her angry, it was the way he looked: gray, worn, old, ill. However, he was still Graeme who did not give a flicker of surprise but dropped his eyes to her feet and said, "I say, what a charming pair of shoes."

She had her luggage brought up by the taxi driver, who, like most people serving her, was ready and willing to carry out further orders. There were three flights of stairs, narrow, steep, and dark, and they walked in procession up to Graeme's flat, with Baby resting at the landings and Graeme urging her on with "One more."

"Doesn't anyone else live here?" she asked, looking at the padlocked doors.

"Only during office hours," he replied. "I say, you're not intending to stay, are you?"

When they arrived at the top, the taxi driver also looked dubious as to the suitability of this lodging for someone like Baby and, after she had paid and tipped on the scale he had expected, offered to fetch her and her luggage anytime she wanted. Graeme urged her to accept—"There's only one wretched little bedroom here," he said, which made her get rid of the driver and walk around the flat. It was worse than she expected: a bachelor's lair where he had crouched for thirty years with all his possessions, which were mostly books and prints overflowing from drawers and shelves, gathering dust. Rain-smeared windows looked out into a courtyard hemmed between brick walls. The kitchen was a hole with a slimy sink and dirty glasses in it and a battered, blackened coffeepot.

Watching her expression, he said, "I told you it wasn't a fit place for you to stay."

"No. Nor for any human being."

She was in his bedroom now, which was the worst, yet also the best in so far as it was, in its own idiosyncratic way, the most comfortable. This was obviously the place where he spent most of his time and had dug himself in. It was also the only warm room—indeed, it was stifling with some sort of heater he kept on all night. The bed of course was unmade—probably he had just crawled out of it to go down and get his milk; his reading lamp shone over the pillow and his open book; more books lay on the blanket and some had fallen to the floor.

"When did you last have these sheets changed?"

He groaned but seemed to enjoy telling her some long story about a Mrs. Parrot who had "done" for him for thirty years but had recently had to retire on account of her kidneys, handing him over to her daughter Penny, though only theoretically since Penny had a lot of trouble with her live-in boyfriend and was rarely available. "So there's no one," Baby interrupted this tedious recital.

"No one," said Graeme, with what sounded like satisfaction emanating from the depths of this filthy, cozy room that he inhabited in his own special way.

"And you don't care to answer the phone when anyone tries to call you, anyone being for instance your wife, or your daughter, or your grandson."

"I've been away," he said. "You could sit down for a moment if you wanted to—there's a chair in the other room that's not too bad."

"Where have you been?"

"I daresay you're tired after your flight. They're dreadful, these overnight flights, knock you out completely . . . Well if you must know I've been in hospital."

He had been there for six weeks. He had had a heart attack. He was very reluctant to talk about it but over the next few days she managed to get information out of him, bit by bit. Those were strange days and nights that they spent together in his flat. He tried to make her go to a hotel but at the same time seemed not unwilling for her to stay—he went so far as to try to find some clean sheets and even made an attempt, soon given up, to spread them on the sofa. He watched her open her suitcase and said "I say" in appreciation of the dainty things that came out. His bathroom had a strange geyser contraption that needed expert handling, so that he had to fill her bath and check up on her while she lay in it—to make sure she didn't blow up, he explained, as he peered around the bathroom door. She made him shut it immediately, but when she came out, she knew from his complacent smile that he *had* looked his fill at her plump, soft, aged body floating in the water, which she had made fragrant with her bath gel. He fed her on Indian curries—it was his usual arrangement, he said, he simply phoned the Star of India and they sent up whatever he wanted; they were even thoughtful enough to provide paper plates to save him the nuisance of dirty dishes. Mostly he ate propped up in bed reading his book—he said he could not imagine a more sybaritic existence than eating curry in bed on a rainy day in London while reading Tod's *Annals of Rajasthan.* But in her honor he turned on the gas fire in his other room, and in the evenings they sat in front of it, she in his leather chair and he on a cushion on the floor. She wore a flouncy robe of deep rose—"I *say*"—and he never got out of his pajamas; both held paper plates of curry in their laps.

He told her about his heart attack as if it had happened to someone else. And in a way, he explained, that was how it had been. The attack had occurred just as he had got out of bed to fetch his milk. It was of course an hour when he was completely alone in the house and could expect no help till the employees from the offices downstairs arrived at ten o'clock. But it took him much longer to attract their attention, which he could only do by rapping on the floor, for the telephone was too far for him to get to. He didn't know how long he had lain there before he was found and an ambulance called. Those hours were the strangest of his life, he said—and he had spent some very strange ones in the course of his career. But these were completely different in quality from any previous experience: he had lain there passive to the point of indifference, letting himself be floated into another dimension, which might not prove unpleasant. "Interesting" was the word he used to describe this sensation or adventure.

"Yes and if it happens again?" she asked indignantly.

"Ah," he replied. "Perhaps I shall advance somewhat further the next time." Her indignation swelled into outrage, she opened her mouth to scold but before she could begin, he said, "There's a little piece of popadum stuck to your denture. Looks rather charming, actually."

That night he tried to climb in with her where she lay sleeping on his sofa. She fought him off—"at our age," "a sick old man like you," and so on—but he persisted; he said he only wanted to hold her. And that was what he did, wrapping his long, nerveless arms around her plump body in its silken nightie. It seemed to give him immense pleasure; by the street-light penetrating through his threadbare curtain she could see his face—worn down to the bone, stubble in the hollow jaws, but his mouth open and his eyes closed in rapture. After a while she said, "This sofa is going to collapse with the two of us. I'm surprised it hasn't already"—for it was very old and sagged into a hole in the middle.

"Oh this sofa has stood up to plenty," he said with the most irritating self-satisfaction, so that she kicked him out at once.

Afterward she couldn't sleep. She was still confused on New York time, and more and more uncomfortable as the thoughts tumbled around in her head regarding his boast about the sofa. She knew that in his younger days he had been very promiscuous, hardly ever went to a party without bringing home a woman, or it might just be someone he met standing in line outside a cinema, or at the next table in a restaurant. Imagining him with these strangers on this sofa, she felt as though she were sinking down into the pit in its middle, so that she couldn't bear to stay there for another moment but jumped up, snorting to herself in disgust.

He had the light on in his bedroom, and she went straight in there. He was propped up in bed reading a book, with the lamp beamed straight down on him. He gave a peculiar impression of youthfulness—like a studious schoolboy, with huge spectacles and a little tuft of what was left of his hair sticking up on his head. When he saw her, he asked, "Can't you sleep?" and invitingly opened the cave of his grimy bedclothes for her.

She turned from him in exaggerated disgust and at once stumbled on one of his tomes scattered over the floor. She kicked it as violently as she could with her slippered foot and faced him in fury. "How much longer are you going to live like this?"

"That is hardly up to me."

"No," she said. "It's up to me. That's why I'm here. I'm taking you home with me."

It was his lifelong practice, honed to a pitch by his profession, never to show what he felt or thought about any situation. His utmost response was one of mild surprise—which was what he registered now, pushing his spectacles up into the wrinkles on his forehead. She had the opposite tendency of building up the expression of *her* emotions, so she continued with exaggerated vehemence: "And if it happens again—not that it will, but *if*—next time you'll lie here a whole week before anyone finds you."

"Oh don't worry," he said lightly. "Those girls downstairs look after me pretty well."

"What girls downstairs?"

"Working in the offices. They've even offered to look in on me over the weekends. There's one absolute charmer from Chelmsford, a Tess of the D'Urberville type—strong, strapping I might say, honey-blond—"

"I see. Then if there are all these charmers taking such a tremendous interest in you, how is it that I find you in your condition tramping up and down three flights of stairs to get in your milk bottle?"

"Exactly what they say. They say if you'd just wait, we'll bring it up, but you know I have to have my morning cup of tea the moment I wake up—so incorrigibly English—"

She wiped the smile off his face by shouting: "You're coming home with me! Do you think Renata would ever forgive me—yes, Renata! Your daughter Renata! Remember we have a daughter? And that she is worried sick about you and her last words to me at the airport"—after just a second of hesitation, she made them up: " 'Bring Daddy back with you.' "

"Renata said that?"

"Yes." She defied him to call her a liar, which he flatly did. "I don't believe you," he said—with a matter-of-fact acceptance that saddened Baby, who knew how much he would have liked to believe her.

"Well don't believe me but it's the truth." She approached nearer his bed, even sat down on it. "And Henry too was terribly anxious about you." Here she could speak more confidently. "He likes you very much. I think he esteems you." When Graeme gave an incredulous laugh, she went on: "No really—and in so many ways he takes after you: when I came in just now and saw you with that *book,* you could have been Henry sitting up in bed all night reading, reading. I tell him you'll ruin your eyes, you'll have to wear big ugly spectacles—" She framed her eyes in these imaginary spectacles and Graeme took off his own. "Oh but *you* only wear them for reading," she said, "and only now—when you were young, you could see further than anyone, especially what you were not supposed to see. Eyes like a hawk," she reminisced, half to herself. His eyes had been piercing, keen, blue like clear water (now they were washed away as with many tears, though no one had ever seen him shed a single one); and their gaze had had the far-ranging quality of a bird of prey, hovering just above the world, ready to swoop down into it to take what he needed.

"Maybe if Henry hadn't—wasn't—you know—he might have been more like you. I think he would have been. I think he would have been very active."

"With girls and everything?"

"I find it completely incomprehensible how, at your age, and in your condition, your mind is still on all that business. Yes maybe I mean 'with girls and everything,' but I'm sure when Henry reaches your age he is not going to make an idiot of himself lying in bed drooling over some girl with platinum-blond hair—"

"Honey-blond," Graeme gently corrected. "Don't go," he caught at her hand as she made to get up. "Talk to me."

"I don't want to talk to you. I've never wanted to talk to you because I know that every word that comes out of my mouth confirms your opinion that I'm the stupidest woman you've ever met in your whole life."

"No, no, nowhere near the stupidest—"

"And if I were the sort of person who could be given an inferiority complex, you would have made me into a classic case. You certainly tried hard enough. Let go of my hand," she said but that only made him hold on to it tighter, nor did she tug very hard.

"No one could get you down because you always come bouncing right back. That's what I like about you. That's what I've always liked about you."

"Oh my goodness, do you mean to tell me at this late date that there is something about me that you actually like?"

After a thoughtful pause, he said, "Well, I suppose you're the only woman I ever married."

"What a triumph for me!" she said, sarcastically tossing her head.

But in fact it *was* a sort of triumph for her when she came back with Graeme—he described himself as her vanquished captive tied to the wheels of her chariot and dragged across the Atlantic; yet he seemed to be relieved to be there. She had a partition put up in Kavi's room so that one half of it remained a workroom for Henry and the other half, adjacent to Carl's closet, became Graeme's bedroom. He soon had it just like his London bedroom, with a permanently unmade bed in which he lay propped up under a reading light and with books piled on his blanket and the floor. He fitted very easily into the household, which was indeed highly flexible due to the characters of its members. Mealtimes were spontaneous rather than regular; a daily help did some cooking, Baby some more, and there were usually supplements from a caterer. Everyone except Baby was too much taken up with their own concerns to pay attention to domestic details. This was especially true of Carl and Renata, who appeared almost physically enveloped in a cloud of distraction or abstraction—so that they were hardly aware of the addition of one more member to their household. Only Baby realized that Graeme was put out by their daughter's nonchalance. "Oh hi," was all Renata had said when he arrived.

"She's glad you're here," Baby interpreted, and when Graeme looked wry, she pointed out, "Well *you*'d rather pluck out your tongue than tell someone you're glad to see them." But she herself knew it wasn't the same: Graeme's indifference was deliberate, it was a manner, whereas Renata's was an ingrained quality—she genuinely didn't care.

Eight

IN THE COURSE of his work on the Master's papers, Henry had begun to open the journals the disciples had kept as a record of their development. The Master himself had apparently never bothered to read them, and Henry, opening the neglected bundles, realized why. Although obviously written with intense sincerity, their only interesting feature was their sameness. Henry was surprised to find that, when people reached into their inner depths, they all came up with the same material, fascinating no doubt to a depth-psychologist or an anthropologist but too impersonal for someone like himself—or, apparently, the Master who had so unceremoniously tossed them aside. After reading about a hundred of them, Henry gave himself permission to do the same. Although they were baring their souls, these followers remained the same shadowy presences he had already encountered in photographs.

Of course, in the photographs it was because they were so entirely eclipsed by the Master himself. The center of every group portrait, he was a striking contrast to the others—in his English suit, and his face with its black mustache and oriental cast of features glowing above his starched white collar and silken necktie. The pale figures standing around him—he alone was seated—wore strange costumes of their own devising: tunics or smocks, cravats like Bohemian artists, and some of the women in flowing white Botticelli dresses, with headbands; all wore sandals. While the Master smiled, they remained very solemn; their odd costumes gave them the air of a troupe of acrobats—not in the least gay, but forlorn, and ghostly.

The Master believed—it was part of his message—that people had to learn to survive in whatever situation they happened to be thrown. He himself could do *anything*—carpentry, house painting, repairing a watch, he could always make a living for himself and had done so for years before his movement got going; and even afterward, whenever funds were low, he would go out and earn money to put everyone back on their feet. And because he himself could do this—because he was such an expert survivor—he expected the same from everyone else. But most of his followers were too finely nurtured for such enterprise; and it may have been the reason why only those with private incomes, like Cynthia and Elsa, could afford to remain with him. Those who had to put his theory of self-reliance into practice tended to sink, and as far as he was concerned, this was the necessary consequence of not learning to swim. Mme. Richter, for instance, only just managed to scrape a living for herself, her daughter, her granddaughter, and ultimately her great-granddaughter Vera: she never got anywhere near establishing the Master's movement in New York, which was the reason she had been sent there. Her failure blocked her progress with the Master and ultimately led to her break with him.

Henry discovered a whole packet of her letters to the Master among his papers, some of them written in French and others in Russian, so that Vera had to translate them. Vera was so moved by them that afterward it was difficult to tell which were Mme. Richter's tears and which her great-granddaughter's, smudging the rust-brown ink. Yet the majority of the letters were undauntedly cheerful; after years of struggling, Mme. Richter was still writing how well they were getting on in New York, what wonderful new prospects were opening up, how she had been introduced into the homes of millionaires living on Fifth Avenue to teach their children. And along with piano lessons, she would be introducing them to the ideas of the Master, so that soon the day would arrive when lectures and support for him could be arranged in New York. She also wrote about the progress of little Sonia—wistfully regretting that he could not see the child grow up and hear her first lisping of Mama (there was no mention of Papa). The correspondence was one-sided—from her side—but she appeared not to have expected anything else. Only sometimes there was an outpouring (this was always in Russian) in letters that were all written at night—she refers to her daughter asleep on the bed behind the screen—while her heart was so full (of him) that she could not sleep but felt herself tossed like a frail bark on an ocean of passion. She knew this was wrong, for he had taught them that his absence was a presence, but she so desperately longed for him and needed some assurance that he thought of her sometimes, even if it was no more than a line scribbled on a piece of paper at a café table. And when such a line came, she was so overwhelmed (this was again in Russian) that she pressed her lips to his beloved hands a thousand times —it was always his hands, never any higher or lower, though they had at one time been lovers.

There was no indication that he had read these letters any more than his students' work journals—some of them were still in their envelopes, and her great-granddaughter was the first to slit them open. It was also Vera who divided these early letters from another, different batch. As the years progressed but her financial prospects did not, Mme. Richter became somewhat importunate: at first apologetically, still promising another American millionaire, but in the meantime there was not even enough money for winter shoes for her granddaughter, for little Irina, let alone her own or Sonia's. Later letters became more importunate —desperate, with no note of apology but demanding, even reproachful. Some of these had notations in the margin in red pencil: Attn. C.H. (presumably Cynthia Howard)—send £25. Whenever such a sum was received, its acknowledgment was accompanied by requests for more and bigger sums—till in the end there were no more notations in red, the letters became more and more reproachful, and then they ceased altogether and Vera tied them together with gold thread.

Vera's mother, Irina, remembered and passed on a scene from her childhood: it was when her grandmother Mme. Richter had ceremoniously burned all mementos of the Master, including his photographs, in the fireplace of their lodging. The fireplace had been disused for a long time, and a volley of black smoke had rushed into the room like an emanation of the devil. Mme. Richter had gathered her daughter Sonia in one arm and her granddaughter Irina in the other, and raining kisses on their hair and faces, she told them that from now on the three of them were alone in the world. Mme. Richter, who died when Vera was five, survived the Master by six years. Vera remembered her great-grandmother as immensely old and shabby as a pauper; but in spite of the tough spirit that made her go after every dollar she could get to bring home to her children, she had retained the courteous, aristocratic manner of her pre-Revolutionary girlhood.

Vera herself had never known what it was like to have enough money but looked as if she had always had it. She was like those girls whose families had been in America for several generations —they might be Anglo-Saxon, Irish, or Jewish, but with the common denominator of having grown up against a background of money. Although in Vera's case this ingredient had been missing, in everything else she was an American girl of good family. She was fair and fine—everything about her was fine: her features, her hair, her hands and feet; her complexion was of the most delicate tint. At the same time she had a robustness of mind that often surprised Henry. She was, for instance, so robustly outspoken about the Master that Henry asked her, "Then how can you bear to spend your days rummaging around in his remains?"

"Oh I do it for the salary you pay me."

"And if someone else came along and paid you more?"

She didn't commit herself, so that it embarrassed him to continue the conversation.

Still, there were days when she would suddenly push aside

their work, shake back her hair so energetically that sparks seemed to fly from it, and say she had to get out into the open. When he said he would go with her, she agreed happily; but he was always aware that he hampered her—that what she really wanted was to charge along the street, skipping a few steps and running some others. Moreover, he was aware of Renata watching them—if not in actual fact, though that happened too, then always in spirit—so that he felt doubly lamed. Sometimes he told Vera to go on her own, pretending he was too engrossed in his work to break off; and after she had gone, he longed to be outside with her, though he guessed it was a relief for her to be without him. And it *was* a relief, and yet she felt sorry to leave him behind, stuck among old papers; and one day she suggested, "Why don't you let me take you in your wheelchair . . . Oh don't be so proud," she said at the expression on his face, and he blushed under his beard but he wouldn't let her. It was years since he had used his wheelchair outside, though he usually moved around the house in it; he felt he had worked too hard at rehabilitating himself to give in now. So she went alone and he stayed back, thinking how nice it must be outside; and on the third day, when she for the third time suggested the wheelchair, he agreed. That was a joyful outing—it took some maneuvering to get the chair into the tiny back elevator, but once out in the street, Vera managed to get them moving at the same speed she would have walked by herself. Henry felt that he was not in the least impeding her but that they were scudding along like leaves blown over the earth, clouds over the sky. Even when they turned the corner into the avenue, crowded with people and shops spilling far out over the sidewalk, she guided their way so skillfully that he continued to feel as free as in a field or meadow. Sometimes they paused—it might be at a fruit and flower stall to admire the display, and once they bought a red apple each and a bunch of yellow daffodils, both these items wet with what might have been dew but was actually drops of the water with which the Korean owner had washed them down.

When Renata discovered that Vera was taking Henry out in his wheelchair—for the excursion was repeated—she wanted to do the same. But this was not a success at all. Renata grew impatient quite soon, and so did he, for their progress was much slower than he was used to with Vera. It was also more clumsy, and by the time they got to the avenue, he was receiving so many jolts that he asked her to turn back. "Why?" she said. "Don't you want to go around the block?" He said no, and this upset her so much that she got the chair jammed between a group of passersby, who tried to suppress their impatience out of respect for his condition. Renata failed to notice, she pushed the chair through and argued with Henry: "You always go around the block with *her,*" jolting him along more fiercely. Then he put the brake on and refused to let her push him any farther; and she walked off and left him there in the middle of the sidewalk among the crowd. By the time she came running back, he had steered around and was on his way home, propelling himself along with an energy fueled by rage. She ran beside him, pleading, but he wouldn't reply or even look at her, and the most he would allow her to do was help him into the back elevator.

Henry envied Vera her ability to shake off the effects of the Master's papers the moment she had finished her day's work on them. Perhaps this was because her relationship to the Master was quite simple—she hated him. He may have been her great-grandfather but she carried no trace of him; whereas Henry, who was probably *not* his son, looked out into the world through the Master's slanting, hooded eyes. Mostly he agreed with Vera in deploring the Master and his influence, but he could not dismiss him as absolutely as she did. And while he may not have appreciated his methods, or his character, he did respect his message. Vera teased him that this was because he himself was in need of a message, and if he had encountered the Master in his lifetime, might have been converted into one of his disciples to run around doing menial tasks for him.

Henry had no difficulty with the Master's teaching. As far as he was concerned, it was so simple that it was almost not worth stating: all it said was deny your self, overcome your self, transcend your self. But this truism, so age-old that it was ingrained in human as distinct from other forms of life, was delivered to a succession of generations who had been taught the opposite: indulge your self, express your self, exalt your self. The new formulation had not brought happiness—far from it—so when the Master came along and said try the opposite way, there were many ready to follow him. He presented his rule as based on ancient manuscripts long hidden away in monasteries; these were so far up in the Himalayan mountain ranges that they were inaccessible to every human foot but his own—who had been transported there by means he was not ready to reveal, or did not judge others ready to receive.

Henry, however, discovered that it was a way he had taken himself. He had not had to be transported to any mystical peaks; all it had taken in his case was a car accident and the consequences to himself. No, he did not need the Master's message: it was his papers that filled a gap for him. During his years of confinement, when he had had to educate himself as best he could, he had longed to take up something that would be a task for him, a life's work. He had had no idea what this might be, but now it seemed to have been presented to him with the Master's papers. And the work satisfied another need that had so far been denied—for adventure, exploration, a going out into the world. Hobbled physically, it was only in the mountains of the mind that he was free to roam. So he roamed among the Master's papers to extract his message from the mass of verbiage and anecdotage in which it had become embedded. He also gave a brief account of the Master's method of teaching and the groups who had formed around him. He tried to express everything in a simple prose, submitting himself and his material to the technical discipline (this was the hardest part) of compression and clarity.

His monograph was published by a press specializing in books of an occult nature and distributed by them through their own catalogues and through bookstores dealing with a mixture of mystical, mythical, theosophical, astrological, as well as classic theological and philosophical texts. These bookstores were usually small, quaint, overstocked, smelling of incense, and tucked away in unexpected corners; but they had their counterparts in many countries—though only in highly developed ones—so that Henry's book was diffused more widely than he had expected. He and Vera became involved in dealing with requests for more information relating to the Master and his work. There were inquiries from many places, from people wanting to revive the groups that had once flourished but had died along with those who had founded them. Everyone seemed to be waiting for a lead—or leader: books, letters, messages, and answers to inquiries were not enough; what was wanted was contact with a living person who would give guidance in the way the Master himself had done.

Apart from Graeme, Henry had not shared his awareness with anyone that he himself had been cast in the role of the Master's successor. It wasn't only that he knew himself to be entirely unfit for it, he thought everyone else was too—unless they had the mixture of impudence and charisma (Vera added charlatanism) that had characterized the Master. And if someone like that should come along to lay a claim, Henry thought it would be his duty to oppose that person; not because he wanted the position for himself but because he felt it would be better left unfilled. Yet that seemed far from the hopes and expectations of the people who wrote to him. Some of them stated outright that they had heard the Master had appointed a successor: but in answer to requests for more information on the subject, Henry always said that he regretted he had none and Vera typed out his letter with terse satisfaction. The two of them were united in fending off all suggestions; but Carl, who often sat in the room with them working on *his* papers, felt that some door should be left open. Once, when Henry had dictated such a letter and Vera had typed it out and was licking the envelope, Carl turned around to them and said in his shy, hesitant, yet intensely hopeful way: "But if there is a need?" Henry and Vera saw none.

Reading in bed on the other side of the partition dividing his bedroom from their workroom, Graeme heard much of what was going on. Mostly he found it profoundly uninteresting, but whenever there was mention of a successor to the Master, he became uneasy. He was aware that Henry would never of his own accord divulge that secret; so that Graeme, as the only other person to share it, wondered if he should die with it untold. The thought of dying had come to live in Graeme ever since he had lain on the floor of his London flat. It was a constant and by no means unpleasant companion, rather like a wife of long-standing —rather like Baby was to him nowadays. The idea of "something happening" to Graeme was never far from Baby's mind either, and it made her fuss over him in a way he intensely disliked. She knew she was irritating him, and it was partly why she was doing it: Graeme irritated, sarcastic, was for her Graeme himself, and she did not intend to let him sink into being a bland old man.

Nowadays, when Henry wanted to have his evening game of chess with her, she was often occupied with Graeme. "Go ahead, I won't disturb you," Graeme would say and help them set up the chess pieces. But he did disturb them—either by offering unwanted advice to Baby, who was a much better player than he had ever been; or just by being there—suddenly, her bishop poised over the board for an important move, she remembered that Graeme had not yet taken his medicine. Her concentration was so bad that she lost several games to Henry, which was almost unprecedented and for which she blamed Graeme. Henry realized that he had become displaced as the center of her attention and gracefully yielded up his time with her to his grandfather. He liked the picture they made together in her red sitting room, crowded in by her gilded objects, reflected in the great mirror over the mantelpiece left over from the undivided Kopf house: Baby's head bent over a piece of sewing on which she was charmingly engaged, Graeme reading in one of his thumbed volumes of poetry that had accompanied him all over the world.

Sometimes Baby asked him to read aloud to her—at first he said she wouldn't like it, and anyway he read very badly. It was true that he didn't read well, but she did like it: he had forgotten that she was used to listening to poetry, having grown up with a poet father. Kavi had recited very differently from

Graeme, with much expression intended to extract all possible emotion out of the lines. Graeme read tonelessly; and compared with Kavi's poetry, which was mellifluous, full of exquisite images, and ending in rhymes tied on like little bows, what Graeme read was harsh in feeling and form, expressed in metaphor that preferred to be ugly and set in verse that was blank like a wall. But whether the mood was bitter as in Graeme's favorite poetry, or surpassingly sweet as in Kavi's, the content, Baby discovered, was the same—how short was human life, and evanescent. Instead of listening, she would surreptitiously study Graeme and his hollow cheeks with stubble in them. When Graeme looked up and caught her melancholy gaze fixed on him, he was annoyed: "I said you wouldn't like it"—and in spite of her protests, he went on reading silently to himself, his lips moving, which made him look as if he were mumbling like a very old man.

There was no need for them to sit silent together, for they had plenty to talk about, sharing a present, with a daughter and grandson in the same apartment, and a past. And it was while recalling this latter—specifically, her mother Elsa and his aunt Cynthia—that he came out with the secret of Henry's succession. He told Baby about Elsa and Cynthia's last will and testament in the course of discussing his own—such as it was, he added, for he had little to leave. She had protested she didn't need to know about it, and anyway what made him think that she was going to outlive him? He admitted it was a guess on his part, based on his assumption that she was indestructible. At that she became sententious—alas, all of us were all too destructible, and how quickly, she said, suffused by experience and poetry, it was all gone, how the strongest people disappeared in a flash: look at Cynthia and Elsa, and the Master himself, choked in a few minutes on a piece of meat. "But not before arranging for instant renewal," said Graeme and, having said that much, felt the urge to continue.

Baby blew up instantly: "Are you trying to tell me he died so that Henry could be born? . . . I've never heard such rubbish in my entire life."

"Exactly. Neither have I."

Baby frowned and laughed together. After a while she said, "I know for a fact that his intention was not to die but to come to New York. To be with me."

"How interesting." He countered her tone of coquettish triumph with his own characteristic one of supreme calm. "And how old would he have been at that time, do you know?"

"Who cares! He was ageless. He said he'd take a suite in some hotel and would I come visit him there."

"What did you say?"

"You don't commit yourself to a man you've just met. You leave it at maybe yes—maybe no—or simply maybe."

"And how old were you?"

"You know very well how old I was twenty-five years ago," she said tartly, which put him in a better mood again.

"Oh yes. And I know what you were like then. And I know what you're like now."

She was pleased with this salute from him. They relaxed with each other; they felt almost united, each having let the other into a secret—though Graeme suspected that his would not remain one for long.

Here is a view of Henry that Baby had when she looked out of her front window and saw him pass by on one of his solitary outings: short, dark, bearded, dragging one hip and leg, he often wore headphones and appeared to be absorbed in the music pounded into his ears. But actually, he had confessed to her, there was no music, he wore them to shut off whatever was going on outside his own head. "And what's going on inside that's so wonderful?" Baby had asked him. But after Graeme's revelation, she looked at him differently. The very evening that Graeme had informed her of the Master's legacy, she hovered around Henry's door in a manner that told him she had something she was burning to impart. This led him to engross himself entirely in the pages of his book—he was so much Graeme's grandson in this and other ways that Baby's new respect evaporated immediately. She said, "I simply cannot understand why you have to imitate your grandfather in everything when there are much better people you could try to be like."

"Oh yes? For instance, who?"

"For instance, the Master." Then she could not help blurting out: "Did you know that you're supposed to have his soul?"

When Henry made a great show of laughing at her, she laughed too—because it did sound ridiculous. But next moment she said, "Then why are you looking at me with his eyes?"

Henry dropped them. "I'm beginning to wonder," he admitted, and after a while, *"You* didn't sleep with him by any chance, did you?"

"And if I had, how would that account for you?" Henry had to agree it wouldn't; she kept on looking at him. Overwhelmed with pride in him, she kissed him—saying, as usual, "When are you going to shave that thing off?" But she sighed with deep satisfaction in him. "I always knew you were someone special."

"But *so* special?" Henry asked her.

At once her own doubts revived—for it was not easy to accept the idea that the Master's soul had found its habitation in Henry.

Graeme was right: Baby couldn't keep her mouth shut for more than a day. Soon Renata and Carl had been informed, and neither of them had any difficulty accepting the idea of their son's election. For them it was only the fulfillment of something they had expected. Renata walked around with an air of exaltation; at first she said nothing to Henry but darted glances at him that made him ask Baby: "What did you tell her?" And then, with a groan: *"Why* did you tell her?" He knew his life with his mother would become more difficult, and so it turned out.

Two days after she heard the news, Renata waited for Vera to go home. Then she darted into Henry's room, and standing with her back to the door as if barring entry to anyone trying to come in and between her and her son, she said, "Do you think Vera is the right person to help you?"

"Why, what's wrong with her?"

Careful not to antagonize him, she was uncharacteristically mild. "She's so young."

"Yes, a whole year younger than I am."

"But she's so immature. She understands nothing about you, or your work. She doesn't know who you are."

"Who am I, then?"

She was standing over him, wrestling with her strong emotions. In an attempt to defuse her, he spoke very calmly: "What's your interpretation of all this business with the Master? Whenever I ask you, you say he's not my father, that Carl is—"

She sighed; she said, "We're not even married."

"I'm aware of being a bastard," Henry said, "but what I never have understood is why it should have been so very objectionable for you to get a piece of paper, if only for my sake."

"Oh I don't know, Henry—we're so unsuited." Even she, with her limited sense of humor, had to laugh at this statement as soon as she had made it. She went on, "And marriages never do work out in our family—look at Kavi and Elsa, and Baby and Graeme—what disasters." She fell silent, and he could practically see the thoughts going around inside her and tying themselves into a knot out of which she finally extracted this thread: "I tell you what we could do, if you like." He waited. She said, "Carl and I could get married. It's only an idea, of course, and if you don't like it, we'll say no more about it ever again."

"Whose idea was it?"

"It was Carl's," she said, shooting a quick look at Henry, who assumed an expression as blank as his grandfather Graeme would have done in such a situation.

After a while he said, "Carl asked you to marry him?"

She nodded; she appeared overcome with shyness.

"When was this?" Henry questioned her, feeling responsible for his parents and whatever might have taken place between them. And she was very ready to tell him, accepting his right to be fully informed.

It had happened on a day when she was particularly unhappy about Henry's friendship with Vera: "I watched you in the street with her and you looked so happy."

"Oh I'm sorry. I'm sorry I looked happy."

"You were different. Not the way you are with me. With me you're always—like now."

He realized he was frowning. What she said was true: he never could be lighthearted with her, the way he was with Vera, or with others, such as Baby. Renata made his heart heavy, she was like a burden on it.

"I was sad," she continued. "I didn't know what to do so I took my camera and went out. I walked in the opposite direction from you, not wanting to meet you and see you with her. What can I do? It's the way I feel, I'm telling you honestly. So I walked and I took a few pictures, nothing special, I've thrown them away."

She had walked many blocks, following the avenue as it degenerated farther into closed storefronts with people living in them, past the flyspecked little window of a clairvoyant, ethnic eating places, more homeless madmen mumbling as they grabbled in the trash cans overflowing at each corner. She had sat down to rest on the steps of an ornate temple with statues and a golden dome belonging to a sect that, like everything else in the neighborhood, had decayed and closed down. The Doric columns were plastered over with posters advertising other sects, photographs of holy men, half peeled off; also of entertainment events, a jazz group, and a middle-aged comedian. Here Renata reclined, a soda pop she had bought on the way by her side; no one glanced at her, for she looked no different from any other vagrant, or a person wandering in her mind. One of the people who passed in front of the steps was Carl—she was not very surprised to see him. Perhaps he had deliberately followed her; or it may have been chance—it had happened before that they had come across each other in their separate wanderings. It had happened with others too, quite unexpectedly—not so long ago, while crossing Park Avenue, Renata had seen Baby in furs waving to her from a cab, and twice she had passed Graeme standing in line outside a cinema. These meetings confirmed Renata's impression of the city as something like a forest where people wandered along solitary paths, sometimes encountering each other in a clearing.

Carl had come up the steps and sat beside her. He too seemed to belong in these streets, for he had the same vagrant quality as Renata. Both were tall, bony, and ill clad. But, unlike her, Carl no longer felt at ease sitting exposed to public view; he craved shelter. "Have you got any money?" he asked her. She reached into the pocket of her jeans and came up with some crumpled notes she had forgotten about and had put through the laundry. Carl smoothed and counted them and said there was enough for them to go to some eating place so Renata followed him, not forgetting to take along her half-drunk can of soda. They found a narrow place where a rough, rude man contemptuously shoveled pizzas in and out of an oven as though they were lumps of coal, and two or three people sat at the bare tables, dejected and ashamed with loneliness. Carl ordered all sorts of toppings for his pizza—it was easy for him to ignore the man's surliness— and carried it to the table where he spread a paper napkin and sat down opposite Renata and talked to her about Henry. It was as if it had been London before Henry was born and the two of them had been in a café where she bought him a meal and he spoke to her about his ideas. What was different now was that Carl's ideas had merged with those of the Master, and instead of only one manuscript as yet unpublished, there was an entire literature and a movement waiting to be revived. It seemed to him that all this had grown out of the seed he had himself sown and tended. Tremendously excited by his success, he transmitted his ardor to Renata—something he had not been able to do since their youth, so that she too glowed with the cold flame that had then illumined them. Carl felt it was up to them to kindle the same enthusiasm in Henry. He told her about the letters that had come from different places, inviting leadership, and the disappointing message Henry and Vera had sent in reply. Renata's face, briefly illumined, went blank. "It's her fault."

"No," said Carl, "it's ours. Yours and mine." He looked around, not wanting to be observed in any intimacy—the lonely customers were covertly watching them, perhaps envious of their togetherness, and the server squinted in hostility to see Carl actually enjoying his pizza. Carl left his chair and slipped in beside Renata on the upright bench on which she sat against the wall, under printed guidelines on how to save a victim in case of food suffocation.

"He needs us both," said Carl. "Not singly but together. As a couple. As parents: mother and father."

"But he thinks you may not even be his father."

"Was Joseph the father of Jesus Christ? Of course this is only a comparison. The situation is not the same but the principle is. For the sake of the outside world—the Philistine as well as the believer—there has to be a spiritual and an actual dynasty, yes a spiritual father and also an actual one. I'm proud to be the latter," he said and laid his hand on Renata's. She was so surprised she drew hers away, but he followed and captured it again; his hand like hers was cold. Then he asked her very formally to marry him—"Renata, will you be my wife?"—and she had looked the same as she did now while telling Henry about this occasion. Carl took her shy silence for consent and pressed his chaste lips against her chaste cheek (the server furiously thrust in another pizza). Joy and other strong emotions arose in Carl and he spoke to her in German: *"Meine Geliebte,"* he said. *"Meine versprochene Frau."* It was the first and last time he ever spoke to her in this language, which went back to his most sacred memories: to the times in his childhood when his father had taken him out on the balcony of their flat to see the wonderful canopy of stars above them. His father—who had been a high school teacher, an idealist like Carl himself, a philosopher in its exact meaning as a lover of wisdom—had named the stars and told him about the planets and the universe; and he encouraged him to ask more questions—"Ask, Carl, always ask"—and never to stop asking them.

For their wedding at City Hall Renata wore a frock. It was one of several that had hung unworn in her closet for years, but since her figure, apart from becoming more gaunt, had hardly changed, it still fitted her as well as it ever had done—which was not very well, for she had no idea what to do with clothes beyond letting them hang on her. Carl too appeared unwonted and uncomfortable in the new suit Baby had bought for him; Graeme had helped them choose it, and it would have been elegant on anyone used to wearing good clothes, but on Carl it looked as if handed down by more prosperous relatives. Afterward Baby had arranged a little celebration in a favorite restaurant of hers—it had been a favorite in the Kopf and Keller families for generations, so that Baby herself as a child, preceding Renata and Henry, had gone there for Sunday brunches and birthday teas. It was dense, plush, in menu and ambience very central European (though now owned by a midwestern conglomerate), and the waiters and some of the clientele were still shouting in their original accents. A round table had been prepared for Baby's party in the center of the restaurant under a light fashioned out of pink and red satin with colored streamers dangling from it. They were hemmed in by other tables in the center and down the sides of the room, all packed with people in a festive mood, leaving very little space for the waiters who could only get through with their trays and their hors d'oeuvre and dessert carts by emitting warning cries like porters on a crowded railway platform.

Besides the couple, the wedding party consisted of the bride's parents, Baby and Graeme; Henry, the bride's son, and presumably the groom's; and Baby had also asked Vera and her mother Irina as part of the family. Irina was weeping; tears were her natural response to all occasions. No one was sure whether they were happy tears or the reverse—the former might have been expected at a wedding, but with Irina nothing was ever unalloyed by sorrow. She wept over the past, not her own but her grandmother's, for Mme. Richter had carried her memories around like a set of holy icons and passed them on, enshrined in their cultured personalities, to her daughter and granddaughter. Only her great-granddaughter Vera was free of them, which seemed to make her light in body and spirit—a quality greatly admired by Henry who knew himself to be the opposite: squat and dark and burdened by the memories of a past that she had shaken off.

Renata, though resigned to being married, was not radiant. She had her usual air of discontent, which had nothing to do with Carl, but as everyone knew was more a divine discontent endemic to her nature. In contrast, Baby sparkled with her jewels, and high spirits; it was she who looked like the bride—looked, in fact, as she had done when she was Graeme's bride in his mother's garden on an English summer day. Probably nothing she had then expected had come to be, yet she carried on as though the cornucopia of her hopes had been abundantly filled by life in general—and by Graeme, her off-and-on husband, now seated next to her, old, gray, and sick, mumbling to himself (probably lines of poetry but it could have been any old man's mutter). She nudged him and called out, "Aren't we going to have any speeches?"

"Yes yes a speech!" It was Carl who scrambled to his feet before anyone could forestall him. It seemed that all his life he had been waiting for just this moment to address them, and also anyone at adjoining tables who would listen, and all around the restaurant, and indeed, if possible, all around the world. Bony, balding, and fervent, he stood in his wedding suit and expounded his philosophy. It did not matter that it was incomprehensible, for clearly it was something he believed in and lived by to his own satisfaction. After an exposition, which went on so long that Baby, though glad to see him happy, was devising a tactful way to make him stop, he turned to Henry to address him directly. He exhorted him to carry on his father's work—he didn't specifically mention who the father was, and in urging devotion to his work, was sincere and selfless in not caring whether it was he himself or another.

Nine

BABY SAID, "What do you think about Carl and Renata?"
"There's not much to think," Graeme replied. "They're
both insane."

Baby made a resigned gesture. However, there was their
grandson to consider, endangered she felt by his parents' ambi-
tion for him. "Do you believe any of it? Could it be?"

"You mean, could he be descended from what's-his-name—"

"The Master."

"That's not his name." Graeme said this in a way he had that
suggested private hinterlands of knowledge.

"Why, what do you know about him?" Baby took him up
sharply. "You don't know anything about him. You never even
met him."

"I didn't?" said Graeme with his secretive smile.

"You kept very quiet about it if you did."

"Well you see I never got to know him as intimately as you.
He never found me so irresistibly attractive that he made a
rendezvous (unfortunately not kept) to meet me in New York."

Although Baby was dying to know how and where Graeme
had met the Master, she knew it would be fatal to show curiosity. How childish he is, she thought—but with satisfaction that

he was still able to savor his little victories over her. She even humored him a little by asking, "Did you meet him in London?"

"I met him in India," Graeme said, and returning to Henry, "He's not taking any of this seriously, is he?"

"If he is, he is too much like you to let us know it . . . But in some ways he is *not* like you, and maybe he does take it more seriously than you would, or I, or," she added, "the Master"— which opinion Graeme neither contradicted nor affirmed, but as usual kept his own counsel.

That same night Graeme suffered some pains that had become familiar to him. He groped for his pill, always at hand, and while it melted under his tongue, he lay waiting for what might happen next. When nothing did, he thought, Not this time. He was relieved, but also somewhat disappointed, as though a promise were not being kept. He had begun to assume—almost to take for granted—that everything he perceived was a veil, a flimsy piece of gauze that it would be the easiest thing in the world to tear aside and enter into the really solid dimension behind it. Now he realized that it was not so easy after all—that he was more deeply embedded in his weakened body than he had thought possible, so that even the implosions that occurred within it could not shake him free.

Next morning, when there was no sound from his room for a long time, Baby cautiously entered. She saw him lying on his bed, his face turned to the wall, one hand limp on the covering sheet. She approached him; she put out her hand to touch his. She shook it, then his arm, his shoulder, she called his name. She woke him up; he turned his face toward her and opened his eyes and looked straight into hers. He managed to smile and to say, "Better luck next time."

Relief rushed over her—"How can you talk like that, how dare you!" and at the same time she fell on his shoulder and for a moment buried her face in it.

However, he felt it was time to impart to his grandson whatever knowledge he had relevant to the Master and his teaching. One day, when he was feeling better than usual, he offered himself for an outing with Henry. Henry liked accompanying his grandfather, who went at the same pace as his own; neither of them could walk far, and they soon hailed a cab to drive them. It was Graeme who chose their destination—a restaurant high up over the city where he used to take first Renata and then Henry on his visits to New York. The place had not changed since that time but continued to thrive on its appeal to nostalgia. The general style was of the thirties, with geometric motifs outlined in triple-colored fluorescent lights; later in the evening an orchestra would be playing tunes from that era. In addition to the old-fashioned ultra-modern interior, the main attraction was the view through the wraparound windows over the fabled city: superstructures reared mightily into the sky, while Gothic churches and turreted apartment buildings sat on the ground, like miniature models built to illustrate a variety of architectural styles.

If Graeme had chosen the place in search of some lost time— and he thought he had—his expectation was not fulfilled. He wondered aloud at his own lack of nostalgia—of pleasure or regret about anything; Henry suggested that perhaps Graeme was too far from his true home to be stirred to such sensations in this place.

"My true home," Graeme repeated. He narrowed his eyes at the brilliant view, in an attempt to convert it into the soft pastures and dripping trees of his homeland, but continued to feel nothing except the pleasant stimulation of his drink, a medically prohibited vodka on the rocks.

He began to talk to Henry about his meeting with the Master. This had been many years ago, and in India. Looking back at it now, Graeme thought of it as the best year of his whole life. "It was the year before I met your grandmother," he told Henry, adding, "I'm mentioning this as a matter of sequence not consequence." But it *had* been a good time for him—the war was over, he was about to be discharged, and in the meantime he was free to roam around India. He had sought out the Master in response to pleas from his aunt Cynthia. Just before the outbreak of war (the second one), the Master had mysteriously sunk out of sight. There were rumors that he had been interned in occupied Holland, and that he had escaped to Lisbon, finally that he was in Buenos Aires. None of these turned out to be true. It was not until the last year of the war that a report began to circulate that he had surfaced in India. At the time Graeme was wandering around between India, Burma, and Ceylon on the sort of missions that later became his standard mode of operation. Contacting him via a family friend in the War Office, Cynthia begged him to locate their Master, reputed to be somewhere in the Himalayas. Her letters—she sent several in quick succession—made Graeme smile: that in the current state of affairs she thought he had nothing better to do than go in search of her spiritual guide, and also that he was expected to find him among the snowbound peaks and gorges of the Himalayan mountain ranges.

However, he did find him, more or less by chance. ("There is no chance," said the Master later—but with Graeme he said it tongue-in-cheek, in parody of the sort of thing expected of him.) One of Graeme's Indian interests was the study of wood-carved temples, and having heard of a remarkable example in the Kulu valley, he made his way there via Mandi. It was a most enjoyable trip; and before returning to Delhi on the next stage of his journey home, he crossed a few more valleys and mountain passes to visit an army comrade stationed in a cantonment in the foothills. One very social evening, over their whiskey sodas in the mess, Graeme and his fellow officers discussed their imminent withdrawal from India. Most of them could not think what India would do without them, and the general opinion was that their place would be taken by a new conqueror: Russian, or Chinese, or even, joked one of them, a whole army of crusading holy men—"like that fellow who's taken Hobson's house up on Swan Point."

Graeme leaned forward. "What fellow would that be?"

His informant yawned at this turn in the conversation. "Some crackpot who says he's been living in a cave near Gilgit. He's not even Indian—the devil knows *what* he is—and the harem he has living with him all look like Scottish schoolteachers."

Graeme didn't ask any more but let the talk continue on the subject of their departure from India. Unlike most of the others, he regarded it as a victory for his generation of idealistic cynics who loathed the *type* of empire-builder—they had been his fags at school—even more than the idea of empire itself. Later Graeme somewhat changed not his mind but his feelings on the subject. Not that he wanted any of it back but for the vacuum it had left for his own class of Englishman, whose education and skills, and the character formed by them, had become redundant.

Next day he inquired his way to Hobson's house. Hobson had been an Englishman in the Indian Civil Service, and on his retirement, he had chosen to stay in India, in the house he had bought outside this hill cantonment. On his way there, after threading through the usual small bazaar, Graeme passed several other bungalow-type houses belonging to other retired British officers, or to wealthy Indians who had learned to live just like them. Hobson had died two years earlier and lay buried in the old Christian cemetery on the slope of the mountain. The house had been rented by this holy man of mysterious origin who had moved in with his followers—when Graeme arrived, two of these were working in the garden leading up to the front ve-randa, and they really did look like Scottish schoolteachers. The assiduous way in which they pruned and weeded, wearing gar-dening gloves, was very familiar to Graeme; the flowers they tended were also the same as in his mother's garden—hollyhock, flox, petunias, and foxglove. However, their manner was not like his mother but like the followers whom he had met around Cynthia—mild, patient, and spiritualized—so that he at once felt that the mysterious holy man would indeed turn out to be Cynthia's Master.

Graeme was received immediately: as usual, when surrounded only by his adoring followers, the Master was bored, and eager to see other visitors. And when he learned that Graeme was Cynthia's nephew, he got up and embraced him like a son. This was not altogether comfortable, for the Master was smeared with coconut oil, which Graeme feared might come off on his British officer's uniform. He had seen many photographs of the Master in Cynthia's house, but he would not have recognized the figure now before him. Having laid aside his English suits, the Master wore only a togalike ochre robe that left large orbs of him naked. Probably he had always been fat—he loved food—but now, with huge areas of flesh exposed, it could be seen just how fat. Yet he told Graeme that he had spent the last few years—the entire war—meditating in a Himalayan cave, sustaining himself on fruits and a few handfuls of rice. He gave no account of how he had managed so magnificently to thrive on this meager diet, but he did explain what had led him to his ascetic withdrawal. It had been for humanity, he said, the human race, which had reached such an impasse that it could be saved only by invoking higher powers for a renewed infusion of spirit. The Master could make such statements in the most matter-of-fact manner, waving his hand holding a cigarette; and, also deadpan, he went on to say that fortunately he had managed by his strenuous meditation to contact these powers and to draw down the current of their energy through the medium of his own psyche. It was not until he was entirely successful—that is, till the war had ended—that he had felt free to leave his cave and return to a more normal way of life. After this explanation, he regarded Graeme through his slanted, hooded eyes, as if challenging him to laugh; and when Graeme didn't, the Master himself did and invited him to stay for dinner.

Graeme enjoyed his company so much that he remained in the cantonment for a few extra days, during which he regularly visited him. The ambience of the house was a curious mixture. The Master had rented it from Hobson's heirs with all its Anglo-Indian furnishing intact. The dining table remained laid with bottles of tomato ketchup and Major Grey's mango chutney, and there was often a smell of scones that the followers were baking for tea. Two of them really had been Scottish schoolteachers, who had come out as governesses to Indian princesses; there was an English officer (a former Buddhist), and a German archaeologist, caught by the war in India, who had undergone a spiritual conversion during his internment as an enemy alien. These were all caught in the web, not only of the Master's teaching, but also of his luxurious way of living—a lot of rich Levantine cooking went on, which the Master, now that he had concluded his retreat, was the first to enjoy, along with his liqueurs and cigarettes.

It was the Master's habit to speak far more freely with outsiders than with his own followers. He told Graeme all sorts of things—for instance, that in his youth he had been a spy for the Russians in and around Afghanistan.

"Did you believe him?" Henry asked his grandfather.

"I did and I didn't," reminisced Graeme pleasurably. The lights of New York sparkled through the restaurant window while in memory Graeme saw himself sitting on Hobson's veranda—in the great silence of the mountains, under the stars shining pure and steady and seemingly much nearer than the electric lights flickering in the cantonment town. "But that was the way he wanted it—that you shouldn't know whether to believe or not believe him. He really enjoyed mystifying or downright fooling people."

"Not unlike yourself," Henry pointed out.

Graeme shrugged this away—neither denying nor affirming, just as the Master himself might have done. He did not tell Henry that the Master had set up a sort of permanent wink with him, in recognition of some mutual understanding. Graeme had liked it, though not sure what he was supposed to understand by it. He was at that time—and, in various ways, for the rest of his career—an intelligence officer, and when the Master declared himself to have been a spy, he might have wanted to inform Graeme that he knew all about his game. Yet at the same time the Master gave the impression that his own concerns went far beyond this activity—he seemed sometimes to deny any such involvement at all, and when on one evening he had related some fracas with a British agent in Kashgar, the following day he spoke of his discovery of a long-lost text of secret doctrine in a monastery located in the same place.

"Do you think he possibly did both?" Henry asked.

"Very possibly. And he spoke about both in the same tone— as making casual conversation over his after-dinner Armagnac, or whatever it was the Scottish schoolteachers kept pouring into his glass."

"And were they part of this conversation?"

"By no means. They hovered at a respectful distance till he hollered for them to come around with the drinks again. No, what he was telling me was highly confidential stuff, absolutely top secret, though why he should have chosen me as his confidant I couldn't begin to guess. Now, why should I be the only person in the world—as he led me to believe—to be told that his real name was Nasir Salah and that he was born in Tabriz, the son of a carpet seller?"

"But I knew that," Henry answered. "It's one of the versions of his autobiography we've been translating—that particular one was in French, as far as I remember."

Graeme laughed. "What were some of the other versions?"

"Oh don't ask," said Henry. Then he said, "Do you think he was serious about anything at all?"

"Yes I do think that," Graeme said. But he failed to specify what this might be. Instead his gaze moved outward again to the galaxy of silver lights on the heavenly darkness of the New York sky. Sixty-five stories below, the city shone and blazed like a shimmering ocean flowing in all directions. It reminded Graeme of the great ring of pure and endless light that was his favorite description of eternity. Nowadays it was lines like these that mostly played around in his head. He tried out some different ones—like that favorite of his earlier years, about the bird's flight from darkness into darkness. But he no longer found it as apposite as he had done in his youth.

Next day Henry asked Vera to get out the Master's autobiographical accounts. There were, as he had told Graeme, several versions of them, all contradicting each other but with the common factor that every one was hard to believe. In one, he was born in Tiflis, the son of a shoemaker, and as a small child had caused such a sensation (by speaking in tongues? by prognostication? the accounts differed) that he had been sent for by the Czarist court at St. Petersburg. In another, as the son of a prosperous horse dealer, he had accompanied his father's caravan to Kabul where he had encountered a mysterious emissary and followed him back to his Tibetan monastery to be initiated in secret doctrines. And so on and so forth. Henry laid these accounts aside: they may have thrown light on the Master's personality, and certainly his sense of humor, but none on his biography. The Master's early years—his ancestry, his provenance, his education, and his name—remained obscure.

But if nothing much could be deduced from their content, the form and method of their composition told something about his later way of life. There wasn't a single one that ended as it had begun—not even in the same language, for an account written in French might suddenly switch to Russian, and then to English, and maybe back again. Some of the pages had been typed, but mostly they were handwritten, and the calligraphy changed as often as the language. Evidently the Master had moved from country to country, from secretary to secretary, whirling from one center of his movement to another. It was well known that his arrivals were always sudden and unexpected, as were his departures, keeping his followers in a continuous state of expectation. Henry had assumed that this was a matter of policy with him—to some extent due to his general restlessness (he did get bored very quickly), as well as to keep everyone alert. But after Graeme's revelation, it occurred to Henry that there may have been a third reason, which was one of necessity: that the Master did not always want to move but sometimes had to. If he had really been, as he told Graeme, a Russian spy in certain sensitive border areas between India, China, and Russia, then he might not have been a welcome presence in London. This would account for his sudden, hitherto unexplained departure from England just before Elsa's arrival there, and his reluctance to return until many years later—until, with the independence of India, he was no longer persona non grata with the British government, and his English followers were able to get him an entrance visa.

The most authentic account of his early years came to Henry not from the Master's own papers but from the memories handed down by Mme. Richter to members of her family. Mme. Richter had first met him at a German spa, where she had gone in search of a cure for the terrible headaches that had begun to plague her some years after her, so far, childless marriage. Her husband, who was much older than she was, had been unable to accompany her, and she had joined an agreeable circle composed mainly of ladies and bachelors. Like Mme. Richter herself, they were all well off, cultured, and, in the case of the ladies, married to husbands who did not understand them (M. Richter, though devoted, was entirely unmusical). The Master had arrived at this health resort as tutor-companion to the children of a Viennese industrialist—two rather delicate boys, whom he was strengthening through long walks and healthy diet. His regime followed a well-known German system, supplemented by esoteric breathing exercises and secret herbal remedies that he had brought from some obscure place very far away.

He soon became influential among the members of Mme. Richter's circle, helping them with their medical and other problems. He was skilled in massage, which he practiced on Mme. Richter so effectively that her headaches almost entirely disappeared. In order not to interrupt her cure, she extended her stay at the spa, although her husband wrote many letters pleading with her to return. It was not until world war broke out (the first one) that she went back to Moscow—accompanied by her masseur, who became a member of the Richter household for almost four years. During that time, he established his reputation as a healer and performed some remarkable cures (he was the first person to use hypnotism for opium and alcohol addiction). It was at this time that he revealed his extraordinary array of talents and business skills. He dealt in antiques and jewelry; he imported carpets and exported furs; he built up a number of home industries, training some indigent girls to make paper flowers and others to copy corsets. People wondered about the protean nature of his sources of income and even more about what he did with the money. He lived entirely free in the wealthy Richter household and was never known to pick up a check in the cafés where he sat surrounded by his patients, students, and admirers. Moreover, in contrast to the later dandified figure, his appearance at this time was exceedingly shabby: his shoes were broken, and no one knew what he wore under the greasy overcoat that he never took off.

Later it turned out that he had saved everything in order to deposit some amounts in foreign banks and turn others into portable assets such as pictures and jewels. So it happened that when during the Revolution the Richter family and all his other patrons had to flee the country, leaving behind their estates and most of their wealth, he was able to gather them into a band of pilgrims and lead them through the confusion of Red and White Russian front lines to Essentuki and Tiflis and Constantinople and finally to Berlin and then to Paris. He supported them with the money he had saved in Moscow, and when that was gone, he started up his business enterprises again. He led them like a ringmaster—it was from this time that he took on some of the aspects of such a person: in his sweeping mustache, his flourish of manner and dress, and that glint in his eyes, cunning and amused, of one whose business it was to make others jump to the crack of his whip. Their journey took three years, during which time most of his followers left him, many of them because they quarreled with him, others because they could not stand the physical and even greater psychological rigors he imposed on them. The half dozen or so who stayed formed the nucleus of his future communes. They included the Richters—although M. Richter only made it as far as Constantinople where he died, worn out by the journey and unable at his age to bear such loss and deprivation. Mme. Richter, on the other hand, had become as robust as a farm woman; she no longer suffered from migraines, especially after her little daughter Sonia was born—with hair as blond as Mme. Richter's had been and eyes as dark as those of M. Richter's family (who had some German-Jewish ancestry), though slanting in a way that was not Jewish but from somewhere else.

Whenever the subject came up of the Master being Vera's great-grandfather, she said, if he was, he didn't do anything for us; on the contrary. Henry pointed out that it was due to him that the Richters had survived at all, but then Vera's eyes flashed blue fire and she said no, it was due to Mamenka, which was what she had called Mme. Richter. Mme. Richter was over ninety when she died, but right till the end she was their principal and often sole support. For many years they had lived in the front parlor of the German landlady's house, but by the time Vera was born, the house had been sold and they moved into a succession of apartments that were on very cheap leases because the building was about to be torn down. Vera was born in one of these short-term lodgings, and both Mme. Richter and her daughter Sonia died in another. Irina and Vera continued to shift from place to place, always renting out part of their accommodation to people who needed a temporary place to stay—different refugees newly arrived from different countries, single mothers, or women in the process of divorce.

But now, with her earnings from her work on the Master's papers, Vera had taken an apartment of her own, just for the two of them, herself and Irina. She was fiercely proud of it, and determined that from now on she would always earn enough to enable them to have a place to themselves. She was also glad to relieve her mother of the necessity of earning a living. Irina was of a dreamy disposition, prone to headaches, and work had never really suited her. Now, thanks to Vera's salary, she could stay home, busy only with making little embroideries—a coin purse or a cushion cover—to present as gifts to Baby and other friends whom she visited. For she had kept up that tradition of Mme. Richter's, of taking tea where she had once given piano lessons and the tactful passing of a little envelope at the end. These visits were terribly embarrassing for Vera and a constant source of contention between mother and daughter, but Irina derived too much pleasure from them to give them up.

When Henry thought about Vera and her work with him on the Master's papers, he envied her ability to go home and forget all about it. He remained behind, surrounded by those papers, simultaneously oppressed and excited by them; and always oppressed by his parents' expectations. And far from drawing to its conclusion, the work was taking on new momentum. More and more people heard about it, read his book, which was now in its second printing, wrote to inquire; here and there independent groups were beginning to meet to discuss the Master's ideas. Henry had also received offers for further publications, this time from a large mainstream publisher and for two volumes: one on the Master's teachings, the other on his life. Even if he ignored his parents' larger ambitions for him, many years of work lay ahead of Henry—many more years of living in the Master's presence.

When he talked about his doubts of continuing with the work to his grandmother, her first thought was of Vera. "What'll happen to the child if you fire her? Well, what is it except firing someone when you tell them their work is finished?"

"I didn't say it was finished. I said I didn't know if *I* could finish it."

"It's been so nice to have her here all day. Just think what it would be like if Vera didn't come anymore."

Henry said, "I really can't continue with something I no longer believe in just to keep Vera employed."

"Why not?"

"Are you asking why not Vera or why don't I want to continue?"

Baby evaded the question. "It's lovely to have a young girl in the house. It makes such a difference, like having your window open or shut."

Henry silently agreed with her. He remembered what she had said the next day. It was very hot, but Vera persuaded him to let her turn off the air-conditioning, which she disliked, mostly because she disliked being sealed in behind closed windows. She was wearing some sort of linen dress that opened down the front and she kept undoing more buttons, revealing the upper swell of her breasts; and she stretched, showing two dew-damp patches under her arms, and yawned too, not out of boredom but that lethargy that weighs down youthful limbs with too much vitality.

Suddenly he asked her, "Supposing I gave it up—what would you do?"

She was surprised. "I thought you liked it."

"In some ways—but I don't know that I believe in it as entirely as I ought to." She shrugged, and he said, "I know for you it's only a job."

"Yes but one I very badly need, and if I didn't have it, I wouldn't be able to pay the rent or anything."

Henry continued to think about his dilemma, and Vera's, after she had gone home, and it became so urgent to him that he felt he had to talk more about it with her. He took a cab to her place, where he had not been before. It was in an area for which ambitious plans had been drawn up but not carried through because funds had run out. Only Vera's apartment block had been completed, a thin pastel tower springing like a tall weed out of streets run to seed. The building kept itself aloof from its neighborhood. It had a security system and a lobby with strip lighting but not yet many tenants—most of the apartments had been empty for the three years since the building had been completed: the area not having come up to expectations, no one wished to sign a lease for them, except people like Vera who were glad to take advantage of the drastically reduced rent.

Henry announced himself over the TV security, so that when he emerged out of the elevator, Vera had had time to recover from the surprise of his arrival. But in any case she was taken up by other emotions—she was in the middle of a fight with her mother, who sat damply holding a crushed handkerchief. To get over his embarrassment, Henry looked around with exaggerated interest and complimented Vera on her apartment.

"Yes we have this nice place," Vera interrupted him hotly, *"and* I earn the money to pay the rent, so what need is there—"

"They want to give!" Irina wailed in protest. "They'd be hurt if I didn't take it!"

Henry understood that their quarrel was over the little envelope that was passed on as a matter of course every time Irina came to visit Baby. He was impatient with Vera for questioning this family tradition, but to distract her, he asked her to show him around the apartment. This did not take long—there were only two rooms, one of which Vera had fixed up for her mother and the other for herself. The building was so thin, tall, and insubstantial that it appeared to be swaying in the wind; already cracks had grown in the whitewashed ceiling and walls, giving warning that it might be about to totter and fall. But Vera had no sense of transience; she was proud to have established herself here. The place was full of light, for it was so high up that it appeared to be isolated in the sky among clouds.

"We don't need that money," she told Henry again as they stood together in her room. Henry liked being here with her instead of in his own place among the Master's papers. It made him feel freer to discuss the work they did together and his doubts about it. She said, "Well, Henry, I do need a job so if you decide not to go on I'd have to start looking around."

"Would it be very difficult for you to find another job?"

"Are you trying to tell me I should be looking?"

"No I'm only saying supposing, *if* I don't go on—"

"I'd hate to think," she interrupted, "that you'd go on for even a day, a *minute,* on my account. Because you needn't worry about that at all. Because I can always find something."

"Have you looked?" he said, too quickly to sound casual.

"Not actually, but people have asked me."

"I didn't say I wasn't going on," said Henry.

"No," said Vera, "but maybe I really do need a change."

"From me?"

"Not from you. Of course not, Henry . . . And I wouldn't ever leave until you found someone to take over from me."

"There's no one like that and never will be."

"No one! Never!" Vera echoed sarcastically and louder than they had been talking up to now, so that her mother called from the next room:

"Vera, you're not quarreling with Henry?"

She came to the door and Vera stepped away from Henry and said at once, "No, I'm quarreling with you because you're so horribly stubborn and never listen to me."

Her mother came up to her and softly took her hand, murmuring the sweetest endearments. "I mean it," said Vera, both frowning and leaving her hand to be fondled.

"I don't know what to say to this child," Irina appealed to Henry. "I love to visit with your dear grandmother, talking about my darling precious Mamenka and how she adored you all. And then my Vera scolds me and says I shouldn't go."

"I never said that, and you know it! You know what it is that makes me so angry and ashamed." And Vera blushed—right up to her eyes, the way she always did.

"I go to see my friends and my child is ashamed," Irina said to Henry. "How many friends do we have in this world, she and I, that we can't go to them with open hearts."

"And open hands," Vera muttered, not for Henry to hear. But he did, and felt himself to be a constraint on mother and daughter—without him, they would have relieved their feelings more extravagantly and more quickly. Now Vera turned on him: her eyes sparkling in her flushed face, she took a chair and compelled him to sit, for she knew it was painful for him to stand too long; but her thoughtfulness carried some of her present anger against her mother, and probably a bit against him too, for being there as a witness.

As he settled himself laboriously on the chair, Henry felt Irina regard him in the "oh poor boy" way he had long since learned to live with—in her case, laden with sorrow for the suffering in the world, of which she and her family had always carried such an unfair share.

Aware of his stoical discomfiture, Vera felt more anger against her mother. "I don't know why we have to talk about it before Henry. It must be terribly embarrassing for him."

"But he's our family! There's no embarrassment in a family!"

"Oh yes there is," said Vera. "You know how I feel when you go there—and to other places—" she broke off, biting her lip; there *were* other places, her mother took them in rotation and made notes in a little diary as to when it was whose turn.

"All very old family friends from the time of Mamenka," Irina defended herself. "They would be hurt and offended if I stopped visiting with them. Mamenka went regularly, she was expected

—long after the children didn't need piano lessons anymore, and the grandchildren too had gone away. And when she was ill and too weak to go, she'd send me, and however much I said, 'Oh no, Mamenka, it's snowing outside and so cold and I have no boots,' she'd be very strict—'No, Irinichka, hot or cold, these are our friends who have the right to expect our friendly call.' It was the way she was brought up, when people left cards on each other," Irina explained to Henry, proud to belong to such a tradition. "Vera is a very clever girl, much more than I ever was, but she forgets sometimes who we are."

"Who?" Vera teased, not requiring the answer she had grown up with.

Her mother took her literally; she went into the next room and soon reappeared with a photograph which she thrust at Henry. "This is who," she said. "And you can see for yourself— look, it's my Vera completely, completely Vera."

The photograph showed Mme. Richter in the earliest years of her marriage to the wealthy M. Richter. Henry gazed at the portrait with interest but found it difficult to see Vera in the young woman seated on a curved carved sofa beside a round marble-topped table on which was placed a bouquet in a vase. The photograph was almost a hundred years old and had brown stains like liver spots on the cardboard in which it was set. It wasn't only Vera whom it was impossible to trace back to the elegant lady in the picture but even more the Mme. Richter they all remembered, who had looked and smelled like a pawnbroker.

Irina appreciated the respectful way in which Henry gazed at the photograph; she sat down next to him and fondled his hand as she had done Vera's. "I can be quite frank with you," she said. "And I'm very, very happy you came today so that we can have a real heart-to-heart talk."

"Oh no please, Mummy." Vera was standing above the two of them, smiling down at them.

"But it's about you, darling: everything in my heart is about you. Of course I'm glad she's working with you," Irina returned to Henry. "I know you care for her and look after her, but it's not for her whole life."

"Then what's for my whole life?" asked Vera, tenderly mocking.

Her mother continued to address Henry as the more serious person. "I want her to be with a good family like yours but not only as a working girl."

"Mummy, Mummy, you sound like you're proposing to Henry for me," Vera groaned in what she pretended was embarrassment but was really amusement as at something absurd.

Irina was truly shocked. She gave Henry another of her pitying glances, making it clear to him how very little he entered into her calculations. "Henry knows I'm talking to him as a friend, as a family member, someone who cares for you as I do and is worried about you, day and night thinking what is to happen to Vera." She burst into tears—her general tears, but also for being so misunderstood. Vera melted at once, she knelt on the floor and put her arms around her mother to comfort her. The two of them were now completely engrossed in each other, Irina protesting that everything she did and said and thought was only for Vera, and Vera repentant, asking forgiveness, with only a glance to spare for Henry—almost of reproach, as though he had tried to come between them.

When Renata was a girl, Baby, who could hardly wait for her to form romantic attachments, was foiled by Renata's complete indifference. Now too she would have loved to discuss with her the interesting possibility between Vera and Henry but instead found herself having to refute any idea of it.

This is the way Renata usually spoke of Vera: "What's she doing here? What use is she to him?"

"Poor girl, she needs a job," Baby would reply. And to soothe Renata's angry heart: "He's only working with her, darling. You know how it is when people work together, they don't really get involved in any other way."

"I don't know that," frowned Renata. In fact, she thought the opposite—that the primary contact was through the mind, and if anything followed, it was as a mere corollary.

In search of someone more like-minded with whom to share

her thoughts, Baby invited Irina to a tête-à-tête lunch. But here too the subject did not develop along lines Baby had anticipated; instead she learned about a chapter of Richter family history—or rather, two chapters, both hitherto kept secret. She had taken Irina to a place that was a favorite with many of her friends because it reminded them of the cruises they took in winter. The decor was as airy as an island café and the waiters in their white uniforms looked like naval officers. The drinks were colored and came in tall glasses topped with little parasols—a playful note that disguised their potency. Irina, taken in, sucked at hers as at a particularly luscious ice-cream shake. The effect was swift and startling.

Like a burner lit under a test tube to change the chemistry of its contents, the South Sea Island drink drove Irina's blood and made it boil. The Irina whom Baby had always known, who accepted checks and made gifts of her embroideries, turned out to be a mask under which the real Irina seethed at every slight leveled at her poor appearance. And aside from the injuries within her own biographical span, there were those reaching back into the past. She spoke of fathers: in this connection, she passed the Master over completely and acknowledged only M. Richter, who had provided a handsome house in Moscow for his wife's musical soirées. When she spoke of him, Irina straightened her shoulders, and her eyes, no longer lowered, flashed proudly into Baby's face.

But this pride was extinguished when she came to speak of her own father. Here Baby became very interested, for she had never heard mention of him or his identity or even his existence. It turned out that his name was Werner and that he was their German landlady's son. Irina now spoke with a rage as uncharacteristic of her as pride. He had taken advantage of his position in the house to insinuate himself into the Richter family. Otherwise, what chance would he have had to enter such a refined circle—this Irina had often heard as a child, when bad feeling had broken out between Mme. Richter and the German landlady. These quarrels, usually sparked off by something domestic like a bathtub left with a dirty rim, were conducted in a manner characteristic of the two protagonists: by the landlady in a tangy German expressing contempt for the pretensions of those who didn't have two cents to rub together, while Mme. Richter remained tight-lipped and courteous, and so deadly that the landlady was left oozing tears like a sausage releasing its fat. She was right to be upset by these insinuations, which unfairly included her son. Werner was not in the least like his mother— this was what made her treasure him so, his mutation from herself. He had charm and flair and wave upon wave of blond hair; he dressed well and danced well, was always in good humor, and with manners so perfect that they appeared inbred. He was welcome everywhere, and most of all in his mother's house where his visits were sporadic but prolonged. Toward the end of them he was so bored that he hardly got out of bed and could be seen at noon in his pajamas, yawning and rubbing his beautiful hair; it was as though he were there not exactly as a captive but as one who had to wait out something. Mme. Richter's daughter was demure, fair, and slight—a typical *jeune fille,* but her slanting eyes added an exotic note that must have been piquant to a young man cooling his heels in his mother's house.

Baby ordered another drink, and this time Irina wasted no time with a straw but drank deep from the glass before continuing to talk about her father. Yes, she had known him, he had come to the house in his old way, irregularly and staying for long stretches of time. She had not cared for him; his charm did not work on children, and he never brought her any presents. It was owing to him that they all finally had to vacate the house; his mother had been forced to sell it to get him out of some trouble he had had in Philadelphia. The Richters moved with another refugee family into a railroad flat and were mostly out of touch with their former landlady. Only sometimes she sent them photos of Werner cut out of the social pages, where he was observed at a black tie benefit, smiling with his hostess and a fellow guest. But later he got into more trouble, no one knew what, though there were rumors of a prison sentence; anyway, he disappeared out of the social pages and out of the lives of the Richters.

Baby now suggested finishing their meal with coffee and dessert, but Irina preferred another potent pineapple drink, to give her strength to carry on with her story. She confessed how, after finishing high school, she had longed to take some course—bookkeeping or physiotherapy—but it was never possible. Her mother was too delicate and sickly to work, so it was Irina who had to help her old grandmother with giving the piano lessons and collecting the welfare and other checks that kept them all going. On weekends Irina would wait for her elders to fall asleep to have an hour or two when she could leave the railroad flat and walk by herself in the street or the park. She was already thirty years old, and nothing had ever happened to her and she hardly knew anyone except her grandmother, her mother, and the refugee families with whom they shared the rent on their accommodation. So those solitary walks she took were exciting to her, not because of anything that happened but for the thoughts she had about things that might happen. Sometimes these were so thrilling that her cheeks flushed and she broke into a run. However, if anyone tried to speak to her, she averted her face and fled; but few people did, for her shy loneliness made her appear awkward and grim.

The young Irishman was lonely himself, so he persisted. Irina had never had anyone so eager for her company, or anyone so ready to do all the talking. Within five minutes she knew he came from Belfast where he worked in the post office; that he was visiting a cousin in New Jersey who would get him a green card and a job with the telephone company, if he liked it here and decided to stay. And he thought he would; he appreciated the way the sun was always shining, and it made him realize that he was tired of living in a place where it never shone. Yes, he was sure he would stay, he said; he took her hand and she left it in his, and soon he was swinging their clasped hands as if they held a child between them. They had turned into Central Park and walked up and down little hillocks and winding paths and under a bridge and over a bridge. It was a Saturday afternoon—a sunny summer Saturday—and a concert of country music was going on and there was singing through loudspeakers. They didn't join this concert but wandered into lonelier spots till they came to a dell where there was only one other couple, stretched out on the grass.

Irina and the Irishman sat under a clump of trees where moss grew; soon they were lying on this moss. Irina was looking up, past the ear of her companion; she saw the tops of the trees where they merged and became lacy like a veil through which light poured, sky-blue turning into green as it descended through the leaves. The sun had released all the odors stored within the grass and trees, and green moisture oozed from every pore of the earth. Irina always liked to think that Vera had been conceived on that day and not on the following one, when it had rained. They had taken shelter under the same group of trees but nevertheless got wet; nor was there any music on that second day, the concert having been canceled because of the weather. It rained for most of the week, which was perhaps why the Irishman didn't come up from New Jersey as he had planned. He didn't come up on the following weekend either, although it was sunny again, and more beautiful than ever; but perhaps he had grown discouraged by the climate and decided that, if it was going to rain here too, he might as well go back to Belfast.

Ten

FOR ALL her pride, Vera was inconsistent—partly due to Baby, partly to her own overwhelming desire, so that she gave in to temptation. It had to do with Baby's jewelry, of which Baby had a great deal. She had always loved it. There were some pieces she never took off—several rings, sapphires and diamonds, that had come to her from the Kopf and Keller side of the family; these in fact she couldn't take off, because with age her fingers had swollen around them so that they were now wedded to her flesh; and there were sets of gold bangles, some inset with precious stones, that Kavi's family had saved from the wreck of their fortunes. Other pieces—earrings, necklaces, bracelets, brooches, hair ornaments—she kept in inlaid boxes that overflowed onto her dressing table and into its drawers, so that she only had to dip in her hand to pull out some glittering ornament with which to adorn herself. The more valuable pieces she kept in her bank vault, and whereas in earlier years she had made regular trips to retrieve them for some special occasion, nowadays she had almost forgotten about them, or at least had tucked them away into a corner of her mind where they glittered along with other precious memories. When Renata was small, Baby had assumed that in the course of time everything would be

worn and enjoyed by her; but as her daughter's personality un-
folded, Baby realized that, though Renata would inherit everything, she would only keep it locked up, passionless but posses-
sive, the way she kept her money. The most she would ever wear
was a string of balsam beads, not for their ornamental but for
their spiritually healing quality.

Like a woman with a store of love unused, Baby longed to
bestow her treasure where it would be appreciated. One day she
called Vera into her bedroom; she opened first the top drawer,
then the next and the next. Vera gasped with all the pleasure
that gushed from Baby's own heart; and when Baby fastened a
string of pearls around her neck, Vera, smiling and shining,
couldn't stop looking at herself in the mirror. "No it's yours,"
said Baby when at last, with reluctant fingers, Vera made to take
it off. On that first occasion Vera protested vigorously and had to
be persuaded; on the second—for both took immense pleasure in
the repetition—she gave in sooner, on Baby's untruthful assurance that it was just costume jewelry; and after that it became an
accepted habit between them that, whenever Baby beckoned her
into the bedroom, Vera would emerge with some new piece
shining on her person and joy in both their eyes. They never
spoke of this transaction to anyone, and it might have been
regarded as a secret between them if Vera hadn't quite openly
worn whatever was given to her.

"Is that new?" Henry would say.

"Don't you recognize it? Baby gave it to me."

"It suits you," was all he said, as though he didn't care very
much about the piece itself or who gave it to her.

This assumed indifference was to cover up the pleasure he
derived from her physical presence. Vera carried a delicious fragrance, quite different from all Baby's fragrances, which were
also delicious but expensive and imported. Vera had principally
her own young-girl smell, its freshness compounded of her
shampooed hair and whatever she chose to spray on herself by
way of floral colognes. Once a month there was another smell,
with which Henry was familiar from his mother and had always
disliked; but with Vera it was not sour but healthy, natural,

young blood flowing. Vera thought a lot about her clothes, but once she wore them, she forgot about them, letting them become part of herself, so that each fold of her dress followed the movements of her body. And she moved a lot, not because she was restless but because she was active, and every time she did, there was a jingle of jewelry—a real gold jingle, for she now only wore what Baby had given her. This sound, light and fine, enveloped her as her smell did—in fact, these two delights of the senses were inseparable, as when a breeze releases the scents of a flowering tree in which birds are also rustling and chirping.

Graeme was as quick as his grandson to notice Baby's gifts to Vera. "I say!" he exclaimed, his eyes at once appraising the new acquisition, along with its effect on Vera.

When she asked, "Do you like it?" he answered with enthusiasm: "Of course I do, I always have done," for he knew each of Baby's ornaments as intimately as he did each of her characteristics. He never gave any indication that he wasn't tremendously pleased to see his wife's jewelry transferred to Vera. But he took it up with Baby—not the first or second time it happened, but when it had gone on for several months. "Are you planning to give her the whole lot?" he asked Baby, so abruptly that she could easily have pretended not to know what he was talking about. But they had got beyond such prevarications with each other.

"I can't resist it," she frankly explained. "She looks so lovely —jewelry suits her so, and she doesn't have anything, poor child. And it's not as if it's going out of the family because she is family—think of it, how far we go back, with poor Mme. Richter . . . And then she does so much for Henry. Here, this is getting cold." The reason she had come into Graeme's room, as she did every evening, was to slip a hot-water bottle under his covers. Although he turned the heat up very high, making his room as stifling as his London den, he could never get warm enough and wore a scarf permanently knotted around his neck. His feet especially always remained cold—how well she knew those large, white, cold English feet! Now he quietly submitted to her hot-water bottle, though at first he had kicked it out, as an affront to his manhood.

"Did you see her this evening in my mango earrings? Wasn't she enchanting? Enchanting," she said, clapping her hands and smiling in a way that made him smile too, but at Baby herself. "I watched her going out and her friends oohing and aahing as soon as they saw her—oh they knew the difference between *my* earrings and that handmade stuff they hang all over themselves. Still, they look good, don't they, and probably they have a nice time though I don't know what they do in those cellars they sit in and their dirty lofts. When I ask her, she says, 'Oh you know,' and I guess I do know—at that age just to be together generates all that electricity." She grasped his toes through the blanket and shook them.

He said, "And Henry? They're together all day—don't they generate electricity?"

"Henry is different. His personality is different."

But for once she regretted Henry's personality. She felt that, by being too rational in a situation where reason was not called for, he was hindering Nature from rolling out her bigger guns.

When Graeme lay awake at night, often till the early hours of the morning, he was aware of his grandson on the other side of the wall, as awake as himself, silently burrowing around in the Master's papers, seeking out whatever might be hidden there. This activity was not unlike Graeme's own had been—he too had preferred a burrowing mode of operation, in his case not in papers but in reality, which he loved. He had had two principal passions in his life—his work and his relations with women; both had been as much under cover as he could manage, so that no one knew about either in their entirety except himself, and the one pleasure left to him was to keep it that way.

His favorite memories were of occasions when work and women had coincided. There had been any number of female couriers with whom he had enjoyed himself in brief, inconsequential encounters, though these were somewhat spoiled for him by their commonplace settings: the lobbies and swimming

pools of international hotels, and amid their sheets, which, however tumbled, remained stiff with professional laundering. But
there were a few happy occasions when he could more deeply
infiltrate the foreign city to which he was posted. Among his
contacts were, besides higher-ranking officers, clerks with access
to papers he preferred to have in his possession rather than in
that of his French, Swedish, or Russian counterparts. There was
one marvelous night in the humbler section of an oriental city,
far from the diplomatic center where he carried on his official,
above-ground business. He was not unfamiliar with these streets:
he made a point, as soon as he arrived in any city, of acquainting
himself with its general layout, as well as its quirks and alleys.
But hitherto he had seen these particular streets only in the
daytime, when they were overlaid with the activities of shops
spilling out on to their sidewalks, pregnant housewives with
children hanging on to their garments, rickshaws, stray dogs and
cows, and washermen ironing sheets on boards laid out at crossroads. But on that occasion, when he had come on business
rather than a random survey, it was night and the entire maze of
streets lay asleep as under a spell. Moonlight pouring from above
transformed them into a shimmering landscape, so that even the
very ordinary government quarters, new though cracked like
ancient monuments and with washing strung out on crooked
balconies, appeared enchanting. The smell too had changed: instead of the everyday city fumes mixed with bad drains and
rotting vegetables, there hung the faint but piercingly sweet
odor of mysterious bushes that flower only in the night.

Graeme had come by appointment and prearranged signal,
but as soon as he had walked up the stone staircase to an upper
floor and rapped on the designated door, he realized that his
contact had failed him. When he was not admitted as promptly
as he had been promised, he pushed very gently against the door,
which gave slightly before it struck against a barricading chain.
The rasping sound made by the chain alerted someone inside
who had been waiting—not for Graeme, it was made clear by
the sharply intimate query in the local dialect, but for an over-
due member of the household. Graeme softly inquired for this

same person, and the woman who had answered came to the door
so that he could partly see her, and she him, through the opening left by the chain. He understood her to say that the man he
wanted was not there and to comment on his absence with some
pungency, but when Graeme asked humbly if he could wait,
there was a moment's pause in her invective. He was aware of
being measured through the gap, weighed as to his greater potential of danger or excitement. Then with a gesture of recklessness—he realized at once she was a reckless woman—the chain
was unfastened and the door flung open so wide that not one but
any number of men could have poured in. There she stood, short,
squat, and defiant, without her veil and in the crumpled cotton
tunic and trousers that evidently served as her day and night
clothes. She was not at a loss for words—all to do with the
failings of the missing husband he had come to find. Although
unable to understand her, Graeme could guess at those failings:
his contacts were usually people who needed money rather desperately to support their bad habits. This one anyway had a wife
ready to challenge him, and in his absence to turn on Graeme,
who put up his hands in self-defense and retreated a few steps,
laughing; she followed him, working herself up. He admired her
spirit—he liked being attacked as someone else's husband—and
from there he went on to admire her. She was homely, with
pockmarked skin and a coil of greasy hair hanging down; but her
low-cut tunic dipped into a wonderful cleft promising huge
mounds to be explored by anyone ready to plunge in there. She
was soon aware of Graeme's gaze lingering on that place—had
they met under ordinary circumstances, it would have been
veiled and hidden from his eyes. But now nothing was ordinary:
they were in her family living room, turned for the night into a
marital bedroom with two string beds set out side by side, each
spread with a mat and a single sheet. Evidently she had been
lying on her sheet, for it was tossed around and crumpled. She
put back the chain on the door and closed another door leading
to an adjoining room, where perhaps some children slept and an
old grandmother. The window had bars on it and its glass was

open to let in whatever cool air there might be, along with the moonlight and the fragrance of the night-flowering bush.

Graeme, at that time in his late thirties, had reason to consider himself experienced with women of the West and of the East. He knew this about the latter: that the more secluded, the more repressed, and the more ignorant they were kept, the readier they were to break out—and with a wildness that was astonishing and of course delightful. And if they had reached an age where they were no longer really young but not quite middle-aged—though aware that this was not far off—then their abandon could rise to heights that belonged in the realm of fable or fantasy. This was the case with his present partner: he had suspected her recklessness but now learned its full extent. At one point she screamed so loudly that he put his hand over her mouth, which annoyed her and she beat it aside and went on screaming; perhaps, if there were children, they slept very soundly and the grandmother may have been deaf. The fact that they had no language in common nor any knowledge of each other beyond the carnal helped them over the usual restraints of human contact. There was also a sense of urgency, for the husband might return at any moment. When he did, muttering outside and fumbling with the lock until stopped by the chain, the guilty couple were regretful but not in panic. Pulling her trousers up and her tunic down, she made her way to the door at her own pace; and before unfastening the chain, she let loose some more invective to confound the man outside and give the one inside time to arrange his clothing. When the husband was at last let in, he was already crushed, and now confronted not only by an angry wife but also by Graeme, who had taken his place on a cane chair and, crossing his legs and tapping one foot in the air, pointed at his wristwatch to indicate a time far in advance of the appointed hour.

Graeme's work took him into widely different milieux, and not long after his encounter with the clerk's wife, and in the same country, he attended a banquet at the President's palace held in honor of a visiting English cabinet minister. Earlier that day, along with members of this dignitary's delegation, he had sat in on a high-level conference—a purely formal and very dull affair, for the real decisions had been taken weeks before at a much lower level. While the English delegates were so disciplined that they did not even have to try to stifle their yawns, the President, who was a very old man and knew he did not have much longer in office, felt under no constraint to pretend to listen but sat amusing himself with balancing a rose on his bald head. The banquet promised to be an equally somnolent occasion. It was the third Graeme had had to attend in the same place in as many weeks, and since it was a country with a prohibition on liquor, he had prudently fortified himself beforehand. The surroundings were grand but the guests were not. A mixture of British civil servants and local peasant politicians, they sat stiffly at the long banquet table, overwhelmed by the enormous chandeliers, the golden plates, the goblets full of pineapple juice, and the tall palace servants in majestic uniforms standing behind their chairs. The only pleasure to be derived from these banquets, at which there was no kind of human interchange, was the purely subjective one of knowing oneself to be sufficiently important to have been invited. There was always a dearth of women guests, and on a previous occasion Graeme had found himself seated between two men, a deputy minister and a joint secretary—which was not amusing but on the whole preferable to a wife who said nothing because she knew no English or a woman politician who never stopped talking because she knew everything. But this time Graeme considered himself lucky, for he was seated next to the President's niece. At that time she was not yet important—she was known only as the Niece—which was how she had fallen to his lot. She was as pleased as he was— "At last someone to talk to!" she exclaimed when it turned out he was familiar with the work of certain poets she was crazy about. Altogether she was crazy about literature and music and art, but her conversation soon strayed from these subjects to their fellow guests, whom she declared to be boring and backward. She herself was certainly very different. She had gone to school in Switzerland, followed by a language course in London, had cut her hair short, and did not veil her face or even her neck and shoulders. She drew the eyes of most of the peasant cabinet ministers at the banquet table but she was contemptuous of them. She concentrated all her attention and charm on Graeme; her back turned on her other neighbor, she appeared to move closer and closer to Graeme, touched his sleeve with a painted fingernail to emphasize her opinions, and allowed his manly whiskey breath to play over her face.

In her way she was as reckless as the clerk's wife. She invited Graeme to lunch with her at the government villa allotted to her by her presidential uncle. He found himself alone with her, for her son was away at school and her husband had departed some years before. She was as frank about her husband, even at this first lunch, as she was about everything else. Although it had been a love match—she would rather, she said, have jumped down a well than submit to an arranged marriage—it had not worked out, for her husband had not shared her interests. That was why she felt drawn to Graeme, she said, because she had known at once that he was one of the rare souls who spoke the same language. He took this as invitation, but when he tried to follow it up by saying something gallant, she drew right back into talk about literature, protesting how she hated politics and her political family and longed to be a writer or an interior decorator. He managed to draw her forward again with a poetic quotation about public and private faces but spoiled it with too personal a reference to her own face. So it went on for a while, and he found it really delightful to be flirted with so chastely. The invitation to lunch was repeated, and the same thing happened the next time and the next. Then Graeme became a bit impatient—he was not used to wasting his time in these matters —and turned the conversation to the subject of love and sex, in a purely theoretical way of course, which was received well. They talked freely and, after some time, less theoretically. At last, after coffee and when the servants had retired to their afternoon siesta, she allowed him into her bedroom where she continued to talk as freely and boldly as before, but there he found her recklessness stopped short; for, unlike the clerk's wife, it turned out that she didn't like anything about sex except to discuss it.

From his point of view it was an unsatisfactory affair—but in later years it was the only one Baby really got to hear about. This was because the Niece became very famous as a political leader: yes, she who had despised politics and loved only literature had allowed herself to be persuaded to stand for office; and having once tasted power could not bear to relinquish it. Years after she was assassinated, when Graeme was a sick old man being cared for in his wife's New York apartment, a young woman came to interview him for a biography she was writing about the Niece. She considered the encounter to be historical—in fact, congratulated herself to find still alive the man who had been the great love in the life of her dead subject. For that was how he was featured in the secret diaries to which the interviewer had been granted access. Graeme knew about the diaries—they weren't all that secret, at least not to him, for the Niece had read him long extracts during their hours together. They had been mostly about her feelings, both positive and negative—the former for a beautiful sunset she had seen illuminating the walls of the old city fort, the latter for the crass and materialistic people she met. But she had never read him the passages relating to himself; nor was he allowed to see them now—the interviewer guarded them jealously as a scoop for her own publication. But she gave him to understand that they were the most torrid in all the diaries, and moreover continued for many years after he had gone away. This saddened him, for he had not had such feelings for her at all, and in fact remembered her less poignantly, in spite of her later fame, than he did (for instance) the clerk's wife, or any number of flimsy girls whom he had come across acting as intermediaries for someone's shady deals.

But Baby brooded profoundly about the Niece—and also about the interviewer. She accused Graeme of flirting with the young woman, claiming that he couldn't keep his eyes off the thigh exposed by her skirt—which, in any case, said Baby, was too short for someone with not very good legs. Then she switched to the Niece, congratulating him on so successfully keeping this historic affair a secret from the world as well as his wife. Unexpectedly he did not counter with the superior smile she hated so much, but quite seriously assured her that the lady was as completely out of his mind as she had been out of his sight, except when her picture appeared in the newspapers—for instance, on her election, her state visits, and on her assassination. He was truly puzzled to discover himself as a leading character in her diaries; for whereas he had realized that his occasional afternoons with her would not have gone undetected —the servants who had so discreetly withdrawn would have seen to that—he had not suspected that they could ever have been considered anything but minor in comparison with her other affairs. But apparently there had been no one else. He didn't even know her all that well, he told Baby, and frankly she was not the type of woman he would have wanted to be involved with very closely: he couldn't, he said, handle anyone so *subjective.*

"Yes of course," said Baby. "You can only handle idiots like me."

"Well at least with you one doesn't have to listen to all sorts of psychology and nonsense."

This may not have sounded terribly complimentary, but all the same Baby felt flattered. Married to him on and off for almost fifty years, she realized she really was his type; and moreover that he trusted her enough to talk to her with a frankness that was quite foreign to his nature.

He told her not only about his meeting with the Niece at the banquet and the following afternoons, but also about one last encounter long afterward when she had already attained historical stature. He had remained what he was—or rather, had diminished, for he was close to retirement and still no higher than a middle-ranking diplomat. He was considered an expert on her country, which was how he had come to revisit it in the train of an English parliamentary delegation. He had followed her career with amused surprise: right from the time she had let herself be persuaded, for the sake of her country, to be elected from a safe seat. Everyone except herself was aware that she was being manipulated by powerful politicians, who thought to use her till the time was right for their own purposes. But once she was in, it was impossible to get her out. However much she may have hated politics and yearned only for a private life as a writer or interior decorator, power turned out to be very much to her taste. By the time he met her again, she had reached the highest office, and it was generally known by what progressively more ruthless methods she had attained it. Graciously she had granted Graeme a private interview. Of course it wasn't very private, she was too busy for that, and he had to share the time with a Polish artist who had come to paint her and an American journalist working on an in-depth profile. These two sat on either side of her, not unlike a manicurist and a masseuse, while Graeme was allotted a chair facing her. Although many years older than when they had last met, she had kept herself wonderfully well and, aided by professional skills, had greatly enhanced her style. She still spoke in the same soft feminine lilting accent, which gave no hint of the methods she had used on her opponents, and the sort of things she said to Graeme and simultaneously to the American journalist—for private and public were no longer differentiated for her—were also still the same: how her personality was such that all she really wanted was to read, reflect, and devote herself to those she loved.

"She *stank*," Graeme told Baby in a tone of such disgust that for a moment she took him literally. It wasn't that—on the contrary, he said, she was exceptionally well-powdered and perfumed, cosmetics wrapping her in a rosy cloud, like an angel or another superhuman being. Nevertheless, beneath all that daintiness he had recognized the stench he knew well—of power, or the love of power. The major part of his working life had been spent in countries where power was new and raw and attainable so that there were many out to get it. He had often been— always in some humble capacity—in the presence of dictators, and in all of them he had sensed that exaltation he recognized in her. It was truly exaltation, for she felt herself raised above other human beings; and this made her sparkle—all the dictators he had known had sparkled, with shining eyes and medals and teeth as healthy as a shark's—and gave her that beauty he had been surprised to read described in magazine articles. For in her youth she had not been beautiful; her nose was too long and appeared longer because of her morose expression. Graeme realized he had been summoned to witness her transformation and to revise his memories of her in her youth and unimportance. Seated between artist and journalist, a globe of the world at her shoulder, she radiated triumph at him.

"One gets used to people changing. They grow old and gray, for one thing, and wrinkled—present company excepted," Graeme gallantly remembered whom he was talking to.

But Baby said, "Yes yes," impatient for him to go on talking in that reflective, inward-looking way as though she were part of himself.

"Or they get sick," said Graeme, "and become transformed that way. But *her* transformation came from this wonderful fountain of triumph and power springing up inside her that made her radiant and beautiful."

"And I suppose you were dying to go to bed with her again."

"Haven't you listened to *any*thing I told you?"

"Or she with you: since we now hear how you were the great love of her life."

"I wonder," said Graeme. "I think it was the sort of thing she had to confide to a diary since she was keeping one. It was all in her head, sex and every other natural feeling, of which I don't believe she had any very strong ones—till she felt power. But then! I tell you, it was a physical force in that room. It made me come out in a cold sweat—no, not of desire, don't worry, unless it was the desire to get out of there and breathe some clean air. But that wasn't all that easy—you had to wait out your time till some minion tiptoed in to remind her of her next appointment. 'Oh what a bore,' she said then, all girlish and informal. She gave me her hand to shake and I was even encouraged to hold it for a moment. No I did not," he answered Baby. "I gave it back as soon as possible. That made her smile—she thought I was overwhelmed—which I was, although not in the way she thought. I loathed her," he concluded, slowly and emphatically. And he did not retract when Baby rebuked him for speaking this way of someone who was dead—and moreover dead in such a terrible manner, shot while watching a parade of patriotic schoolchildren. But Graeme said that, if she had consented to die at all, this was the way she would have chosen: in a public place, her slain corpse on the front pages of the world's newspapers— "And not like the vulgar rest of us," he said, "dead of a common or garden heart attack."

"Be quiet," said Baby, secretly crossing fingers on both hands.

Henry had not shared his doubts about continuing his work on the Master's papers with his mother. There was never any need for him to tell her anything, for Renata was abnormally quick to sense any mood or intention of his. So one evening she appeared in his room. She was shy, not looking him in the face, her attention fixed on closing a button on her denim jeans. She said, "I want to tell you something. About the Master."

"Oh the Master," yawned Henry. "I think I'm quite tired of him, and can you wonder, what with digging around in his papers day and night."

"It's about you and him. If he's your father or not. Shit," for she had in her nervousness pulled off the button and now had to hold on to the waistband.

Henry stared at her. "You always said he's not."

"What do I know?" And as he stared at her more—"I was so young, I didn't know what was going on."

"But you were pregnant already."

"That's what *he* said. Do you have a safety pin?" She took one herself out of his desk drawer—she knew better than he what he had, she had a complete inventory of everything about him.

"So now you're telling me it was more than a massage."

"I don't know," she said candidly—in the present tense, for it was clear that she was no more knowing now than she had been then. After a while she continued, "Anyway, he goes so far back with us that he might as well be family. Right back to Elsa; and of course to Kavi who met him in India."

"In London," Henry corrected.

"Was it in London? Are you sure? I thought I remembered

Kavi telling me about this first meeting in Bombay—yes, it *was* Bombay, I'm sure now because it was at Safiya's."

Henry had never heard of Safiya and didn't even know if it was a place or a person. "Oh a person," Renata said. "I think she was a famous silent film star."

"You think or you know?"

"I know, I think," Renata replied.

Henry tried to make her recall everything she could about the time and place of that first meeting—but at first all she could come up with was the time and place where her grandfather had told *her* about it. This had been in the Indian restaurant where Kavi used to take her in the afternoons, in those latter years of his when he had felt nostalgic for India. It had been before the great explosion of Indian restaurants, and there had been only two or three in the city; but these were as Indian as could be, pulling out all the stops with carved brackets, plaster-of-Paris arches, and godlike figures entwined in erotic poses copied or actually pilfered from temples. Classical ragas on the sitar were played by a musician who was an engineering student making up his tuition fees. But after three o'clock, when all the lunch guests except Kavi and Renata had left, and the engineering student was enjoying the meal that was part of his salary, the waiters put on records of their favorite film songs. Kavi enjoyed them too, for though they were from recent films he had not seen, the themes were the eternal ones of his own poetry. And sometimes he did recognize a lyric, in some potpourri of loved old songs rendered by a new playback singer: including once a song made popular by Safiya, and how it made his young heart leap in his eighty-year-old body! He sang along in a voice that wheezed and cracked and then failed altogether, so that he could only sway his head and press both hands to his heart, as though to prevent it from bursting.

That was when he had told Renata and everyone else in the restaurant about Safiya. Some of the waiters had vaguely heard of her, though she was generations before their time—mainly because of her daughter, who had also become a famous film star, and then her granddaughter (she too was now dead), who had been the most famous of them all. But for Kavi and his contemporaries Safiya had been the reigning queen. He recounted how they used to visit her where she lived with her mother and an assortment of relatives in a big baroque house on a hill overlooking the ocean. She loved to surround herself with young admirers; she gave them tea and macaroons, while she herself drank apricot brandy from a tiny glass. She said they were too young for alcohol—and they *were* very young, Kavi had only recently begun to shave. She said she herself needed it to help her bear the burden of life, although they noticed that the more she drank the heavier this burden appeared to become: so that, after several glasses, she was shedding tears—sometimes for a particular cause, such as the calumnies a rival actress was spreading about her, but more often in general about the fleeting nature of youth, fame, and love. For she had already begun her decline and knew it; the sweet dimpled plumpness that was such a part of her appeal was spreading out into fat—later she would become like her mother, who lay, mountainous and groaning, on a chaise longue, with a woman servant fanning her. But mother and daughter both retained and would till the end their eyes of deep dark velvet glowing against a petal-soft skin so much fairer than anyone else's. For they were not Indian but from Baghdad and spoke to each other in a language their visitors could not understand. Although they had lived in Bombay for many years— Safiya's mother had brought her there when she was only five years old—they retained all their differences: down to the cooking smells emanating from their busy kitchen, of their scented pilafs, so subtly different from the Indian variety, and the honey-eyed flaky pastries they baked.

Not all their houseguests were from Baghdad, but they were all from some undefined region stretching from Kurdistan to the Black Sea. It was not always clear in what language they were speaking, but they seemed to switch easily from one to the other and to be fluent in all of them. The women stayed around the house, wearing slippers and long dresses with tight bodices that also served as brassieres; while the men—quite formally dressed in tropical European suits and shoes—were in and out on all sorts of business and commerce. Safiya did not introduce any of them to Kavi and the other youths who came to visit her. Shutting the folding doors of her drawing room against the rest of the house, she entertained her admirers either in the room itself, with its plush sofas and fleshy plants, or out on the marble-paved veranda where they could enjoy the cool breeze and the sight of the ocean ornamented with a diamond necklace of electric lights and a tiara of stars. No one ever dared open the folding doors once she had closed them—except one of her houseguests, whom she introduced as her cousin (but they were all understood to be her cousins). He seemed not to notice the uneasy silence caused by his entrance; and while they waited for him to go away, he drew up a chair for himself close by Safiya, crossed his legs, and smiled amiably around their circle.

He must have been a young man at that time, but to Kavi and his friends he appeared immeasurably older than themselves. He gazed slowly from one to the other, as though he were simultaneously measuring them and inviting them to come up to his measure. He had a very black mustache and pewter-colored, slightly slanting, hypnotic eyes; but if there was anything sinister in these features, it was neutralized by his dapper attire of cream-colored shantung suit and matching waistcoat with a gold watch chain; also by his smile which, in contrast to his penetrating gaze, remained blandly social. Oblivious of their stricken silence—"Please don't let me interrupt your symposium," he kindly rallied them. Safiya, as nervous as the young men, said something to him in one of the languages they spoke around the house. He answered her in English—a rebuke to her for using a language not understood by her young guests. "Oh no, but I'm so interested! Fascinated! I want to know what the young intelligentsia of today are thinking, what are their solutions for this sorry world we all have to live in. I'm completely out of touch—naturally, in the place where I've been," he explained to the young visitors, leaving them to wonder: Where had he been? In what desert, or on what mountaintop? Or maybe in prison? He made them uneasy, but also excited. When no one spoke, he crossed his legs the other way. "Let me guess," he said. "I think you were talking about—wait: Nature? The stars up there? The universe? About nice feelings? I think some of you write poetry. For example, you," he said, pointing without hesitation at Kavi. Safiya let out a cry and made a protective gesture toward Kavi: he was her favorite, perhaps because the youngest and a poet, she liked to cradle his head or to pinch his downy cheek. She called him her Bulbul, her nightingale.

"But I'm not doing anything to him," her cousin protested. "I'm only asking to hear a little poetry, just a few drops of verse to trickle into this dry soul. You wouldn't grudge me that," he appealed directly to Kavi who, abashed, looked for help to Safiya. Intercepting that look, "Now I'm sure," her cousin said, "you've written some piquant verses for her, to celebrate her beauty and the sleepless nights and other difficulties it has caused you. Of course you regard me as a coarse, unfeeling fellow —no no no no, but that's what I am, compared with all of you, who are poets and lovers, sitting here so nicely nibbling—what are they? Macaroons? May I? I love to dip them into—no, not tea, I'll have whatever is in that little glass. Ah"—he leaned back so that his watch chain stretched across his stomach—"now I'm completely in the mood to enjoy your charming composition."

Kavi wanted to and didn't want to. Again he glanced at Safiya for guidance, but she was no longer capable of giving any. She was perspiring heavily and waving her little fan into her face. Then Kavi looked back at the cousin, who twinkled his slanting eyes at him in such benign encouragement that Kavi opened his mouth like a bird that could not help but sing. However, what came out no longer sounded as it had done only half an hour earlier, before the cousin had joined them. After only a few lines Kavi began to halt and then to hurry; he no longer felt proud of what he had written but just wanted to get it over with as soon as possible. This was by no means the fault of Safiya's cousin—he sat riveted with attention, leaning forward with both hands planted on his knees; and when Kavi was through, he did not stint his applause, clapping his hands together in such a way that they made a particularly loud and hollow sound. He encouraged the other friends to join in, which they did halfheartedly, although before they had been as enthusiastic as any poet could desire. And Safiya didn't clap at all or say anything, she just perspired and fanned.

After that, as if he had only been waiting to be introduced, the cousin—or the Master, though he was not yet known as such —took a lot of interest in Kavi and the other youths. He waited for them at a corner leading up to Safiya's house, waylaying them on their way to her. It was a busy intersection, but he was a conspicuous figure who could not be overlooked: impeccably dressed in his shantung suit, in the street he also wore a panama hat, with black band, which he raised to the friends. He invited them to accompany him to a very special kebab place; some of them accepted, others continued on their way to Safiya. Kavi belonged to the latter group, but next day listened avidly to the others describe the fabulous evening they had spent with him. The following day the cousin again stood at the crossroads, raising his hat to invite them, this time to eat spicy roast chicken. Kavi once more declined in favor of Safiya, and the cousin, not at all put out, raised his hat in farewell and led away those who had accepted—a larger group than on the first invitation. But the third time Kavi too followed the cousin, and after that he did not return to Safiya.

Every evening the cousin led them to a different treat. It was amazing how well he knew and was known in the deepest mazes of this city in which he was a stranger. Although he spoke only a broken and very idiosyncratic version of the local language, he was greeted everywhere with shouts of welcome, tables were wiped off, and a little boy deputed to wave the flies away. The proprietor himself hurried to prepare the specialty of his house —if it wasn't kebabs or roast chicken, it was Bombay duck, or buttermilk pounded out of sweetmeats, or a multilayered cream puff, or a flat bread as huge as a table. Another place attracted customers with a phonograph that had very famous musicians from faraway Lahore singing through its horn. They also visited a house famous for its singing and dancing girls, where the cousin was well known in one of the rooms rented by a mother and her daughter, exponents of the Kathak school of dance. It was always the cousin who paid for the amusement; although the young men were all from wealthy families, he would not allow them to spend anything. Taking out a wad of money, he peeled layers of notes from it—many more than necessary, which may have partly accounted for his popularity wherever he went.

These evenings stretched far into the night, or the early hours of the morning. They passed in a flash and always in great excitement—about what? What did the cousin talk to them about? If they had been less excited, they might have noticed that it was not he but they themselves who talked—with the same fervor as they had done at Safiya's, but not on the same subject. Kavi found himself revert to the theme of his earlier days, before he had known Safiya; and just as she had inspired him to write of love and its loss, now it was again his country's loss of freedom that made his verses weep. The cousin approved and applauded; it was he who first applied the epithet of "Poet and Patriot" to Kavi. But once he repeated a line from the latest poem: " 'If your country bleeds, O Kavi, how can you stanch the crimson teardrops of your heart?' " the cousin quoted, smacking his lips with pleasure. Then he continued, "But if something is bleeding, if blood is flowing, don't you try and do something about it? Like for instance stopping it? Calling a doctor? Or even buying a packet of plaster, or tearing up a sheet for a bandage? Wouldn't that be the sensible thing to do?" They agreed it would be; they declared themselves ready to do whatever was needed, even in opposition to their families. One of them admitted that he had proposed joining Mr. Gandhi's movement, had already bought a railway ticket to Ahmedabad, but when his mother heard of it, she had threatened suicide, so that he had had to abandon his plan. However, at the name of Gandhi, the cousin made the same dismissive gesture as did their families at home. That was not the way, he said: sheep to be led by a sheep. A wolf, that was what was needed: and not one but many, many wolves—yes, all of them, he said, gazing around their circle with his hypnotic eyes. Were they ready to become wolves? he asked. To put on that rough fur instead of—

here he stroked the silk sleeve of the nearest friend and seemed to like it, murmuring "Best quality French import" in a soft voice, which however hardened again as he admonished them, "Remember: never bark until you can bite, and never bite until you can make your teeth meet," and he showed them how, snapping them into the air (he still had his own teeth then).

A few evenings later he said he wanted to introduce them to some particular friends of his. He hired a horse carriage and crammed them all into it to drive far out to a new suburb. It was a dark and deserted place, for not many plots had as yet been built on, and there was no street lighting. The great attraction of this new housing colony must have been its proximity to the ocean; the sound of its waves was not audible from this distance, but the putrid smell of fish hung up to dry on the beaches gave the air a marine quality. The house to which the cousin took them stood alone in a waste of empty plots, with here and there a skeleton of construction glimmering under the stars. If it was a secret hideout, it was perfectly situated, engulfed in silence and solitude.

Inside, its darkness was relieved only by some candle stumps, for there wasn't even a kerosene lamp; one bed with the strings coming loose and a steel trunk were the only furnishings. The visitors sat in a circle on the floor with their hosts—a man and a woman, a couple in their early thirties though it was unlikely that they were married, for they were not the type to submit to such a bourgeois ceremony. They may even have been brother and sister—they looked alike, both short and dark-complexioned, with spectacles and protruding teeth and skin pitted with smallpox scars. They spoke to each other in Bengali but to their visitors in an English that was literary not in the sense of English but of Marxist literature. However, they were not Marxists —they made that clear at once: Marxism was too slow a process for India, which needed bombs to blow everything up and start again. Kavi and his friends thrilled and shivered, while the cousin watched them with amusement. In his light suit and shoes and panama hat, he illuminated the room more than did the candle stumps—and also with his personality, for everyone,

including the hosts, was turned toward him as if for enlighten-
ment. He gave a little speech to explain why they were here.
Introducing Kavi and the other friends, he said that these young
men were all idealists and patriots who, in their ardent wish to
set their country free, were willing to stop short at nothing.

"At nothing?" repeated the host.

The cousin invited the friends to confirm his statement, and
when they had done so in eager chorus, he continued: "So far
they have expressed their noble aspirations only in noble
speeches and literary effusions, but now they know the time has
come to serve their country with more than words."

"With our lives!" Kavi burst out—for which the cousin lovingly pinched his cheek, just the way Safiya liked to do.

"So you wish to give your lives," said the host. "Very good.
But have you any idea what that means? You're perfectly right,
yes—it means to die: but to die while you're still alive." His
voice was steady, but the match with which he lit his cigarette
shook. It lit up his fingers, which were stained with what they
took to be nicotine though later figured to be some chemical
used in making explosives. "To be worthy of our cause," he said,
"you have to become saints and ascetics. Like those worthy gentlemen of old, the revolutionary of our times must have no interests, no feelings, no attachments, no property of his own, not
even a name."

His woman partner nudged him to pass his cigarette to her.
As she inhaled, a little spot of fire glowed around her mouth. She
concluded his definition: "That's what we mean when we say the
revolutionary is dead to life."

"He's dead *in* life," emended her partner.

But only a few days later both of them were really dead. Their
photographs, taken much earlier when they were students in
Calcutta, were printed in the newspapers; so was a picture of
their house, or what was left of it after they had accidentally
blown it up along with themselves in the course of making
bombs to explode the British Empire. The cousin disappeared
overnight and was not heard from again. When the friends went
to ask about him at Safiya's, she put the chain on the door and

screamed at them through the crack that she didn't know them, had never known them, and what cousin? she had no cousin. Panic seized the friends; scattering in different directions, they took care not to meet each other again, renouncing their friendship. Some of them went abroad—this was the time when Kavi enrolled as a student at Cambridge University. It was later learned that two of the friends had been sent to Moscow to be trained as terrorists; but when they were returned to India, they vanished along with the red rubles entrusted to them to put their training into effect. On the whole, Kavi preferred to forget this episode; he felt he had been in danger of taking a wrong turning.

Eleven

WHEREAS the Master's message was easy enough to grasp, he himself remained elusive. And maybe, Henry thought, it was at that very point that one *could* get hold of him, just there, where he was at his most elusive and ran away: for that was the one constant factor about him, that he always ran away from people and the situations he had set up with them. This applied especially to his followers—and Henry, having read so many of their letters and journals, was beginning to share some of the Master's feelings.

"Yes, they irritated him horribly," Graeme confirmed. He described a meal he had eaten with the Master in the dark and cavernous dining room of Hobson's house. Some expert Indian servants, who wore whitish uniforms and appeared to have come with the house rather than the Master's entourage, walked around the table, silent on bare feet, to offer dishes of mutton curry and rice. The Master and Graeme sat at one end, while the followers were crowded together at the other. They took no part in the conversation at the upper end but listened in hushed respect, careful to make the least possible noise with their silverware.

The Master spoke of the Himalayan cave where he had spent

the previous five years. He didn't go into detail, and when one of the Scottish schoolteachers ventured to ask a question about his mode of life, he waved her into silence. What did all that matter? It was enough to know that he was high up in an icebound cave, beyond all vegetation and birdsong. As for food, he said, digging into the bottle of hot lime pickle held out to him by the turbaned bearer, he often forgot to take it, and perhaps would have spent the entire time without sustenance if devotees had not left offerings at the mouth of his cave. At least, he assumed it was devotees—anyway, food was always miraculously there when he remembered to be hungry. He had nothing to cook or to make a fire with and did not need one, for although he wore only this same robe, which left his legs, his arms, one shoulder, and half his chest bare, his body kept its own comfortable temperature by means of a certain yogic exercise he had learned from other ascetics. Now it was Graeme who interrupted to ask a question, for he had heard of this exercise—it was called *tumo*—and was curious about it. But again the Master emphasized that all this was entirely irrelevant because "You see, Mr. Howard, Mr. Graeme if I may call you so, when you get to that height—and I don't mean only literally, as so many feet above sea level—when you get there, you have long left all the senses and their sensations behind you."

"And then what happens?" Graeme had asked.

At that moment the bearers carried in the last course—an English pudding, sitting squat on its dish, made from a recipe of the previous owner's mother. They offered it of course first to the Master—but "Not now!" gasped one of the schoolteachers. For the Master was smiling in a very special way, as if about to divulge some very special information. Even Graeme, a skeptic by nature, felt the quality of that smile, though quite unable to describe it, not then and not now, half a century later, to his grandson. "It was more like a girl's than a man's, especially an obese and masterful man like him—a girl thinking of something very lovely—or, wait, no, like my mother at the age of sixty when she saw all the full-blown flowers in her garden that she had sown in the spring." Anyway, the Master had continued to smile, calling back the servant with the pudding to which he helped himself—and still he smiled, at the pudding yes, he loved everything with sugar, but also at other things beyond and at the same time including it. But he did not answer Graeme's question; he could not. Instead he sang a little verse—no one understood the words and they did not even know in what language it was; but it seemed to express the essence of some uncharted joy, or perhaps this was not in the words but in the Master's smile and in his voice which gave a little skip, a little dash into unknown territory, and then broke off as if unable to go farther, and into that echo-filled silence he waved his spoon before eating what was on it.

"You've both got him all wrong," said Baby, who had entered with a dish she had cooked for Graeme. "I keep telling you: he was absolutely normal and only wanted the same every man wants. Yes, I mean women," she replied to Graeme, "along with every other nice thing."

Graeme conceded her point to some extent. "The moment the meal was over," he reverted to his meeting with the Master, "he shooed them all away—told them to go and meditate or something, while he and I sat on the veranda and drank apricot brandy. A bit too sweet and sticky for me, but he liked it. His cigarettes had a sweetish smell too. He smoked one after the other and waved them around in the air so that the smoke wafted up to the mountains and the stars. That's what he really loved—no, I don't mean only the brandy and cigarettes, I was thinking more of the mountains and the stars. That's why he kept running away from people, because he didn't want to be dragged down from up there. Dragged back."

"Oh he set you a good example, no wonder you liked him so much," said Baby. "Because that's all you ever did, run away from people who needed you."

"If you're referring to yourself, you have the last laugh: because here I am, captured, bound, and delivered." He peered at the plate she had set before him. "What is it?"

"Whatever it is, you asked for it."

It was true, he *had* asked for it. Nowadays he only wanted the food he had eaten as a boy at his prep school, so Baby found herself mashing a lot of potatoes and baking tapioca puddings and other things she hadn't even heard of but had to look up in a book.

When Henry heard his grandparents speak of the Master, it seemed to him that it was of a person whom one could actually know. But for his parents—though both had known him too—he seemed to be an Idea; and moreover one that they both felt they had to serve. They were intensely eager to do so, Carl in a theoretical way—never had he composed so many incomprehensible manifestos—while Renata for the first time in her life tried to be practical. This was in response to the growing interest in the movement manifested in the immensely increased volume of correspondence. To deal with it, Carl and Renata had entirely taken over Kavi's old bedroom, leaving Henry and Vera to make do with Henry's own room; and Renata had engaged a secretary, an overweight, zealous woman called Marjorie who believed in the Master's work and was willing to accept a very low salary. (All future helpers would be of Marjorie's type, and even when the movement became exceedingly prosperous, its workers remained either voluntary or underpaid.)

Now they urgently needed more space, and Renata began house-hunting. First she went by herself, then she called in Carl who, although wanting a house as much as she did for their activities, lacked the stamina and the patience to search for it. They made things more difficult for themselves by walking everywhere or taking the subway, even in the rush hour; and Carl irritated Renata by going around whatever house they were being shown saying "Perfect, absolutely perfect for us"; he did this partly because he really believed it—one place looked as good as another to him—and also because he tired quickly of any practical business and wanted to get it over with. Finally Renata dispensed with him and took her mother into her confidence.

Baby was at first shocked that Renata should want a house when they were all so comfortable together in the apartment;

but she understood quickly enough and asked, "What does Henry say?"

"He doesn't know," said Renata. She scorned to admit to any secrecy between herself and her son but worked herself up against him. "He can be so stubborn. He still thinks we can carry on in one room with one untrained secretary."

"Vera types very fast and knows so many languages."

But Baby liked the idea of going around the city looking for a house to buy. Of course for her there was no other mode of transport than her usual limousine service with her favorite chauffeur who pampered her with a lap robe and personal conversation. Renata sat beside her, miserable because she considered it wrong to sail through the streets, as safe and sealed as if in an aquarium, instead of being jostled and panhandled out among the crowd and having one's shins kicked. But Baby adored driving through the city—at least the nice parts of it—even the streets that had been completely changed since her youth, with the old houses replaced by glittering office palaces of black glass. The sky had remained the same, clear as water and with little woolly wandering clouds in it; and the trees planted along the sidewalk seemed never to have grown but remained slender saplings enveloped in a pale green haze of new leaves, some of them with blossoms of pure pink entirely untouched by city grime.

Baby was surprised how many of the old houses were still left to buy. They stood awkward and unwanted among the pinnacles of new developments; most of them had been on sale for years, and some had made halfhearted attempts at converting into apartments. They all smelled of mice and seemed ashamed of the real estate agents who showed them off and told lies about them. Baby knew their interiors well—her own house had been very similar before Elsa had had it remodeled. Sometimes she thought she recognized a house and had been in it, maybe for a children's birthday party. One place, a huge old turn-of-the-century relic overlooking the Hudson, she thought might even have belonged to a relative: she seemed to recall visiting a sickbed there, a very old uncle in a nightshirt attempting to smile when she was brought up to him and to grasp her hand—she bravely gave it to him, unbuttoning her little white glove, and felt the last faint warmth ebbing within his dry skin.

There was one house she was certain that she recognized, in spite of the attempts at alteration it had suffered. It was the house belonging to the German landlady where Mme. Richter had lived with her family and other refugees. Now it was almost back to its original structure as a one-family house, probably built for some mercantile family not unlike the Kopfs and Kellers. No attempt at modernization or partition seemed to have worked and everything had been torn out again, leaving holes in the parquet flooring where supports had been bored into it, an unconnected, brownish gas stove, and a tap sticking out of a half-tiled bathroom wall. Baby stood in the middle of the large front parlor and remembered her visit here with Kavi when Mme. Richter, surrounded by her fellow lodgers, had lain suffering in bed behind a curtain sagging from its length of string. She folded back the wooden shutters from the French doors to step on to the little wrought-iron balcony she knew was there; but when she tried to go out on it, the key wouldn't turn and she could only look through the glass panes at the view opposite, which in Mme. Richter's day had been another Gothic brownstone but now was quite a smart hotel with an awning and a doorman blowing a whistle for cabs. Baby thought everything changes and then comes around again—so it seemed to her: an impression confirmed by Renata stamping around taking Polaroids with the same energy her grandmother Elsa would have shown, likewise in the service of the Master.

It may have been that she really thought this the most suitable house they had seen so far, or that she was tired of searching —but Renata decided that Mme. Richter's former rooming house was the one she wanted to buy. She could now no longer postpone letting Henry into her plans: apart from anything else, she needed his money to supplement her own for the first mortgage payment. Renata was unskilled in subterfuge; it never occurred to her not to come straight out with her intentions. Only with her son it was different—there was too much mined terrain between them—so that she mused and pondered on how to broach the subject to him. This process was not a silent self-communing, but a muttering to herself as she walked around the apartment; or she opened the door where Henry sat working with Vera—she stared at them both, her mouth opened as though about to say something but closed instead over gritted teeth.

If Renata knew nothing of delicate approach, Baby knew everything. She began with a meditation on the Master, how closely intertwined he was with all of them; and when Henry looked at her with his anomalous eyes, inquiring what she meant by intertwined, she swept a careless gesture through the air, scattering sparks from the diamonds in her rings. "I'm not saying that he might be who you sometimes think he is—you could be dark from any number of people, though I must say none of us have ever had those Tartar eyes."

"Was he a Tartar?"

"Who knows what he was, darling, and who cares. And anyway those things really don't mean a thing—you cannot tell who anyone's father was from looking at them, or their grandfather; look at Vera, and there is no doubt that she *is* his great-granddaughter, at least they all said so and they ought to know."

"Is this your secret you want to tell me?"

"Did I say anything about a secret? But now that we're talking about Vera, I might as well say that I don't understand you. If I were you—well, not I, that's silly, but any other handsome young man, yes you are, of course you are, my goodness, not handsome perhaps in a common way but your expression, darling, such intelligence."

"That's from you then."

"It's certainly not from your parents," she retorted. "They're stupid. They don't understand a thing. That's why I'm speaking to you because you would at least have some idea that buying a house worth several million dollars isn't exactly child's play. Yes of course," she answered him impatiently, "why do you think I'm talking to you, that's what they're doing, buying a house. What for? For you, they say."

So the next time Renata hovered around him without being able to come out with her proposal, Henry said, "When are you going to show me that house?"

"Anytime you like," she replied, too relieved that he had the information to wonder how he got it.

She had the floor plan and her Polaroids all ready to show him, and she explained her vision of how it was to be converted into the World Center of the movement. She was so deeply engrossed in what she was saying that she failed to hear him ask, "Was it really Mme. Richter's house?" and he had to repeat it.

"Whose? What? Oh you mean the piano teacher? It wasn't *her* house; she may have rented a room there—this is where we could install a little elevator for you so you could easily get from the copy machines up to the storerooms."

"She lived there for years with her daughter and granddaughter. The granddaughter was born there: Irina," he said. "Vera's mother."

"Well really, Henry, are you interested in this or in a lot of personal gossip?"

"Both are interesting," Henry said. "And it would certainly interest Vera to work in the house where her mother was born."

"In the first place," said Renata, putting down the pencil with which she was pointing at her plan, "I don't care *where* her mother was born." And when Henry was silent, waiting to hear her second point, she got excited. "Why should she work with us—she has no commitment, she only does it for the salary you pay her which by the way is much too high. Marjorie would be very happy to do it along with her own work and for the same pay. We'll have to economize, you know. This house is going to take a lot of money."

"How much?"

She told him and it *was* a lot: almost his entire inheritance from Elsa and Cynthia. "So you see, Vera will have to go. We can't afford her," Renata explained with an air of impartiality.

It was left to Baby to ask Henry for the down payment on the house and the first installment on the mortgage. She had arranged a favorable rate of interest, which she explained to him as well as the amount of repayment he would be required to make every quarter. "Is it all right?" she said. "Can you manage it?" He said yes, and when he went off to calculate his assets, he found he could, but it was as he had thought, it would take almost his entire legacy. He considered this just, for the money had been left to him on the assumption that he would carry on the work of the Master.

Soon everything around him changed while Renata took possession of the other house. She moved the office there—that is, herself, Carl, and their secretary Marjorie, and at once had to take on more staff to deal with the many tasks of their rapidly growing organization. The history of "Head & Heart House" has been written up elsewhere—though not by Henry—and here only the origin of the name might need some explanation. It had been thought up by Carl during a sleepless night—he was mostly sleepless now, he lived in a state of such excitement. When he told his idea to Renata, she said it was "corny," and Henry had to explain that word to him. Carl vigorously denied it. "It's not corny; it's sincere." There was never any question of Carl's own sincerity—it flowed through him almost visibly, like a clear fluid through glass. Probably that was what made him what he has since become (that is, the real leader of the movement, the Master's successor). Right from the start he was an inspiration to everyone. He was the first to move into the house, for he was keeping such long hours, preparing his address to the first general meeting, that it was not worth his going home at night. He moved in a camp bed for himself but kept having to shift it as one by one the rooms were invaded by the workmen swarming over the house. Carl had become very youthful—in spirit, of course, and also in appearance. In his blue jeans and open-necked shirt, he was lithe as a Wandervogel; his long hair —thin now and more gray than blond—was always disheveled, as though a mountain wind were blowing through it.

Everything was being drained into the house and its refurbishment. Henry was pondering what to tell Vera, for soon he would have no more money to pay her salary. He tried to get her to come to see the new headquarters but she never would. He understood that not only had she no interest in digging into the past but a distaste for seeing it overrun by the future that Carl and Renata were imposing on Mme. Richter's old habitat. For while Henry himself remained ambivalent, Vera was not, and once she confronted him. "I thought you said you didn't want any more to do with any of it. Didn't you tell me that I should be finding another job?"

"Have you?"

"Not yet, but I will if you decide to give up."

Henry said, "I thought that's what you wanted me to do."

Vera was too proud to ask "What difference does it make what I want?" But she knew that the time was near when she would have to look elsewhere.

After her day's work with Henry, Vera always had somewhere to go—she did everything that it was customary for young people to do, she was really quite conventional that way; but every night, and whatever might be going on and however much she appeared to be enjoying herself, she would look at her watch and say she had to go home. Their parties were usually in some raw space on top of a warehouse within a waste of streets that she could not possibly negotiate alone. So it was up to one of the young men to find a cab and accompany her—it might be some personable young lawyer or investment banker who, after his formal, interior-decorated office hours, preferred to spend his evenings in other surroundings. They always wanted to see more of Vera, some of them even wanted to marry her, for all unconsciously she fulfilled some sort of traditional, old-fashioned ideal. But as soon as the cab drew up outside her building, she made a dash for the glass doors and disappeared behind them.

Her mother was usually asleep, or just enough awake to say, "Did you have a nice time?" before sinking back into her own deep fears and dreams. Although she knew that Irina hardly heard her, Vera, taking off her clothes and folding and hanging them, told her about her evening; and then, with a sigh, she crept between her sheets and now felt truly at home, at rest, in her bed in this tiny bare apartment she had rented for the two of them and paid for regularly every month out of her salary. She liked to stay awake for a while, just to savor their possession of this shelter, listening to her mother on her couch in the other room snoring a little bit. She also reviewed her day in that other apartment across town and looked forward to the next day when she would be going back there.

But now she had to think what it would be like not to go back. She wasn't much concerned about finding a new job—the young bankers and lawyers were eager to help and several possibilities were open to her; but she thought of them less, in these reflective hours in bed at night, than she did of what it would be like not to see Henry as a matter of course every day. She had gotten very used to him. She had known him and his family so long, that was what held her there; it was, what was it, historical? genealogical? not personal at all—in fact, so little personal that she found it difficult to visualize Henry in his absence. And this though she was with him all day, and moreover had known him since they were children. Maybe what made it so difficult to grasp the idea of him was that there were two Henrys, the one she had known as a child and the young man who had inherited the Master's papers; but this was not the difference between a boy and a man but between Henry before and after his accident. She reflected on his dichotomy in her nightly musings, and it also came up at unexpected moments when she thought she wasn't thinking of Henry at all, like in the middle of a party, or coming home in a cab with an admirer.

She had been both fascinated and scared by Henry when they were small—partly because she had been warned about her deportment before going to the house, the way she was warned before visiting the houses of all Mme. Richter's patrons. Baby always suggested that she should go play with Henry, but Vera was shy and found it easier to stay among the grown-ups, a very good girl with her hands folded in her lap and her feet crossed at the ankles. And Henry too was shy, though he pretended to be scornful; but after some time he laid himself out to impress her —very successfully, for he thought up enjoyable games for her, such as applying all Baby's makeup and tottering around in her high-heeled shoes, and led her into bloody and fantastic realms of the imagination, well beyond the scope of her own little women and secret gardens. She began to wait for the day to come around when it was time to visit Baby—unfortunately only once a month now that they were way past any pretense at piano lessons.

Then Henry went away and never came back to play with her again. She learned about him being taught to move his limbs again in various therapy centers out of the city; and once Baby took her to visit him, driving many miles in a limousine, and by that time he had grown a very black beard and was as scornful of her as he had pretended to be in their early days, so that she came away very sad, mostly for him and his condition but also for herself, that he despised her so. But the next time they met, he was again transformed, and now what stayed with her most was not his beard but his eyes—though strange, they were not sinister but kind like the rest of him. And that was how she thought of him when he was her employer—that he was kind to herself and everyone else, except his mother when she exasperated him, and also thoughtful in a way usually only women are; this was his attitude toward other people, while toward himself he was disciplined and stoical, asking for no concessions and no privileges, as though nothing had happened to him.

Baby kept taking out more of her jewelry to give to Vera— she even went to the bank and got a valuable piece out of the vault. While Vera had learned to accept whatever Baby gave, she now became as reluctant as she had been at the beginning, even though Baby kept assuring her that it was only costume jewelry. Vera believed her about the jewelry, even about the piece out of the vault, for she was naive and unknowing in these matters; but she did not quite believe in the assurance that there were no strings attached. This was an unspoken assurance: if she had spoken it, Baby would have said, "You're not expected to do anything except wear it"; but being very honest inside if not always outside, she would have secretly added to herself, "And to stay with my grandson."

Vera did not often refer to her father, and when she did, it was with complete indifference. She knew nothing about him and cared nothing; for her, he had no name but was just "the Irish tinker."

"The *what?*" Henry said.

"Or something like that," she replied airily. But it amused her to think of herself as descended from a tinker, and it made her feel as carefree as any such traveling person. There *was* something carefree about Vera, and unceremonious—for instance, when she bundled up the Master's papers and dumped them on a shopping cart to wheel them down into the van waiting to take them away to Head & Heart House.

The day arrived when Henry had to admit that he had no more work for Vera; and also, although he did not tell her this, no more money to pay her salary. She could no longer postpone choosing between two job offers—one was with an international fund-raising agency, the other with a multinational computer firm—and to ask Henry for his advice. In fact, she left the decision to him, correctly believing his judgment to be better than her own. During the remaining time until she had to join her new office, she continued to come to the apartment every day. She helped Baby with her correspondence and had long conversations with Henry. The days were bright and clear, and they had a few outings, usually taking his wheelchair. Every time they returned Baby hoped they would have something special to tell, but they never did, though they appeared always to have had a good time and enjoyed each other's company.

Twelve

AFTER VERA LEFT to start her new job, Henry for the
first time felt confined at home and began to wander
around the streets, alone and without his wheelchair. It was a
painful business, but he made himself go through with it. Anyway, it was better than staying in the apartment, missing Vera.
Sometimes he made it as far as her workplace, which was in a
huge new corporate building with a lobby as busy as a public
square—it *was* a public square, an atrium with potted trees and
uncomfortable little chairs occupied mostly by people out of
work. Henry also sat here for a while but only to rest, not to wait
for Vera, though he usually arrived at a time when she would
just be leaving her office. He told himself it was futile to wait for
her, he would only miss her in the crowd of departing office
workers: for whereas he himself, with his crippled gait and his
strange, dark, bearded face stuck out for all to gape at, Vera
merged easily into a crowd, and the only reason anyone might
look at her was because she was even prettier than all the other
pretty girls.

On the first landing of Head & Heart House—one might as
well use the name—there was a large empty wall space. During
the German landlady's time, it had remained empty except for a

calendar hung up to hide a stain; the next owner had acquired portraits of two grim, bony New England ancestors—not his own—but had had no time to hang them before the bank foreclosed. Now the portrait of the Master was there to greet anyone entering the house; but there was still space for another, equally large portrait, and one day Renata took Henry's photograph. Instead of her usual snapshot, she attempted a portrait. She posed and reposed him and dodged around him, squatting to look up at him. He felt uncomfortable—he had never been looked at so intensely, not even by her, and moreover it seemed to him that she was trying to extract something out of his appearance that was not there, or not his.

At last he said, puzzled and irritated, "What do you want of me?"

"Nothing." After a while she remembered, "Oh yes, I do want something."

It was a check for five thousand dollars, to pay for some fittings she had ordered for the headquarters. He wrote it out at once, relieved to buy himself off with something concrete and easy.

A few weeks later, she said, "At least come see your picture."

"What picture?"

"Yours. Mine. *My* picture," Renata said.

What have they done, Henry wondered. Next day, instead of going on one of his aimless walks, he took a cab to Head & Heart House. Workmen were still busy inside and out, so the front door was left unlatched and Henry only had to push it to enter. The entrance hall was unfurnished, the stairs uncarpeted, but everything had been cleaned up and painted white, which made it look all the more empty. But the space on the wall of the first landing was now filled by two large portraits, for Henry found himself hanging there side by side with the Master.

Before letting him examine these portraits, Renata carried him off to view the rest of the place, proud of what had been done, although to Henry it looked as if the house had simply been stripped of everything it had ever been and left blank and institutional. She took him into the front parlor where Mme.

Richter had lived with her family; now it was filled with the files and bundles of the Master's papers and three voluntary secretaries trying to cope with them. They had an air of frustration, for though full of goodwill they were untrained and could not follow the indexing Vera had established nor correlate her translations with the originals, which were in languages they did not know. Renata promised them help, and when she and Henry were outside on the stairs again, he asked, "What sort of help?"

"We'll get some more assistants."

"Will you pay them?"

Instead of answering, she began to descend to the next floor, leaving him to follow as best he could, which was not very well; but she was oblivious of his difficulty, and when he managed to get down to join her on the next landing, she was frowning in thought. She said, "There are so many expenses, I had no idea of everything one has to pay out, quite apart from the house payments, and of course Carl has no idea at all, he doesn't know what money is."

"Do you need some more?"

"I didn't mean to ask you again, but since you mention it, yes."

"I'll write you a check."

Thanking him, she explained, "I need it for the electrician who's sent an outrageous bill for rewiring or something he says he's done."

"I thought you needed it to hire more help with the Master's papers."

"Whatever for, when we have all these volunteers. They can learn, it's just that they're new to the work." When he was silent, she continued, "What's-her-name was new to it too when she started but she learned fast enough so why shouldn't they who have much greater involvement than she ever had."

"Involvement is good but knowing Russian, French, and German is better. Anyway, she has another job."

"So why are you even thinking of her!"

"I think of her a great deal," Henry said.

"Here, sit down, you mustn't stand so long." Suddenly solicitous, she helped him sit on the top step. They were on the first landing, just under the portrait of the Master, and of Henry himself; but they had their backs to them, sitting side by side on the step. Renata linked her arm in his and then her hand in his; if she had not been taller, she might have laid her head on his shoulder. Thus romantically placed, she could say anything. "She's so ordinary; such an ordinary person for someone like you."

"I don't feel all that extraordinary; unless you mean that I'm less than ordinary, which is true. Oh yes it is, don't let's pretend."

"I'm not even thinking of that."

"No? I have to all the time, every time I try in the least to do what everyone else takes for granted. I'm stating a matter of fact," he said.

"I wish you would see yourself as others see you"—and she tried to make him turn around to look at his own portrait hanging behind them.

"You mean as *you* see me."

"It's how you are," she insisted stubbornly.

"It's how you want me to be."

But he did turn around to look. Certainly, he had to admit that she had made him into an impressive figure. In a way, even more impressive than the Master, hanging next to him. For the Master had played himself down in his portrait, assuming the role of a benevolent uncle, with a twinkle in his Tartar eyes. Whereas Henry—as photographed by Renata, developed by her, and finally touched up by her—was portrayed as beyond or above any familial relationship. Even his dress, unlike the Master's English suit with collar and necktie, did not belong to the everyday world; he tried to remember what he had worn when she had photographed him and did not think it could have been anything more exotic than a T-shirt. Only the white edge of it showed in the picture, so that it might have been the collarless garment worn by a member of some sacred order, or by the victim of an imminent beheading, or anyone else in an outer-limit situation.

Renata defended herself. "Other mothers are ambitious for their sons, so why shouldn't I be?"

"Other mothers only want a doctor or lawyer or maybe a President of the United States. No one is as ambitious as you are."

"It's the way you were born. I didn't make it up. You can blame Cynthia and Elsa if you want to blame anyone—no, I don't mean the accident, but it's they who said the Master died so that you could be born. And maybe the accident was part of it too so that you wouldn't be like other people but different. *More,*" she insisted before he could say *less.*

"And so that I wouldn't do anything that other people do, like for instance get married. I *said* for instance," he tried to laugh off the consternation that appeared instantly on her face.

"You're not thinking of that, are you?"

"No, how can I. Apart from other considerations, you've taken all my money, so I can't even offer Vera her job back, let alone anything else."

"You said she had one." He saw her bite her lip and recognized that she was about to start bargaining with him. "I guess if you really feel she might be useful," Renata said, "we could find the money for her salary. You're the principal person here—don't laugh, of course you are—and it's up to you to determine who you want."

"Ah." Henry greeted this with a pleasure that implied she had just made him a bigger concession than intended.

"Though personally," she went on, quickly limiting her terms, "I never thought much of her typing, and if her filing had been better, those poor girls in there wouldn't now be in a mess."

"But I can ask her?"

"Ask her what?"

Instead of answering, "Help me," he said; he held on to the stair rail in an attempt to get up. Clutching the banister on one side and with her on the other, he began to descend the stairs. The effort this cost him did not permit him to make conversation, or even to reply to her question of "You're not going to see her right now, are you?"

If Henry had been other than he was, he might have gone right now. But he never took a decision without scrupulous consideration; this was a characteristic of his, formed during years of confinement rather than inherent. It was about five o'clock when he left Renata, and he could have just made it in time to meet Vera emerging from the office building at the end of her day. He took a cab home instead, and on the way began to work out the implications of any proposal he might make to Vera. But when he got to the apartment, he found two doctors there, summoned by Baby for Graeme, who had had another attack.

Graeme refused to be moved to the hospital, nor would Baby have let him go. During the following weeks, a nurse was brought in, and after Graeme improved, Baby looked after him herself, with Henry to help her. Graeme slept a lot during the day so that his nights were wakeful, and it often happened that when Henry came in to relieve his grandmother, he found her nodding in her chair beside his grandfather, who was wide awake. However, Graeme's recovery was not steady, and there were anxious days of relapse. At the end of one such day, Henry entered the room to find him sleeping but Baby awake. She was kneeling at the end of Graeme's bed and clutching his feet. When she saw Henry, she was embarrassed and tried to get up, but it was difficult for her—however sprightly her spirit, her joints were old—and giving up the struggle, she simply sank back again. And again she clutched Graeme's feet, as though trying to prevent him from running away; she began to cry, her tears falling on Graeme's feet. She implored aloud, "Not yet, please; not this time."

It would have surprised Baby to hear the lively manner in which in his better moments he talked to their grandson. Alone with Henry, Graeme was remarkably cheerful, especially about his own dying. He liked to compare his recent symptoms with those of his first heart attack, when he had been alone in his flat in London. He said the latter had been more interesting because it had gone further. "I really thought I had had it," he confided to Henry. "And maybe if she hadn't come—Baby," he said in the mocking mode he had for that name. "I suppose I was destined for my time with Baby."

After recovering from another attack, he said, "It feels as if it wants to get out. This—" tapping in the region of his heart. "Not sick at all but very much alive. A great deal more alive than the rest of me"—in demonstration he tried to raise a long yellow arm, and failed—"so can you blame it for wanting to get out of this battered cage. A bird, a living bird, escaping and flying straight up—in one straight line." He made a whistling sound as of something being released and shooting upward far enough to disappear.

"Would this be Bede's bird?" asked Henry.

"No, no. That was flying the wrong way round. Not from darkness into darkness, but vice versa. Vice versa," he said, shutting his eyes for a moment, as if dazzled.

He began to wander—not in his mind, that was clear enough, but in his conversation. He wandered over incidents that were remote from Henry—professional assignments and erotic encounters—and then returned to territory familiar to his grandson and interwoven with both their lives. Again and again he reverted to the Master and the few days he had spent in his company. Now he seemed to regret never having sought him out again. But during the busy years following their meeting, there had been nothing he could possibly have wanted from him; and moreover, he felt he had already heard what the Master had to tell him.

"But what *did* he tell you?" Henry asked, never having managed to extract anything like a great message from his grandfather's narrative.

"Oh you know," Graeme said. "How he went up in the mountains and lived there by himself in a cave."

"But what did he *do?*"

"Henry, I asked the same question: 'But what did you *do?*' He said he waited for the lightning. I thought he meant it literally —after all, if one goes up in the mountains one expects to be alone with the elements, lightning and so forth. But no, he said it was from an Upanishad and after he had a puff at his cigarette and watched the smoke rings go up, he recited it for me: 'It is like lightning; it flashes forth, it makes you blink and say *Ah!'* . . . Ah," Graeme said, in a different way, so that Henry leaned forward anxiously.

Graeme indicated that he was all right, but as he usually told lies about himself, Henry was not reassured. "Should I call Baby?" he asked.

"Let sleeping Babies lie," said Graeme, quite fondly for him. He must have been all right, for he went on talking. "After that, I walked back to the mess. It's rather marvelous walking in the mountains at night. People are asleep and all the houses dark, but a bit lower down there is a cluster of lights floating in a bowl of mist and moon that is actually a town but looks celestial. And you would not believe the silence, which is the most alive thing, the most total sound, and for me that night it was all one *Ah!* the way he had said it.

"When I got to the mess, that was dark too but they had left a note for me, 'Come to the club.' I was so awake, I knew I couldn't sleep, so I went. They were having a party—there were farewell parties practically every night for people going home, civilians and soldiers, everyone was leaving. They had balloons and were dancing to a band come down from Simla. I found a partner at once, cut in on her actually—I'd seen her around and liked her. She was different from the other girls who were all officers' daughters with quite grand opinions, mostly about themselves. But this girl—Clara, unusual name, you know I never met another Clara, not in my whole life—no, not one." He paused, hesitated as on a bank where a torrent of memories rushed past. "Yes, Clara," he continued. "She was the daughter of the local hotel keeper, English of course, but still—it did make her 'trade.' You don't know what trade is, Henry—oh you do know? Well, you needn't. So she wasn't quite as grand as the others and could let herself go more. She didn't for instance have to pretend not to be excited about going home—where she had never been, she was born in India, but now her father had sold the hotel and they were all leaving and going to live in Romford, Essex. My goodness, she thought she was going—I don't know where—to some dazzling metropolis: she was so excited, she was literally hopping, her hair flew around and her breasts bounced up and down. She was a plump girl, rosy, dewy —how old was she? Seventeen, eighteen? I'll tell you, when you're young yourself, you just take it for granted that everyone else is too, and of course they are. It's only now that I think of her as an allegorical figure as it were: Youth. Clara. She wanted to know all I could tell her about London and what were the posh places people went to. God knows what I told her, all sorts of rubbish, and she swallowed it all and wanted more, more, so I made up more and more. She got so hot and flushed, she couldn't stand it, we had to go out on the veranda where there were some other couples taking the air. The club was high up and had the best view in town but no one was looking at it. I think I had my back to it and I was blocking it for her too. She was hot—on fire—her cheeks were flaming. I kissed her and kissed her and she couldn't get enough, except she kept laughing, her mouth burst open and hot breath came out . . . I'd better stop this, I'm supposed to be sick; dying, in fact."

Henry gave his grandfather time to recover before asking, "And the Master?"

"Oh the Master—well I said I was going to come and see him tomorrow to say goodbye, but I spent the whole day with Clara, and the day after that I left. I never met the Master again and Clara only once, by accident. I ran into her in a Lyons Corner House—it seems she never made it to the posh places—actually, I didn't recognize her, she had to remind me. Her husband was with her, an unremarkable fellow, but she seemed reasonably happy, though she wasn't plump anymore nor on fire. She said they were there for their wedding anniversary, the third I think she said, but they had to get home so that the baby-sitter wouldn't miss the last Tube."

Henry did not wish to disturb his grandfather any further that night, especially since Graeme had got on to a subject that was less interesting to Henry. Henry had not spent a great deal of time thinking about girls, perhaps because he had only really known one, and he found now that he was not so much thinking about Vera as enduring her absence.

He continued to limp around the city, frequently in the direction of Vera's office building. He lingered around there a little longer every time but did not feel he could really wait for her before reaching a more mature conclusion about his own plans. And he was still afraid of missing her—he even had a sort of nightmare vision of himself trying in vain to cleave through a mass of people to reach her, while she, entirely oblivious of him, went lightly on her way.

However, this could not have happened because Vera was on the lookout for him every day; sometimes she found it difficult to hide her disappointment when instead she saw other friends waiting for her. Similarly, at home when she asked for her telephone messages, there were always several callers but none of them was Henry.

Her mother's favorite occupation was taking messages for Vera on the telephone. If it was a young man, and it usually was, Irina spoke very sweetly; she liked them all indiscriminately and was never sure which one of them was the principal figure in her dreams. But everything that happened there was blurred, and only the dream itself was clear, and the dreamer. Irina saw herself moving in with the young couple—sometimes it was into a penthouse overlooking the East River, sometimes the upper story in a converted brownstone belonging to the young man's parents. Later, when the children came—Irina had no interest in acquiring grandchildren, but she supposed they would come—they would all move to some leafy suburb, or even a little farther, to the Palisades where they would occupy a period home overlooking the river. Irina would join a local group of women her own age, to play canasta or some other card game which she would learn. There would be a masseuse, and a girl to do her nails, and another to wax her legs. She might take up the piano again.

One day Irina entered Vera's bedroom and found her emptying a box she herself had given her on her last birthday, to hold her jewelry: for she had been very pleased to discover that Vera was slowly replacing some of what had been scattered over the years—mostly in forfeit to pawnbrokers. "What are you doing!" cried Irina, for she saw that Vera was stuffing all of it into a little tapestry pouch, handmade by a friend.

"I'm giving it all back," said Vera, throwing in another piece.

"It's ours!" cried her mother.

"No it's not; it's Baby's."

Irina lunged forward and grabbed the bag. She thrust her hand in and came up with a glittering fistful. "Is this Baby's? And this?" for there were some pieces presented by Vera's admirers, as well as some chunky ones crafted by her friends.

Vera carelessly conceded that they could keep those—she threw them back in the birthday box—but that the rest must return to Baby.

There followed a scene regularly enacted in the Richter family. It used to be Mme. Richter—Mamenka—who took the leading role in the fights with her daughter and granddaughter and even little Vera in her earliest years. Now it was Irina who accused and sobbed and beat her breast. She cursed Baby and Baby's family who had always had everything while she herself had nothing. She also cursed Vera, but when Vera cursed her back, her mother could bear no more: she scrambled to her feet and made to throw herself out of a window. This had been more effective in the old days when Mme. Richter could simply climb up on a sill or the parapet of a little balcony. Now Irina had first to struggle with a flyscreen, then to force herself through the narrow opening of her sliding window. However, they had the advantage of living on a much higher floor than in their old houses where they had usually been at ground level or even below ground, in a basement. But the denouement was the same in the present as in the past: Irina only had her shoulders out when Vera began to pull her back. Thus had Mme. Richter swayed on a windowsill while daughter and granddaughter and tiny great-granddaughter had seized her garments—the fabric was so worn that often it tore in their hands—tugging and imploring while the matriarch swore that this time she would not be held back. But, as Irina did now, she had allowed herself to be overruled. Irina and Vera were reconciled; they knelt together on the floor, whispering their love with every kind of endearment (Irina still remembered the Russian ones Mamenka had used); the only moment when they raised their voices was when they almost quarreled as to which one of them needed forgiveness more. Each had only one desire and that was to fulfill the desire of the other: so that Irina allowed Vera to give back the jewelry, and Vera pledged herself to accept the proposal of the most promising of the young men who had asked her. They got off the floor, dusting their knees. They were calm but exceptionally hungry and ready to send for take-out. They never cooked much at home—they were proud to have their own little apartment but lived in it in a casual, bohemian way.

When Graeme had another attack, the doctors thought he could not outlive the night, but in fact it took him three days to die. There was a fully qualified nurse, whose efficiency was hampered by Baby, squarely positioned on a chair near Graeme's head; the only time Baby left her post was when Henry took it over. Then she performed her usual tasks around the house, such as arranging for everyone's meals, and she sat in her little red sitting room and paid bills, dressed as usual in her pretty clothes and with her jewelry clinking and glinting, so that there was no outward sign of her despair.

Nevertheless, as soon as she entered, Vera knew that she had come at a wrong time to return Baby's gifts. The apartment appeared to have closed in on itself, and not only because the air-conditioning filled it with monotonous noise and used-up air. Baby gratefully welcomed Vera—she thought she had come because she had heard about Graeme; and she described to her the circumstances of Graeme's last attack, which had come on very suddenly while Baby was kissing him good night.

This good-night kiss was something new between them. Previously, although they were already spending practically every hour of the day together, they had parted at night as coolly as two people who happened to have been locked up together in a railway carriage. "Do you want anything?" Baby would say, as she got up to retire to her own bedroom. He invariably did—the light adjusted, a pencil within reach, another drink of water; perhaps because he didn't like to see her unoccupied with himself; perhaps—though he would never in a thousand years have admitted it—because he was reluctant to part from her. When there was no more to do for him, she went to her own bedroom, all the time alert and listening. Then she returned once more to see if there wasn't one last thing he might need. She had changed by then into her youthful nightie that outlined her plump figure and left her arms bare; and as she leaned over him to give a last pat to his pillow, he claimed that she had come deliberately to tempt him. She greeted this with a sound that derided them both. She pretended to be displeased when he touched her soft upper arms, but she lingered a bit, in case he felt like doing it again; and once she bent down to brush her lips over his forehead. It was a swift, shy kiss but so exciting to her that she could hardly wait to repeat it the next night. Her heart beating fast, she fussed with his pillow, both wanting and not daring to try out another kiss. At last, like one jumping into water, she darted toward him, and this time her lips stayed longer; and he said, "Yes yes all right," trying to sound irritable but it came out tremulous. The next night the same, and the one after that; but on the fifth night he said only "Yes yes," and after that only "Yes." But on the last night he didn't have time to say anything, and she would not have been sure whether she had actually got as far as kissing his forehead except that ever since she had felt the touch of it on her lips.

Of course she didn't tell any of these details to Vera—or even to Henry, till much later. She only described Graeme's attack—it had been, she said, quick as lightning; yes, she repeated, as though lightning had struck him. "But he'll be so pleased to see you," she lied to Vera, accompanying her as far as Graeme's room. She let her go in alone but stood for a moment in the open door, gazing toward Graeme lying on the bed like a knight on his tomb. He appeared to be gazing back at her; but she was no longer fooled by that, for she knew that his eyes were looking beyond her, or inward, or elsewhere; anyway, not at her. Similarly, once or twice he had called her name—"Baby," he had said quite clearly—but when she came to him, he turned away as though it were not her he had meant but something infinitely other.

Vera too was fooled into believing that Graeme was looking at her in greeting, so she went toward him gladly. At that moment Graeme stirred, no more than a slight movement of the hand, so that Henry, sitting at the head of the bed, started forward the way he did every time his grandfather gave any indication of returning to consciousness. But all Graeme did was sigh and shut his eyes. "He's sleeping," whispered the nurse and did something unnecessary to the bedclothes.

Henry explained to Vera that Graeme had not been in communication since his last attack but seemed often on the verge of wanting to say something. "I thought he was looking at me and smiling when I came in," Vera said. Henry said yes, it always seemed like that, and who could tell, perhaps he was. They were whispering but the nurse shushed them, so they thought it better to go outside. Henry looked back once from the threshold, ready to turn in case Graeme wanted him. He still hoped that his grandfather would talk to him for one last time; that perhaps he still had one last thing to tell him.

Once outside, Henry was his usual courteous self with Vera, asking her about her job and how she liked it and appearing to be interested in her replies. Baby showed the same interest, and if she had known them both less well, Vera would have believed that they were listening to her. As it was, she felt herself shut out, not only from their vigil but from all she had always shared with them before.

Graeme's door opened and the nurse came out to call Baby, who tried to stand up and couldn't—her legs were trembling so fearfully. But it seemed the nurse only wanted to talk to her about the arrangements for her own lunch—she felt like having a little spinach quiche today—so then Baby managed to stand up. She went to discuss the question with the nurse, leaving Henry and Vera alone together. For a moment they did not know what to say to each other; it even seemed to Vera that Henry's attention was wandering away from her, so she burst out: "You never came to see me. You never even called."

He admitted it. "I wanted to, very much, but you know how slow I am. To make up my mind about anything," he added.

And blushing terribly, she said, "Did you have to make up your mind about me?"

"Not about you of course, but what I might have to offer you that was good enough."

"Were you thinking of offering me my job back?"

"Why, would you take it?" She didn't answer, so he did. "No you wouldn't and why should you. It's not right for you; you're much better off where you are." He went on: "And I understand that because, as you know, I wasn't sure myself if I wanted to carry on."

"And now you are sure?"

He raised his hand for silence—listening toward Graeme's room; but he was mistaken, there was nothing. "I wish I were," he replied, "but I think maybe I'm surer than I was."

"*Why?*" cried Vera. She clutched her pouch with the jewels in her lap as though for courage and went on: "All the time we were digging around in those old papers I thought why are we doing this, but it was all right really because it was only a job, and I thought when it was finished, when we'd done it all, then we'd be rid of it and could do something else."

"Yes, *you* could," Henry said. "But I don't share your feeling that it's just another job to be got through before going on to something else because for me there is nothing else. No, I don't mean because of—you know—that's not all that important . . . I wish I could say this in a way to make you understand."

"I do understand," said Vera, lowering her eyes so that her lashes lay against her burning cheeks. "It's what Renata expects of you."

"Oh you know how I am with Renata. She only has to expect

something of me and I'm off in the opposite direction. But this time, in this, it's not so. Because partly it is what I want—not to become another Master, God forbid, even if I could! But to know some more of what he knew. Or maybe only to do something more than just eat and sleep."

"If there was anyone who knew about eating and sleeping, that was him. I think it's all he cared about and it's everyone else who hung all these grand ideas on him."

"Yes but why him? What was there about him that made people turn to him the way they did?"

"Is that what you want? That they should run after you the way they did with him? . . . I know you'd hate it as much as I do for you."

She raised her eyes to his face and saw the expression of kindly concern he had for her whenever he meant to encourage her to tell him what was on her mind. And she was tempted to speak as she had never yet done, to him or to anyone. But she had no words for that so instead she expressed her feelings about the Master. "I hated him before because of Mamenka and everything he'd done to us, and then when I read all that stuff I saw it was the way he treated everyone because he was just a monster. Don't shake your head! You used to feel the same, and if you didn't, then you fooled me."

"That was never my intention."

She made herself get up. Although she would have liked to stay with him longer, she felt that what they were saying wasn't leading anywhere—at least not anywhere she wanted to go. But when he saw her ready to leave him, he became more urgent. "I felt like you up to some point—I too hated all that self-analysis he made people do, like encouraging them to masturbate"—he looked at Vera in apology, for it was not characteristic of him to mention a sexual act in her presence—"but I thought that if I just read a bit more, just went in a little deeper, maybe I'd find something."

"We went through all the papers, we filed them, you edited them, I translated them—and there never was anything."

"Perhaps there will be, if we work at it more."

"Who told you that? Why should you believe that?"

"I think Graeme told me." And again he listened toward the sickroom but, except for the air-conditioners, all was silent in there.

"Graeme! He'd be the last person to care for anyone like the Master. He never even met him."

"He did once—and you're right, after that he chose not to see him again. But I think the Master told him more than he did anyone else, or he received more. Don't go. Why are you going?"

"I have to. I promised Mummy." She was standing, looking down at him in his wheelchair. "Here, I didn't have a chance to give this back to Baby, so will you and tell her thank you."

"What is it?" He peered into the pouch. "But this is all yours. She gave it to you. No, you must take it back, she'd be really hurt if she thought you didn't want it anymore."

"But I don't."

He was looking up at her and was surprised to see her clear eyes clouded. He said gently, "It's only some little trinkets she gave you, you might as well take them." He rolled his wheelchair near her to thrust the pouch into her hands, but she put them behind her back. "Come on, Vera, don't be childish," he pleaded, and again his tone was one of the most friendly concern for her. But as always the expression in his slanted eyes was different—or rather the eyes themselves were different from the Henry she knew. And Vera thought quite fiercely, who needs this, and she felt that Irina was right, it was better to marry someone whose eyes were in keeping with the rest of him, straight, straightforward, so that you knew where you were.

At that moment Graeme's door opened and the nurse called to them to come quickly. Then there was no holding Henry—he thrust the pouch into Vera's hands and rolled his wheelchair as fast as he could toward his grandfather's room. As for Vera, she ran out the front door and down the stairs that led to the entrance hall. Renata was just walking across it, and after almost colliding with her, Vera thrust the pouch into her hands without a word. Renata took it and peered in while walking upstairs, but then she forgot about it, for she heard her mother's voice crying out her father's name.

"Graeme!" Baby called, as though he were walking out on her again and she summoning him to return. But of course she knew better than to expect him to listen or look back.